Shady
Place

a novel by
David A Byrne

To Mom & Dad

for recognizing the old man in me at such a young age.

To Ashley

for putting up with the aforementioned old man with such great patience.

PROLOGUE

Jim paced their bedroom, reeling from what ended up being his last day of work. They always discussed major life-changing decisions. This time, he didn't consult her; he just did it. He quit his job.

He rubbed his hand over the stubble that had grown on his usually bald head and stared out of the second-story window at a rickety old tree house. He hadn't always been bald, but when his hair had started to thin, he'd just shaved the whole thing off and never looked back.

"It'll be fine," his wife said, buzzing around him, packing a suitcase. "You could have retired two years ago if you wanted."

Karen was his everything, and her words of support were always there, but he didn't want to talk about it. He just wanted to move on. "I really need to take that old tree house down."

"I don't think so, mister," she pulled his face away from the window and pierced his soul with her pale-green eyes. "You and the girls built that together; it's not going anywhere." She let him go and continued to bustle around the room.

The girls were gone. They were grown-up and off starting families of their own. Jim and Karen were in their mid-fifties; it seemed as if everything had changed overnight, but he looked at her and still saw the girl he almost didn't have the nerve to ask out thirty years before. Sure, there were lines around her mouth and eyes that hadn't always been there, but she looked just as fresh and exciting as the day they met.

"Do you remember the time they had that sleepover, and you spent the night up there with your radio and twelve-pack?" she asked.

"Yeah, that was a fun night," he said. Of course he remembered; even just the thought of it brought a smile to his face. "Until I fell out."

"You were so drunk, you didn't feel a thing," she laughed, and then she realized what he'd done. "Hey, don't change the subject. We are going on this trip."

"Should we, though?" he asked. "Can we still afford it?"

She stopped packing. "We're fine. We've already paid for it. We *are* going."

"But—" he started.

Karen immediately shut him down, poking him in the chest as she spoke. "No buts. We're going, and we're going to enjoy ourselves. We're getting on a plane to Florida tomorrow, and that's that."

He acquiesced, rubbing the spot she'd poked. She was little, but she was strong. "Fine, but I'm not going to have fun."

"Oh, Jim," she said, touching her head. She tried to turn as she winced, but she couldn't hide the pain from Jim.

"The headaches still?"

"I'll be fine," she said.

"You still have the appointment in the morning?" he asked, observing her in the mirror fastened to the top of her dresser as he fumbled absentmindedly through an open drawer.

"Yes," she said. "But I'm going to postpone it until we get back."

He turned back to her. "Oh, no; you're keeping that appointment. I'm taking you. Besides, our flight isn't until the afternoon."

"OK, OK, I'll go," she said. She pointed to the dresser. "Hand me that sweater, please."

"Sweater?" he asked. "We're going to Florida."

"You know I'm always cold," she said.

"Women."

He turned back to the dresser and spotted the sweater. While his back was turned, she touched her head again; the pain was worse than she wanted him to know. He returned to her, pressing a bikini top to his chest.

"This one?" he asked sheepishly, knowing it would definitely look better on her.

She laughed as she threw a pair of socks at him.

Florida agreed with Jim and Karen. They spent a lot of time just wandering the coast, cruising down A1A in the convertible she insisted on renting. Jim wasn't a cop here. Karen wasn't a nurse. They were just Jim and Karen, two kids without a care.

They wined and dined at beachfront crab shacks. Suds and sun. Maybe there was a reason so many people retired here. The more they saw, the more they liked.

"You know, the girls love it here," Karen said, her hand dangling in the wind whooshing by the car. "And they don't even live by the beach."

"Yeah," he said.

"I can't remember having this much fun in a long time," she said. She touched his hand as he shifted gears. "What do you say?"

"To what? Did I miss a question?"

She smiled. "What if we moved here? You basically just retired. There are nursing jobs everywhere. We could just move here."

He stopped at a red light. An elderly man with a walker trudged across the intersection in front of them. Jim pointed to the man. "What is it they say about Florida? 'God's waiting room'?"

"James Mortimer Phillips!"

He laughed. "Uh-oh, all three names."

Karen was clever. Maybe in another life, she could have played the espionage game, but she chose a life with Jim. She had guided him there without him ever sniffing a hint. Quite the feat considering Jim spent the majority of his career as a detective.

She made it seem like they were just tooling around and stumbled upon it. There was something about it that seemed to fit the bill perfectly. Never mind the months of research she had done to find it.

Kismet.

"This looks interesting," Karen said, pointing to the sign for a neighborhood just ahead. "Let's stop in here."

The sign was pristine.

Shady Place: Active Adult Community 55+

Jim read aloud, then looked to his wife. Her eyes told him they didn't just stumble upon this hidden treasure.

O NE

Shady Place, Active Adult Community, 55+.
Luscious landscapes await! Live the lifestyle you were always meant
to have! Make your friends jealous! Never shovel snow again!

It went on like that for a while, incessant ramblings about how
wonderful the neighborhood was, heaven on earth. The brochure
had become tattered and worn from years of being studied, flipped
through, and overly consumed. Fingerprints smudged the edges. It
was a reminder of a time that still had hope, a time when the future
was still vast and full of promise.

Originally, the pamphlet held vibrant colors in the supporting
images of people having the times of their lives. Vibrant landscapes,
golf, tennis, pools, dinner, dancing; the list was endless. All this in one
happy, shiny neighborhood for adults fifty-five and up. The residents
were all gloriously happy playing games, frolicking, and enjoying all
that life had to offer in the AARP years. All set to the glow of sunny
Florida.

They were actors, of course. None of them actually lived in
Shady Place. Well, maybe a few did. Jim had told himself for years
that these happy people were paid to be that way. No one enjoyed
those things, not in real life. He didn't, so why would they? This is

how he justified putting it off for so many years. Where was the brochure with the people staying home, not interacting with others, cloistered in their own personal caves?

But he already had that.

He clung tightly to the Shady Place pamphlet for years after Karen's death. The last time he would see it was the day he moved there.

"Dad?"

The plea went unanswered.

The tree house sat in the backyard for thirty years. It was rickety and worn, but it had character. Jim had built it for his two daughters. He'd hoped at least one would be a boy, even asked Karen to give it one more try, but to no avail. He may not have gotten a boy, but he did get two girls he loved, two girls he spoiled as much as he could. He gave them all he could, nice things, a nice home, good schools. They got the best Jim had to offer. That day, they got a healthy dose of the stubbornness he'd spent a lifetime cultivating.

They stood at the base of the tree, staring up at their childhood getaway. The duo teemed with frustration.

"He's up there; he has to be," Jenny offered, shaking her head in consternation. She was in her early thirties, the younger of Jim's daughters, a blonde like he once was but with her mother's pale-green eyes. She bounced a baby on her hip, her second, a boy named after her father.

"Come on, Daddy, you're acting like a baby," Heather barked. Jim's other daughter was more serious than Jenny. She was a little older and looked much more like Karen than Jim, but unlike her sister and mother, she shared Jim's dark-blue eyes.

Jenny sighed. "Seriously, we know you're up there!"

"You need to come down and sign the papers." Heather's frustration grew.

A sign of life.

"Go away!" Jim called down.

Perched above them, Jim rubbed his fingers gently over a heart carved into the wooden wall. Inside the crude heart was etched "JP + KP" with a smaller JP and HP below them. Remnants of a happier time for Jim. Clutched in his other hand was the brochure for Shady Place; it was more crumpled and frayed than ever. It didn't really matter if he had the brochure anymore, he was supposed to be leaving for his new home today.

Sentimentality had him reconsidering.

Jim's face had grown tired and the years had seen him add a few more pounds to his frame than he would admit. It was more from neglect than anything else. He was in his sixties now, but his eyes seemed so much older. Not his vision, though; if you asked Jim, his vision was perfect, better than 20/20. He was bald by choice, but it had been so long since he'd let his hair grow, there was no telling what it would look like if it ever made it past a stubble.

Jenny shouted from below, "Daddy, please! The movers are almost finished, just come down! We have a long drive."

"You can't make me," Jim proclaimed, acting the petulant child.

Heather and Jenny were at a loss. Heather decided, "One of us is going to have to go up there."

"I just had a baby," Jenny said, holding her young child close. "Mommy can't be climbing, can she?"

Heather rejected her argument. "Give me a break; it's been six months!"

Jenny shrugged and booped Jim's tiny namesake on the nose.

Heather furrowed her brow and turned her attention back to their father. "What's the problem, Daddy?"

"You're making me leave my home. What do you think the problem is?" Jim said.

Jenny replied, "It's time to move on…"

"You don't even care! This is where you grew up. Where your mother and I…" He stopped.

Heather jumped in; it was time to tag team him. "It will always be where we grew up, but you made a promise…"

At Heather's urging, Jenny kept pushing. "This is what you and Mom wanted!"

"We were supposed to go together," he returned softly, almost in tears.

The silence was deafening.

When Jim made up his mind and dug in, it was for the long haul. The movers were nearly finished, they had a long drive ahead of them, and their poor Realtor was waiting patiently inside. Jenny and Heather had to get him down. Now.

Jenny knew how to end the standoff. "James Mortimer Phillips, you come down from that tree house this instant. This is not a game. We have to get on the road."

Heather raised an eyebrow at Jenny, mouthing *Mom?*

Jenny nodded with a smirk plastered across her face, and baby Jim giggled; his mommy was so silly.

They waited. It felt like an eternity, but it was only a few seconds before Jim leaned over the edge slightly.

"But—"

Not today, Jenny wasn't having any more lip, "No buts! Now!"

He let out a heavy sigh, one word escaping with the deep exhalation, "Fine."

He began climbing down but stopped after just a few steps. He climbed back up a step and tried to pry his treasured wooden plank from the wall. He grabbed hold and pulled, his footing precarious at best. One misstep sent him tumbling to the ground.

The girls rushed to his side to make sure he was all right. His breath was gone, but he pushed the words out anyway. "Would have hurt less if I was drunk."

Heather brushed some grass from his head. "I assumed you were."

Jenny remembered out loud, "Isn't this like the time you were drunk during our sleepover and fell out of the tree house? Remember that?"

He frowned at her, furrowing his brow. *Of course he remembered.*

"That was funny," Heather smirked. "You had more hair then."

Jim was not amused.

🌴

With the stroke of a pen, Jim signed the last of the paperwork to sell the house his kids had grown up in, the first place he and his wife, Karen, had ever lived together. The *only* place they ever lived together.

With his Realtor at his side, Jim wasn't quite ready to relinquish control just yet. The Realtor tried to slide the papers out from under his hand, but Jim resisted, clamping his fist down hard on the last page.

"And that's the last one," the Realtor said, struggling to pull the page away. "If you'll just…" He finally succeeded in yanking the page out from under Jim's hand, garnering a silent, angry glare from the crotchety old man. "Thank you, sir."

"Screw off." Jim got up and walked away without an ounce of courtesy, ignoring the extended hand his Realtor offered.

No sooner than he'd risen, the movers grabbed the table and chairs they had been sitting on and shuffled them out the front door.

Jim plodded his way to the house's threshold before turning back and looking at his empty home. But it wasn't home anymore, at least not his.

Now it was just a house.

He closed his eyes, envisioning all the good times his family had over the years. The holidays, the family get-togethers, the girls growing into beautiful women, into mothers. He spent too much time at work, but he never missed the significant moments.

Most importantly, she was always there. Karen, his rock, the most loving, hardworking person he ever knew. A smile wrinkled the corners of his mouth.

He opened his eyes, and it was over. There was nothing left, only an empty room, a broom and dustpan, and a little pile of dirt awaiting that last sweep into the pan.

"Come on, Pop; it's time to go." Heather put her hand on his shoulder, startling him.

He lowered his head and walked out.

Defeat.

The neighborhood had changed dramatically since they'd moved in all those years ago. It changed, yet it more closely resembled the Philadelphia suburb he'd moved into originally. He was the last remnant of a generation who raised their kids together, but they were all gone. He was the last holdout. All his contemporaries had moved on, and now, it was Jim's turn. For the neighborhood, it was a new generation's turn.

On the street, his sons-in-law lingered around his car—a 1966 Shelby GT 350-H; it had the rarer white and blue paint job. He'd had it since 1980. It was Jim's baby, the only thing he'd ever splurged on in his life. His father rented one from Hertz when he was a boy, and he'd vowed to own one. He still thought about his father every time he looked at it.

Jim watched them argue over who would drive his car first. "Tell me again why the idiots are driving my baby and not me?" "Idiots" was the term of affection he used for the dynamic duo who were his sons-in-law, Kevin and Terry.

"Because we can't trust you to make it to Florida on your own." Heather pointed to her SUV where Jenny was securing baby Jim in his car seat in the back. "It'll be a chance for you to bond with your loving daughters and new grandson. It'll be fun."

Jim glowered at the boys as Heather led him to the SUV. "You said it right the first time; you just want to keep an eye on me." He pointed to Kevin and Terry. "Not a scratch!"

The boys fake saluted him, then hopped in and fired her up. Jim cringed in disapproval. Heather opened his door, put her hand on his head, and guided him into the back seat. He felt like a perp being placed in a police cruiser. "Watch your head."

"Funny," Jim said, but the door was closed before he could get the word out. He stewed in the back seat next to his young grandson, who was sucking on a pacifier.

Baby Jim—*more like Replacement Jim*, he thought. They had the same haircut and eyes. He rubbed the boy's head, then turned his attention back to his daughters. Jim watched Jenny and Heather talk to the Realtor, then they shook hands and parted. It all seemed simple enough, but what he was sure he saw was the Realtor asking the girls what was wrong with their old man.

Is he senile?

Why is he such a dick?

We really fleeced him, didn't we?

He already hated salespeople; the dialogue he invented in his head served only to exacerbate those feelings. The whole transaction was capped off by the Realtor flipping him the bird as the girls walked away.

That one was the last straw. Jim tried to open the door quickly; he grabbed the handle and pulled, thrusting his whole body outward so he'd be at a full sprint when it opened. But it didn't open. Pulling the handle did nothing, and Jim smacked his face right into the closed window with a thud.

Jim rubbed his forehead, snarling like a caged dog, as the Realtor cocked his head at him with a peculiar look on his face. The girls took their places in the front of the SUV, laughing at their father.

"Child locks," Jenny snickered. "But nice try."

"You're holding me captive; this isn't fair," he said. "I know that little shit flipped me off; I saw it!"

Heather spun around from the driver's seat to reassure him. "First of all, watch your language. Second, that little *shit* just set the record for highest sale on this street. *For you.* Show a little gratitude!"

Jim had a tough exterior but always seemed to back off when a woman raised her voice, the result of being raised under the watchful eye of a strong woman. He slouched down in his seat and mumbled to himself.

As they pulled away, he spun around for one last look at his house. His sanctuary. He wanted to complete his punishment. That's what it was. It was punishment for some unknown crime; he was certain of it. He wanted to watch it shrink into oblivion, to wallow in self-pity as his castle faded into the distance.

What he found was that stupid Realtor still giving him that same peculiar look. But this time, the action wasn't an invention of Jim's mind. The Realtor presented Jim with a prominent middle finger and wry smile. It was the only thing Jim witnessed fade into the horizon.

"C'mon, you had to see that!"

Red-faced and sullen, Jim slid back into his seat. He looked to his young grandson. Baby Jim, *Replacement Jim*, gave him a laugh and reached for his head.

"Et tu, baby?"

TWO

There are a lot of quotes about the value of the journey that leads to a destination. Nonsense. Whoever said those things has never traveled a thousand miles in a car with Jim's daughters and a baby.

The journey was long, it held no lessons, and was full of uncontrolled bodily functions from a baby that *should* have slept the whole way. Isn't that how it's supposed to go? Babies sleep in the car, right? Wrong. Replacement Jim barely closed his eyes for a second. When he did, it was to truly savor relieving himself. It was as if he was enjoying the foul odors emanating from his tiny body. Or at least enjoying the effect it had on those around him.

The trip *should* have taken a day and a half. Three able-bodied adults, taking turns, sixty miles an hour on average, just under seventeen hours drive time, plus stops for food, gas, and an overnight. They'd be there by the next afternoon. That's how it played out in Jim's head.

The reality was drastically different, prompting Jim to make three observations:

1. His daughters had nothing interesting to say.
2. Based on the amount of vomit and crap oozing out of him, his grandson should not be alive.

3. Everyone on the eastern seaboard was traveling at the same time as them.

The trip took three days. Three very long days. Three days that felt like three months to Jim, while his home was slipping further and further away.

He tried to make light of his situation; when they reached the highway, he let a rip.

"I can drive if you want," he said.

"Daddy, stop," Heather said.

Sure, he could stop, but what fun would that be? "You can pass on the left…never mind; too late. After this one. Nope, not now either."

"Let her drive, Daddy," Jenny chimed in.

"Are you going to pass these Sunday drivers or what?"

"Daddy!" Heather was getting fed up.

"Fine, fine, just trying to help!" He eased up, temporarily. He tapped his fingers on the back of Jenny's seat. "How much further?"

Heather was close to her tipping point. "I will leave you on the side of the road."

"I'm hungry." Jim grinned almost imperceptibly, completely satisfied with himself.

"Wait, are you…" it dawned on Heather. "Is this for all the road trips we took when we were kids?"

He smirked.

"Damn it, Daddy, you're a grown man!" Jenny huffed at him.

Jim fiddled with the child-locked door handle. "Could have fooled me."

"Enough! I don't want to hear another word." Heather peered at him in the rearview mirror. "Silence. Got it?"

He nodded. They sat in silence for a moment, but only a brief moment. "Heather, darling?"

"What? What is it now?" She was ready to leave him at the closest rest stop.

"I have to pee."

🌴

If you held the brochure up next to the real Shady Place, it would have paled in comparison. The real Shady Place was alive and vibrant. The moment you hit the front gate, there was an impressive four by six-foot stone framed wooden placard of a golfer's silhouette inside a glorious oak tree. The lush landscapes were even greener than the images in Jim's brochure.

The natives were out in force. They always were. Golf carts, pocket pooches, bicycles, power walkers, and glowing smiles crowded the streets and sidewalks.

Heather's SUV rolled smoothly through the guarded checkpoint and into the belly of the beast. Jim watched from the back seat as the locals observed their arrival. Many smiled and waved.

"They're all so," he shook his head. "Old."

Jenny said, "Daddy, you're…"

"You're…" Heather tried to cut Jenny off.

Jim finished the thought for them, "I'm what? Old?"

Jenny backtracked. "No, of course you're not old, you're uhhh…"

"Not giving this a *chance*; look at all the pretty ladies!" Heather brought it home.

Jim made a sour face at a few women; their tiny dogs sniffing each other at their feet. The duo returned Jim's sour face without missing a beat, dismissing him as quickly as they'd taken notice. It was a beautiful day, and no cranky old man was going to disrupt that for them.

"A chance," Jim hadn't stopped shaking his head since the guard shack. "You know I'm going to die here?"

Heather wasn't interested in hearing any more complaints. "Quit it."

"Look, girls, it's my ride. Just let me out here!" Jim pointed to a hearse-led funeral procession moving through the neighborhood. The natives all paused their activities to pay respects to the deceased.

Both of his daughters shouted at him in unison, "Daddy!"

🌴

Collectively, the residents of Shady Place were a diverse cross-section. Mike Johnson, Sanjay Patel, and Tommy Griffin watched the procession receding away from them.

Mike wore a hairpiece; it wasn't a good one, didn't look right, but no one ever said anything, and they just accepted it for what it was. He always had a cigar on him. His doctor told him if he kept smoking them, it would kill him, but he was so used to the oral stimulation that he needed something to take its place. Instead, he chewed on a Twizzler, the rest of the pack nestled behind the cigar he couldn't smoke in his shirt pocket.

"Another one bites the dust," Mike said.

"He was young," Sanjay added. Everyone called him Jay. He was a diminutive little guy, easily a foot shorter than Tommy and six inches below Mike. He sported a lampshade moustache finely groomed to match the width of his lips; it was jet-black and matched the neatly cropped mane on top.

Tommy was the eldest. He was a former champion boxer from Alabama; his face showed the wear of years in the ring. While he still had the size of a heavyweight prizefighter, the distribution of weight had shifted from his upper body to his midsection. His voice carried a slow southern drawl. "Paper said sixty-three."

Mike tested the waters on a theory. "Think there's been a few too many of them lately?"

"Too many what?" Tommy asked.

Mike spoke with a distinctly Philadelphia accent. He tried to curb his use of words that made it stand out, but on occasion, he couldn't help himself, "Youse know, deaths, too young, seems a little—fishy."

"Everyone here is older…" Jay stated the facts as he saw them. He was always as straightforward as he could be, and since English wasn't his first language, he always strove for perfect diction.

Tommy pointed to Heather's SUV as it pulled up to the house next door. "Talk about fishy. Y'all get a load of this."

Heather's SUV came to a rest in the driveway, just next to a prominent For Sale sign emboldened with a rider reading SOLD in bright red letters.

Samuel Thane, who went by Sam, leaned on the front door. He was good-looking and well groomed; young enough that he could have gone to high school with Jenny or Heather. He was slick, but just slick enough not to be off-putting to the normal Shady Place clientele. Khaki pants, collared shirt, and a nice pair of shoes were his uniform; it was too hot in Florida to wear a suit and tie. Besides, when all your customers are wearing flip-flops and shorts, why should you be the sucker in a three-piece.

He knew the tricks of dealing with folks older than him; don't be threatening, ask them questions, be excited, and always, always make them wish you were their son or grandkid instead of the shitheads they had back wherever they came from. Of course, for Jim, there was no level of slickness or nonthreatening behavior that would make him like Sam. Sam was, after all, the jackass who'd convinced his Karen to move to Shady Place.

"Into the abyss," Jim grumbled as he got out of the SUV.

Sam greeted him with a familiarity that made Jim cringe.

"Mr. Phillips! Welcome home!"

"You better have my keys, Thane," Jim brushed past him.

Sam threw his arm around Jim's shoulder. "As cranky as ever, I see! I love this guy!"

Jim threw Sam's hand off his shoulder, then shot him a dirty look. Sam returned a confident wink and led him inside.

Next door, the boys tried to get a look at the new neighbor, but the Realtor was obscuring him. "Looks like another guy; just what we need," Mike observed.

"Reckon he knows about Jerry dyin' there?" Tommy asked.

Mike shook his head. "Doubt it, Thane's all about the sale. That's another one went too early."

"Perhaps you are correct; there have been many who have passed somewhat prematurely lately." Jay was buying in.

Mike knew how to take an opening. "Maybe youse guys should tell the cops? See what they say."

"Your phone broke?" Tommy asked.

Mike danced around the question. "Uhh, well, it's probably nothing…What do youse think the new guy's story is?"

"I am to find out tomorrow. I am to give him a neighborhood tour. His name is James," Jay said. "James something, I cannot remember; I have the paper at home."

Heather lingered outside to greet the moving truck while the others headed inside Jim's new home.

Tommy and Jay bickered back and forth across Mike about nothing in particular. They always seemed to have something to bicker about. He was too busy studying the group next door to care what they had to say. He failed to get a good look at his new neighbor, but it didn't matter. He had plans. He took a big bite of his licorice twist and tossed it aside before popping his unlit cigar in his mouth.

"See you mooks later; I got a date."

This was his first time seeing the house in person. Jenny had video-conferenced a walking tour, but he had never actually stepped foot inside the property. It was not unique; it wasn't what Jim was used to. There was no character compared to the home he'd left back in Philly. Maybe it was because it was so empty or because it wasn't home yet, but it was cold and sterile. The ceramic tile in the living areas, granite countertops, forty-two-inch cabinets, and stainless-steel appliances in the kitchen, none of it felt right.

Jim hated it.

Sam led him through the house, espousing an enthusiasm he hoped would rub off on Jim as he pointed to different features. Jim could barely muster more than a grumble or a dissenting observation about already having a house that he left behind with all the same features. Jenny tried to help Sam massage Jim's psyche, but it was no use. He wasn't interested, and it didn't matter that none of Jim's apprehensions and observations were true, his old house was not this nice, not even close. Jim would never admit it out loud, but this house was better in every way than the one he'd left behind.

"What do you think? It's nice," Jenny urged. "Right, Daddy?"

"It's not…" Jim hesitated, "home."

After the tour, Sam brought Jim to the kitchen, "So we have one more paper for you to sign. You missed it in the closing package you mailed back."

Jim acted surprised. "Oh? I was sure I signed everything."

"Daddy, that's so unlike you," Jenny said suspiciously.

Sam pulled out a pen and stuck it in Jim's face. "Just one last signature, and it's all yours."

Jim slowly reached for the pen, took a deep breath, then made a dash for the front door. Jenny called out as he opened the door, "He's running!"

Terry and Kevin had already arrived and were speaking to Heather by Jim's car when he blew through the front door and shouted, "Keys!"

Kevin was midsentence complimenting the new digs, but Jim was insistent.

"Keys, now!"

Jenny and Sam rushed from the house in hot pursuit, urging Kevin not to hand over the keys, but it was too late.

They dangled in the air from Kevin's hand in slow motion as Jenny and Sam both spit out a prolonged "*Nooooo.*" But it was as if someone had hit the fast-forward button on only Jim. He snagged the keys from Kevin's hand and was in the car with the engine roaring to life and the doors locked before anyone knew what happened.

Heather threw herself in front of the car to impede her father's way, as Kevin threw his hands up in confusion. Jenny punched her "idiot" on the arm for relinquishing the keys, hitting him hard. So hard, it would leave a bruise.

Kevin tried to rub the throbbing away as he complained, "Damn, babe; that hurt!"

Next door, Jay and Tommy were mounted on a golf cart, ready to leave, but things had just gotten interesting. They were joined by at least a half a dozen other Shady Place residents being treated to an afternoon show.

"Daddy, come on!" Heather shouted at Jim, her hands on the hood. He shook his head from inside the car, revving the engine as though he'd actually do anything with her standing there.

Sam stepped through the madness and made his way to the car saying, "I got this."

He knocked on Jim's window. At first, Jim wouldn't even look in Sam's direction, but eventually, he relented. The girls and their husbands looked on in awe as the two spoke.

Terry observed in reverence, "That dude has some balls."

"You're wasting your time," Heather tried to move things along, but Sam simply held one finger in the air at her, *hang on*. Before too long, the engine was off, and Jim was exiting the car.

A furor ran through the group until Heather voiced what they were all thinking, "The hell?" It would take a minute to collect their jaws from the ground.

Jim brushed past the group without a word. A satisfied Sam triumphantly trailed Jim, but Jenny recovered and stopped him.

"Hold on. What did you say to him?" she asked.

"He's not my first runner," he laughed.

"Let's go, Thane, I don't have all day," Jim called out to Sam from the house. "And I want that damned sign out of my yard before you leave here."

"Yes, sir, Mr. Phillips; right away, sir," Sam replied, continuing toward the house, but he turned back when Heather grabbed his arm. The group pleaded for an answer.

"Would you characterize your dad as cheap?" Sam asked.

The group hemmed and hawed; of course Jim was cheap, so much so that it begged the classic question *How cheap is he?*

"He got his panties in a wad when I told him he'd lose his deposit if he didn't close," Sam smirked and walked away. That was it. The thought of losing a few grand was enough to keep Jim in line.

"Yeah, that'll do it," Kevin said.

Jim popped back out of the front door and wagged a finger at Kevin and Terry, "And don't think I've forgotten about you two. Inspection in five."

Kevin and Terry looked to the Shelby then back to where Jim stood. They both ran to the car at the same time.

Jim returned to his sons-in-law, lining them up for inspection. He always reminded them of a drill sergeant, but he had never served. His father served in the great war and beyond, and he instilled respect and pride in ownership in Jim. It had left Jim with a great reverence for the structure of the military, the order of it all.

Terry and Kevin had checked and double checked to make sure Jim's pride and joy was spotless. They stood beside the car while Jim paced back and forth. For someone who hated attention, Jim had no qualms about making a scene.

Jenny shook her head and went inside, "You're ridiculous. I'm going inside to supervise the movers. Maybe you can help when you're done screwing around out here."

Jim took several passes around the car, inspecting every inch. Occasionally, he rubbed a spot on the paint, then shot a quick glance at the boys to keep them uneasy. It was all for show, but Jim was enjoying the theatrics. They fidgeted as the exercise dragged on. Jim got in and checked the odometer, then peered around the interior, checking the floorboards and the glove box. He got out and stepped in front of the boys—the "idiots." They were both taller and bigger than him, but neither was as imposing.

"Did you follow all posted speed limits?" His question was directed at Kevin.

"Yes, sir," Kevin said.

Jim stayed trained on Kevin. "High test gas?"

"Yes, sir," Kevin repeated.

Jim glanced at Terry, then back to Kevin. "No deviations?"

"Umm," Kevin hesitated. "No."

A crack in the resolve had caught Jim's attention, and he turned to Terry. "No deviations?"

"We, uhh," Terry squirmed.

He already knew the answer. Jim had placed a small GPS device under the passenger seat of his Shelby. He spent an unhealthy amount of time on the trip south staring at an application he'd installed on his cell phone that allowed him to monitor the exact position of his baby at all times. Yes, he knew exactly where they had been, when, and for how long, but he wanted to hear it from them.

Heather couldn't take any more. "They went to South of the Border and bought fireworks because they're man-children! OK,

Daddy? Can we go inside now?"

Jim stared at Heather for a moment; she'd ruined his fun. His big reveal. He turned his gaze to the boys. They grew increasingly uneasy the longer he didn't speak. It was a tactic Jim had used during interrogations. The two began to rattle off excuses, something about a waiver and road flares, but it was useless. It was really for safety; you see? Jim didn't want to hear a word of it.

Finally, he spoke. "Illegal fireworks?"

"Are they illegal?" Terry questioned.

Kevin shrugged. "I don't think so..."

Jim presented the boys with a longwinded diatribe about the dangers of unsupervised use of explosives, a soliloquy on how irresponsible it was of them as fathers of young children and the example they were setting for his grandchildren.

"You should know better," he concluded, turning his back on them. "They stay with me."

Heather rolled her eyes at her father and directed him inside. "Daddy, why don't you go help unpack so you can decide where things should go."

The boys hung their heads as Jim passed by. They were genuinely upset about disappointing their father-in-law, but more so about losing their fireworks.

"Ummm?" Terry mocked Kevin's answer.

"We, uhhh," Kevin mimicked Terry's response to Jim. "You could have backed me up!"

The two argued to the point of wrestling on the lawn before Heather threatened to turn the hose on them.

She led them inside by their ears. "*Idiots.*"

T HREE

Mike lived a simple life. His house looked a lot like Jim's. Same floor plan. Same tile. Same appointments. Some might call it cookie-cutter. But Mike's was lived in, not hard, but a single man had definitely been there for a while. The furniture was sparse, just enough to host a few friends, but the liquor cabinet was fully stocked. His small dining room table was littered with newspaper clippings. There was a clean plate and silverware set in the sink. Even though he had a dishwasher, he didn't really need to use it for just a single serving at a time. There were no personal photos or effects save for a small box on the top shelf of the master bedroom closet.

He laid his clothes out for his date. Dissatisfied, he replaced the shirt…twice. It wasn't the first time, nor would it be the last he would do this little dance. Every date with Beverly was important to him, but it had to appear as though everything was cool. That he was cool. So it was the blue Hawaiian shirt, the one that made his eyes pop and said *I'm here for a good time* but not *too* good of a time. It did have a collar, after all. Yes, that was the one.

It was dark already, but Jim and his kids had unpacked the whole house. The family shared a pizza and laughed about the silliness that had transpired throughout the day. The boys asked Jim for their fireworks back, a petition he instantly rejected. At the end of the day, the girls were happy their father moved to the state they lived in, mostly because they loved him but also so they could keep an eye on him. Well, mostly so they could keep an eye on him.

"Are you sure you guys don't want to spend the night?" Jim uncharacteristically offered. "Plenty of room."

Heather smiled sympathetically at her father. "Terry and I both have to work tomorrow. I think Kevin does, too."

Jenny handed Replacement Jim to Kevin, then sent the boys away so she could say goodbye to her father.

"It's only an hour drive, Daddy; you can come by anytime."

"No, no, it's fine. Just come back next week so we can pick out a burial plot," he quipped. He was kidding, of course. *Maybe.*

Jenny huffed at him, "Daddy!"

"What? You're dropping me off at my last stop," he pushed on. "Give it a few months. Coroner's going to be carting me out that door right behind you."

Jenny used her eyes to plead with Heather, mouthing the word *Help*!

Heather touched her father's arm and tilted her head a little. "You know you're going to be OK, right? This is what you and Mom wanted."

"Yeah, whatever," Jim brushed her off.

"Try to give it a chance, Daddy." Jenny was truly concerned now. "All you did back home was sit around feeling sorry for yourself. You can make friends here. It will be great!"

"I've already passed my expiration date. There's nothing left for me to do," he shrugged and looked around his new house. This was not a *home*. Not to Jim.

Heather grew frustrated, "Sixty is the new forty!"

"Heather, dear, you're so pretty, but math is not your strong suit." He was sincere this time. "I'll give it a chance, for your mother's sake."

"Not for her," Jenny said. "For you."

He agreed to give it a chance, and they said their goodbyes. The girls kissed him and left him standing alone in the doorway. As she got halfway to the SUV, Heather turned back to take one last parting shot at her father. "We're just going to cremate you anyway!"

Not to be outdone, Jim quipped back, "That's even better; you can take turns keeping me at your houses. I'll *always* be there with you!" He grinned and took a step back inside.

The girls looked at each other, then back to Jim, but he had already closed the door.

Jim was alone again. He took a deep breath and looked around his new house. It was full of his stuff, but it was empty. He wandered into the den and picked up a picture of Karen. "What have I gotten myself into?" He smiled at the picture. "Who am I kidding? You'd love it here."

He put the picture down and made himself a drink. A scotch, neat. As he sipped it, he peeked through the blinds at the street outside. He watched as a beautiful woman walked across the sidewalk in front of his house. She glanced in his direction briefly, giving Jim a clear depiction. She wasn't just beautiful, she was stunning, and from the way she carried herself, she knew it.

This was Beverly Stanton.

Jim felt guilty, but he couldn't look away. The heavenly creature floated straight across the front of his house toward his new neighbor, Mike. Jim watched her right up until they greeted each other in Mike's driveway. At that moment, Jim's drink and jaw both crashed to the floor.

FOUR

The night was blustery and wet. Most of the city was inside watching game five of the 2008 World Series. The Phillies were on the brink of clinching their first championship since 1980. Jim was surrounded by a cadre of officers with their attentions split between the game playing through the car radio and the wire recording everything transpiring inside the warehouse.

"It looks like this game is done for tonight folks," the radio announced. "Suspended due to inclement weather."

One officer leaned over to another behind Jim. "Wish we could suspend this raid due to inclement weather…"

"We'll be here all night if we have to." Jim's nostrils flared. "This scumbag has been in business twenty years too long. It ends tonight."

Within the walls of the crumbling building, a mishmash of street thugs and wise guys you might find at a movie audition with the header *Hired Goons* surrounded a tractor trailer. The pint-sized driver, Bennie, was jittery to the point he might piss himself at any second. He found himself searching for an explanation to a question that he really didn't want to answer.

Mike was pacing in front of Bennie, but Mike was different back then; he had more fire, more passion. He was a force to be reckoned with, a leader, the boss. Back then, he went by Mike O'Flaherty. He was the head of the O'Flaherty crime family.

And he was completely bald.

"Why am I here?" Mike stuck a gun in Bennie's face. "I was told thousands of Blu-Ray players. What is that? Four boxes?" Actually, it was an entire pallet, but that was beside the point. "When you came to us a few weeks ago, you said a truckload."

"Mr. O'Flaherty, I-I-I'm sorry," Bennie said. "There was supposed to be—"

Mike cut him off, waving the gun around as he spoke, adding to Bennie's terror as he tracked the weapon with his eyes. Mike leaned over with an exaggerated craning of his neck, "That don't look like a truckload to me. What do youse think?"

His thugs agreed. He leaned in closer to the driver. "You know, our beloved Phils are about to win the goddamn World Series. Where am I? In some shitty warehouse. This guy's probably not even a Phillies fan. What are ya? Braves fan? Don't tell me you're a Mets fan." Mike had to calm himself down. How absurd it would have been for this little weasel to be a Mets fan. "Look, I'm a reasonable guy, so I'm gonna take what you got here, but we gotta rough you up a little. You understand, right?"

Bennie fidgeted and mumbled into his shirt. Mike ripped Bennie's shirt open, revealing a tiny microphone taped to his chest. *A wire.* Mike knew his time was short, so he made the most of it.

"You set me up, you little shit!" He pummeled the defenseless truck driver.

Bennie cried out for help, and it arrived. The doors to the warehouse burst open, unleashing a flood of police officers, Jim leading the charge. Without hesitation, Jim tackled Mike off the terrified truck driver. "It's over, O'Flaherty!"

"Screw you, Phillips." Mike wiggled loose and grabbed his gun off the ground. He turned it on the truck driver, "If I'm going down, I'm taking him with me!"

"Just give it up; we got you." Jim and several other officers had their guns trained on Mike, but he was unwavering. "You know what, go ahead, shoot him. We'll put you away for even longer."

Bennie's eyes fired wide open, and he shook his head violently. "Please don't shoot him!"

"Fifteen years later," Mike laughed, turning his gun toward Jim. "You still think I killed your dirty partner—"

Jim was on top of him before he could get the thought out. He landed a few quick jabs to Mike's face, then reared back for a haymaker, but it wasn't to be. Jim's arms flailed fruitlessly as he was pulled away by three other policemen.

Mike wiped a smattering of blood from his mouth. "Don't worry, Jimmy boy. I'll never see the inside of a cell."

"Get off me!" Jim tried to break away, but couldn't. He huffed, "Asshole."

"Anybody got the score of the Phils game? Wait don't tell me, I got it recorded. I'll watch it later tonight," Mike smirked at Jim as he was led away in cuffs, "When I'm back home."

🌴

When Jim snapped back to reality, Mike and Beverly were gone. He shook his head. "You're losing it, Phillips."

F IVE

Jim spent most nights thinking into the wee hours and never really could turn his brain off. The only way to find sleep was to wear himself out, mentally or physically. The excitement of moving day had afforded him the ability to fall asleep easier than most nights, but it was far from a restful sleep.

*

On any given night, you might find five to ten cops at Curly's Pub, a dark, cramped South Philly hole in the wall. That night was different. Mike O'Flaherty had finally been taken down, and the majority of the force was there to celebrate.

Jim was the happiest anyone had ever seen him. Karen pointed out more than once that he hadn't been that happy on several momentous occasions in their lives, including their wedding night and the births of their children. She could point it out all she wanted, but the fact remained.

He'd gotten him.

Jim clanked a glass to bring the room to attention. He stood up on a barstool and looked around with satisfaction. Then, holding his glass high, he spoke. "Most of you know me as a mild-mannered, quiet guy—"

The room erupted in laughter at Jim's unintentional joke.

"OK, maybe that's not the best description. What I want to say is it's been fifteen years since we lost Frank Peterson. He was my best friend and a casualty of the war on organized crime in this city. When he died, it was a personal low in my life, but last night…last night, when we took down Michael Motherfucking O'Flaherty. We did it for Peterson!"

He forgot he was in mixed company. He didn't use language like that in his home life, but around the guys at the precinct, there really was no filter or decorum. That night was a mixture of work and personal, and Jim couldn't help himself, even on Karen's behalf. She grabbed Jim's arm and gave him a look for using such profanity, but he shrugged her off.

"This bust is the apex of a career devoted to taking down a notorious criminal, and it couldn't have happened without every one of you in this room…" He stopped and shook his head; he was choking up a little. "I just want to say thanks to all of you. For me and Frank. Erica, I still miss him every day."

Peterson's widow, Erica, nodded back to Jim.

He lost himself thinking about his old friend, how they came up on the beat together, shared a car, a poker table, and the majority of his good memories through the seventies and eighties. Their kids grew up together; even their wives were friends. It wasn't until Jim became a detective and left Frank in a uniform that they started to drift apart. Jim had always felt if he had been there that night, he would have been able to save him, that he could have changed things.

It weighed on him, and it was showing on his face as he still stood on that barstool, holding his drink in the air, contemplating. He had managed to swiftly bring the jubilation to somber reflection. Luckily for Jim, a television announcer bailed him out. The Phillies had just won the World Series, and all was right with the world. The room erupted in cheers and high-fives.

He was relieved the attention had been pulled away. "Perfect! I'll drink to that!"

He climbed down to a sea of cheers, handshakes, and back-pats. He tried to disappear into the crowd; maybe he and Karen could sneak out of there. He wasn't in the mood to party anymore. His captain, Kenneth Brown, had other ideas.

Captain Brown was the same age, but he was Jim's superior. A black man who rose through the ranks and played the type of political games Jim could never stomach, he was polished and smooth but still knew exactly how to fit in with his men. Right then, Jim was his main man. The captain grabbed Jim with a satisfied shake of his head. "Hell of a job, Phillips, turning that truck driver. We finally got him. Maybe you'll take that vacation now?"

"I don't need—" Jim tried to dodge the offer, but Karen stepped over his words.

"Yes, we're going to Florida," she said, raising an eyebrow at Jim. "Accommodations have already been arranged."

Captain Brown clapped. "Fantastic! With O'Flaherty out of the picture, I'm afraid this old fool will turn his attention to taking my job!"

"I don't want your damn job. Too much paperwork," Jim said.

"No desk could ever hold James Phillips," his captain proclaimed. "You two have a great trip, but make sure to bring him back. We're definitely not finished with him yet."

"I'll be back; I'm not finished yet." Jim winked at Captain Brown.

"Really? That's quite generous of you..." The captain was confused.

Jim raised his voice as he spoke, "Did you hear that, everyone? Next round is on the cap!"

A huge cheer erupted in the bar as Captain Brown feigned a smile. "On second thought, maybe you should stay in Florida."

The walls were lined with commendations, plaques, and photos of a smiling Captain Brown shaking hands with a who's who of Philly elite, the same schmoozing and political nonsense that had always prevented Jim from wanting to be anything more than a detective despite endless offers for promotion.

Jim slammed his fist hard on Captain Brown's desk, rattling the nameplate he was just a little bit too proud of. "No way! No goddamn way he walks!"

"It's not walking; it's witness protection," the captain said, trying to calm his irate detective as he repositioned the nameplate. "He has a lot of information. A lot of really bad guys are going—"

Jim gave exactly zero shits what his captain had to say. "Racketeering, extortion, murder! He is the bad guy! He should fry for everything he's done!"

"Jim, calm down. It's the best—"

No dice. Jim was finished conversing. "Forget it; I'm finished."

"Jim, we got O'Flaherty off the street..." his captain pleaded.

Jim shook his head and dropped his gun and badge on the captain's desk, dinging the expensive mahogany. "Save it. I never want hear to that name again."

The gash in the wood was deep and pulled the captain's attention long enough for Jim to escape. He was out the door before Captain Brown could process what had just happened. "Phillips! Jim, come on! Get back here!"

It was useless; Jim had already crammed himself into an overcrowded elevator and was on his way out. It was the last time he set foot in the building he had spent his entire adult life working in.

His dreams tortured him. He thought he'd left those times behind. They rarely crossed his mind anymore. So much had happened in his life since then that they felt like fragments of someone else's history. Like the television show you watched and can remember the vague outlines of the plot, pieces of the overall story, but you know you were never really there, that it hadn't happened to you.

But he was there. It did happen to him.

S IX

Mornings in Shady Place were alive. The secret was that it was still cool, especially in the summer months, when the blistering hot sun made it oppressive to be outside in the afternoon. It felt like someone standing on your chest, wringing out a wet towel all over you for good measure.

Whoever planned the streets in the neighborhood was either cruel or had a sense of humor. Every single street, way, drive, and lane started with the word Shady and ended with some tree name. Shady Pine, Shady Palm, Shady Elm, and so on and so on. But somewhere along the way, they must have run out of tree names, because for every street named Shady (fill in your favorite tree name), there was a way, a drive, a lane, and even the occasional place.

Jim found himself on Shady Oak Way, in house number 742.

Most days started the same for the residents of Shady Place. Wake up, take your pills, grab the newspaper, and drink your coffee. Lather, rinse, repeat. From there, they all headed off to their various daily activities. Whether it was golf, tennis, or even pickleball, everyone seemed to have somewhere to be or something to do. The streets bustled with walkers, golf carts, and landscapers. It seemed like there was always a landscaper working somewhere in the neighborhood.

Today, it was in front of Jim's house.

Jim had always been a light sleeper, ever vigilant, ready to jump at any moment, but he was not an early riser. His sweet spot was around nine in the morning. It gave him enough of a cushion to allow for the uneven bedtime schedule he kept while not wasting too much of the morning.

It was seven in the morning when the mower fired up in front of his house, and Jim had just found some semblance of peaceful sleep for the first time all night.

His first full day in Shady Place had begun with a start. His night had been so disjointed and stressful that all he wanted was a few more hours. He tried to go back to sleep, but the mowing persisted. Just when he was almost there, landscapers cruised by his bedroom window, treating him to the humming ticks of an edger getting those tight spots the mower can't reach along the exterior wall.

His loud exhalation indicated his sleep was over. It was for the best, anyway. If he had fallen back asleep, images of O'Flaherty were sure to dance through his miserable mind. He stumbled to the kitchen in just a pair of boxers and a white T-shirt. A nap would be in order later.

His ritual was much like everyone else's. He had an organized pill caddy right by the coffeemaker; a multivitamin, one for his cholesterol, an omega-3, and some flaxseed oil. He kept a few vials of B12 on hand because he had read somewhere that in your fifties, B12 deficiencies can begin to lead to dementia. A shot every few weeks would keep him in check. It was probably bunk, but the energy boost was a welcome side effect.

A simple stroll to pick up his newspaper from the street and it would be a day like any other back home in Philly. He thought things might not be so bad after all. Back home—he would always think of it that way now—the neighborhood had gotten younger around him. They all just left him to his own devices. Keep his head down, stay inside, life was fine, no one ever bothered him. A tried and true strategy he would try to employ in Shady Place.

He took a quick peek through the blinds in his den to confirm the landscapers had moved on from his house. He could see his newspaper waiting at the edge of the driveway. The articles were all available online, but there was something about the feel of newsprint on his fingers he just couldn't let go of.

He opened the front door cautiously. Upon first examination, the coast was clear. There were a handful of neighbors making their way down the street, but he was of no concern to them.

Perfect.

He quickly scooted toward the newspaper at the end of his driveway. He noted how nice his freshly cut lawn looked. It had better, with the monthly fees he was paying. At least he wouldn't have to mow it himself in this infernal heat. It was a big step for Jim relinquishing control over something that important in a man's life, a sign of growth, he told himself.

All he had to do was reach down and grab the paper, then head back inside. Simple. As he reached for his paper, someone offered him a greeting from over his shoulder. He tensed, but ignored it; maybe they'd think his hearing was bad. He lowered his head and moved back toward the house quickly.

The threshold was so close, he was in the clear, no one was going to stop him, but then he saw it. One last glance at his yard yielded a new perspective; something was out of place. He stopped dead in his tracks when he realized what exactly was resting in the middle of his otherwise perfectly manicured lawn. He dropped his paper and dashed to the spot.

"It's shit!" He had everyone's attention now. "Whose dog took a shit on my lawn?"

He scanned the area for the culprit but found only whispers and blank stares. This was unusual behavior for Shady Place to be sure.

"No one?"

Until that moment, he had managed to succeed in his quest to blend in and remain anonymous. But now Jim was turning red, frantically examining the confused faces. He was committed; there was no backing down.

Just a few feet from his yard was an unsuspecting young woman of about eighty, Ruthie, holding the leash of an absent-minded pug named Douglas, or Doug the Pug to his friends. Jim set his sights on Ruthie, but she had no idea why she had landed in Jim's crosshairs. Doug grunted like a little pig as he sniffed the ground around his owner.

Doug must have felt Jim's gaze, too, because he stopped grunting and made eye contact with the newest Shady Placer, the tip of his tongue poking out of his mouth.

"It was you, wasn't it?" Jim accused the unsuspecting creature.

Ruthie picked up her treasured pug as Jim closed in on them shouting at her, "You know, it is common decency—"

He was interrupted by a woman's voice. Strong, confident, and unwilling to tolerate this kind of behavior in her neighborhood, she shouted at Jim, "Mr. Phillips!"

When Jim turned around, he found Linda Stern standing before him with one hand on her hip and the other holding a stack of papers. She was in front of a golf cart in his driveway he was certain hadn't been there a moment ago. Maybe it was time for another B12 shot.

Jim sized up his next opponent. The tight bun on top of her head was paired with conservative attire, a shirt buttoned up to her neck, long pants, and a sweater. *How is she not melting?* Her face was attractive, but wore a scowl and played host to a pair of eyes that could melt a hole through steel. She would prove to be a worthy adversary.

"Yeah?" Jim asked.

Linda was unflappable. "A word please."

"After this lady gets her dog's crap off my lawn."

"Mr. Phillips, I am Linda Stern, with the HOA," she said.

Jim had yet to notice his quarry escaping. "Good, you can make her clean this shit up!"

"As you know, Shady Place is a CID. I've come to drop off the CC&Rs for the neighborhood. I'm sure Mr. Thane failed to do so; he always does. And also to…" she hesitated. "Welcome you to the community."

Sam hadn't given Jim anything; well, maybe he did. There was a pile of papers sitting on his kitchen counter Sam had left with him, saying something that sounded like *blah, blah, blah* to Jim's disinterested ears. They were, in fact, the rules and regulations for Shady Place.

"What? Lady, I have no idea what you just said to me. Was that even English?" He tried to return his attention to Ruthie, but she was gone. "Come on! You let her get away!"

Linda remained unwavering in her resolve. "Mr. Phillips, this is not how we behave in Shady Place."

The idea of making a comment about there not being a *we* crossed his mind, but instead, he went another tried and true route:

he unleashed a stone-cold stare, slowly narrowing his eyes as time passed. Linda's reaction was not what Jim anticipated. She didn't flinch; instead, she narrowed her own gaze in return, until the two of them appeared to be squinting at each other.

A worthy adversary, indeed.

After an awkward moment of silence, Jim wrestled the paperwork from her hand. "Do your job and keep the dog shit off my lawn."

He spun away without another word, showing her his backside on the way to his door.

She was unamused. "This is not an auspicious start to your time in Shady Place. I'll be keeping an eye on you, Mr. Phillips."

"You do that," he said, turning his doorknob.

"And Mr. Phillips," she called to him. He stopped but refused to look back. "Perhaps pants or a robe when you are outside your domicile."

Jim was still in his boxer shorts; he'd never meant to be outside that long. He mumbled to himself before disappearing inside.

Linda didn't make it to this part of the neighborhood that often, and one of her "favorite" residents happened to live next door to Jim. She found Beverly gardening on the side of her property. "Ms. Stanton, I trust you've stayed within the prescribed parameters of the permit you were granted?"

Beverly's garden was full of colorful and exotic flowers, many imported from other corners of the globe. She locked eyes with Linda from beneath a wide-brimmed straw hat. She carried a soft cockney accent. "You want to come measure, Linda?"

She did have a tape measurer in her golf cart, and there were regulations on the amount of square footage a resident could use as a garden. She hadn't written a fine in days, and Jim had put her on a particularly sharp edge, but she decided to let it go. "No, that will not be necessary…today."

Linda turned and left, but if she chose to return, Beverly had prepared a prominent hand gesture she was more than happy to let her measure.

Jim leaned his back against his front door. The ordeal had been far more than he'd anticipated for his first morning in Shady Place. It seemed silly to him that it all stemmed from a simple foray to pick up his newspaper. A newspaper he failed to retrieve.

He made his way to his den and considered a scotch, but decided it was too early to start drinking. Or was it? A knock at the door made him reconsider. There was only one person it could be, so he ignored it.

Knock, knock, knock.

It was persistent and annoying. It had to be her.

Jim threw the front door open brusquely as he said, "What now, Stern?"

It wasn't Stern, though. He found Jay Patel standing on his doorstep wearing a confused half-smile. He was holding Jim's paper. "No, sorry, not Stern."

Jim tried to look past Jay, narrowing his eyes as bystanders pointed and whispered to each other. "Why are you knocking on my door like that? Didn't you get the hint when I wasn't answering?"

"I am sorry," Jay replied. His intentions were pure. "Some of the residents cannot hear very well. Are you mister James Phillips?"

"It's Jim; what's this? Is that my paper?"

"I am Sanjay Patel, but everyone calls me Jay," he said, extending a hand for Jim to shake.

Jim reluctantly accepted the offer, enveloping Jay's with a grip that was so strong, it caused the smaller man to wince in pain. Jay's voice had risen to a higher octave when he said, "Your realtor, Sam Thane, set up a community tour for this morning. Are you ready?"

"What? Community tour? No, I just want to be left the hell alone!" Jim said.

Jay tended to wear his emotions on his face. He was clearly distraught and not sure what to do. No one had ever turned down the tour before. He mustered a soft, "My apologies." Then he reached into his pocket and pulled out a business card that simply read: Sanjay "Jay" Patel, with his phone number. He handed it to Jim. "If you change your mind, you can call me."

Jay walked away, but Jim called him back. "Hey wait, Patel! Do you know who lives in that house right there?"

Jim was pointing at Mike's house. Jay nodded, excited to oblige. "That house belongs to Mike…"

For that brief moment, time slowed down for Jim. He knew what the next few syllables out of Jay's mouth had to be…

O'Flaherty. It was him. He was there in Shady Place.

Right. Next. Door.

"…Johnson. He is a very nice man. I think you will like him."

Jim didn't listen past the word Johnson. That couldn't be right; he mumbled the name to himself in disbelief.

"Would you like me to introduce you?" Jay asked.

"No."

He closed the door without a word, leaving Jay standing alone on his walkway, confused and unsure. The door swung back

45

open, and Jim quickly moved toward Jay, who recoiled in fear until Jim snatched the newspaper from his hand.

"That's mine," Jim said as he went back inside.

SEVEN

Michael Patrick O'Flaherty spent the majority of his life in and around organized crime. His father was a second-generation Irish American who worked in a factory every day of his life after the age of fourteen. He was hardworking and respectable by all accounts, but Mike saw an angry man who drank and smoked himself to death, leaving Mike with no interest in what he considered to be a sucker's life.

He was the middle child of seven, which was only a consideration when he had done something wrong. His mother was cold and beaten down mentally. She didn't so much nurture her children as simply feed and clothe them. She handled the minor discipline but left the heavy lifting to his father. He was never concerned with making his father proud. His approval meant nothing.

Mike was proud to take the first few beatings for his association with what his father called the hoodlums. He knew the connection he made with them meant so much more than anything his own family could ever give him.

When Mike was sixteen, he left home and never looked back. He spent the seventies and eighties working his way up the ranks of the Donnaghy crime family in Philadelphia. And in 1987, when the boss, Anthony Donnaghy, mysteriously disappeared, Mike took the reins for himself. He was thirty-seven years old. No one questioned his ascension to the top; he was always meant to be there. There was nothing, *not one thing*, Mike missed about either one of his parents when they passed. He hadn't seen or spoken to either in decades.

He married a good-looking Germantown *jawn*, (jawn: (n): Philly slang for almost any person, place, or thing, assuming that person is female) and they had a couple of boys.

Those boys were Mike's pride and joy. He had five grandchildren between the two of them, and he loved them with every bit of his heart.

He was at the top of his game, had everything anyone could want, and never saw it coming.

Now that whole life, the money, the power, the family, was reduced to a few photos in a shoebox on the top shelf of his closet.

He tried not to ever look in the box. For Mike, Shady Place was his life. It was a good place to live. He loved it there; he had golf, he had parties, he even had a few friends. OK, he had a lot of friends. Mike was supposed to blend in, but he couldn't turn off who he was. He told himself no one was looking for him, anyway; it had been almost a decade, times had changed, no one cared anymore. Especially him; Mike had a date with Beverly that night.

They would go to some restaurant and chit-chat about this and that. Mostly benign trite conversations that were just filler between Beverly walking over to his house and them returning, usually for a "nightcap" at Beverly's. This had been going on for months. It didn't mean much to Beverly, but to Mike, it was a return to a time when he had someone and something to look forward to. She didn't ask about his past or who he was; she only cared about who he was now and what they were doing in that moment.

Mike liked the finer things in life, and Beverly was that; she was the most attractive woman in Shady Place. The guys had done a list (The List) ranking the most desirable women in the neighborhood, and she sat squarely at the top. Bonnie Park came in a close second, exotic, and even a lesbian, but it was Beverly's British accent that put her over the top. Naturally, Mike wanted the best, and right now he had her. Sort of.

Beverly arrived at Mike's to go on their date and greeted him as she always did, a squeeze and peck on the cheek. She always presented immaculately; hair, makeup, outfit, and accessories to match any occasion. Dinner and a movie were the order of the day, so a simple pair of hundred-dollar jeans and a designer T-shirt would suffice. Mike wore khaki pants and a button up Tommy Bahama shirt, a common pairing for a night out in Shady Place.

"Hello, darling," she said. "Shall we take your car or mine this evening?"

"Why don't we take mine," he said, leading her to his Cadillac. He held the door for her, chewing on an unlit cigar. He never brought his Twizzlers on a date; it just wouldn't be...*cool*.

Jim observed his neighbors from his den, peeking out through the blinds surreptitiously. He narrowed his eyes as Mike led Beverly to his car. He was convinced. The hairpiece was new, but that man was Michael O'Flaherty, right down to his stupid cigar.

It was clear now why he was going by Johnson. A quick Google search yielded the number for the closest US Marshal's office.

No one was in the office who could help him, so he left a number and a brief message: "I think there's someone in Shady Place who's in the program."

Beverly found herself sharing time with several suitors. The dates were all the same. They wined and dined her, but of course, no one wanted to go too crazy on their date; they were on fixed incomes, after all. Beverly fancied herself worthy of extravagance and spoiling, but her champagne tastes were generally met with beer budgets.

There was no shortage of offers. She was happy to take the meals and the company, and every once in a while, she'd even put out. The ever-popular "nightcap."

In general, this did not sit well with the other women in Shady Place. Even the married women labeled her the harlot. They feared the wandering eye of their husbands, but they didn't have anything to worry about. Beverly wasn't after any one man. She simply liked the companionship and enjoyed nice things; especially when someone else was buying.

Mike and Beverly had their date. A congenial dinner at a moderately priced restaurant. The latest action comedy starring that older, but not too old to be relevant, Hollywood star. Then back to Shady Place.

The nightcap.

Beverly did invite Mike in and the twenty minutes that followed were glorious. For him. For her, too, he supposed, but when the party was over, so was his invitation. She thanked him for a nice evening and sent him home. Like she did every time. She was always polite about it and smiling when she kicked him out, but somehow, it felt more like a kick in the nuts.

She sat in bed rubbing lotion on her hands watching him dress.

"Do you want to do something tomorrow night?" Mike put his pants on and straightened his hairpiece.

She gave him a condescending smile, verbally patting the puppy on the head. "Sorry, Michael, I've already got something on my schedule for tomorrow."

"Right, of course." He put his shoes on. "We're not exclusive or anything…"

"We've talked about this, Michael. It's like I said before, *it's nothing serious…*"

He knew the line. "*Just serious fun.* Got it. I'll see you… whenever."

He headed for the door, but she called him back. "Michael?"

"Yes?" He returned to her.

Good little puppy.

"Be a dear and turn the overhead light on, I'd like to read a little before I go sleep, and the switch is all the way by the door." She waited expectantly as he flipped the switch and walked out.

When Mike got home, he thought about his little shoebox on the top shelf of his closet but left it where it belonged. He poured himself a scotch and lit his cigar.

It was still a good night.

E IGHT

After he had a night to sleep on it, Jim decided he wouldn't turn Mike in to the marshals. Guys like Mike never changed; he had to be up to no good. There's no way he was just playing his days out in Shady Place. Not Mike O'Flaherty. So, Jim decided to do what any rational human being would do.

He would watch and wait. Then he would pounce.

Studies show that classical music can help an individual be productive. For Jim, it was a sedative. Instead, he preferred rock music, more specifically, heavy metal. The louder the better. A click of a button on his computer and his Spotify playlist was off and running. The shuffle setting meant he'd get everything from Motörhead to Slipknot in no particular order.

He spent the next few days watching out his front window. He sipped scotch and watched. Mike lived an unremarkable life. He spent a lot of time just standing around in front of his house, chewing on a licorice twist for some reason, while talking to Jay and Tommy or walking over to try to talk to Beverly.

Jim saw the jealousy in Mike's eyes when Beverly would go somewhere without him or someone stopped by to see her. He saw them leave on another date; she meant something to Mike. He would light up at the sight of her. This was of particular interest to Jim.

He jotted all his observations on Post-it notes and slapped them on the wall next to the window.

Jim watched so steadfastly that he was forgetting to eat, shave, or even bathe. It was what he did when he was obsessed. The walls of his den were covered with Post-it notes, but none of them had any significant meaning.

He couldn't go on that way for long. The only food and human interaction he had came from delivery people. Chinese, pizza, or pizza were his only options, so that's what he ate. Unfortunately, no one delivered scotch, so he switched to rum, clear, then dark, then on to the next, until all that was left was crème de menthe. That didn't last long, either. In Jim's defense, he didn't bring that much alcohol with him when he moved, but it was almost gone now, and he was no closer to exposing his archnemesis.

On the fourth day, it happened. Jim poured his last little bit of liquor; his last resort would be to move on to rubbing alcohol. Luckily, he caught a break. Through his shrouded window, he could see a black Escalade with darkly tinted windows, black rims, and virtually no identifying features roll into Mike's driveway. Some might call it murdered-out.

Jim knew this was it; he watched with so much intent, he was worried Mike could feel his eyes burning a hole into his very soul. The exchange was quick but unmistakable: Mike handed a small envelope into the Escalade and was returned a larger one.

"Gotcha," Jim said. He snapped a photo, checked his watch, and wrote on a Post-it note. The first break in his case.

🌴

While Jim cloistered himself, the strangest thing happened. Life in Shady Place went on.

At first, no one really noticed Jim's absence. They even began to forget the antics of his first day in the neighborhood. But Jim was so concentrated on Mike and what he was doing, he failed to notice that people began to point at his house and wonder.

Maybe it was the constant muffled shredding of electric guitars emanating from his den. Or maybe it was the one lonely newspaper in Jim's driveway that was soon joined by a friend, then another, and another. Or maybe it was a combination of the two that led the neighbors to start assuming the worst had happened inside 742 Shady Oak Way.

Maybe Jim Phillips was dead.

NINE

Everyone in Shady Place was a transplant. A few were from Florida, but most were from much greater distances. Sanjay "Jay" Patel hailed from a land much farther than most. A native of India, he'd made his way to America in search of freedom from the life that had made him quite wealthy and famous but left him bereft of the joy one might expect from a spectacular lifestyle.

In Jay's former life, he was world-class cricket player. He played at the highest level for both the Indian national team and Delhi in first-class competition for the Ranji Trophy. The trophies and medals in his house showed the remnants of the life he left home to escape. In America, no one recognized him, no one cared about cricket, and no one would judge him for being himself.

He spent most of his time trying to stay active. He golfed a little, played tennis and softball during the season, but pickleball was his passion. He became enamored with the game when he moved stateside.

Pickleball: a sport played on a badminton-sized court using a paddle and small plastic ball. A cross between ping-pong, tennis, and badminton, the game can be played in singles or doubles and has grown quite popular in recent years.

He was good at it, so good, in fact, he was ranked nationally. Jay fancied himself the best pickleball player in Shady Place, and the upcoming national tournament being held in the neighborhood would give him a chance to prove as much.

Jay's home was simple. When he left India, his cricket trophies, photos, and awards were the only possessions that followed him halfway around the world. He displayed the evidence of his athletic career proudly in a bedroom converted to a shrine to his former glory. The home was otherwise barren of any indication of the man he had been in his previous iteration. The minute he boarded a plane from Delhi to Miami through London, the native soil he'd called home for over fifty years was dismissed as a memory of another life.

The life he left was spotted with moments of triumph and failure. His sporting accolades found him in the public eye, known by millions, but the attention disagreed with Jay. The inability to blend in and live a quiet existence hounded him. No matter where he went, he fell under the scrutiny of an unwavering public eye.

He never took a wife, a fact that was noted frequently but easily brushed aside by an appearance at a major event with a popular model or Bollywood starlet on his arm. The truth was unacceptable; it was illegal, and it is why he left.

For all of the liberties and peace of mind his adopted home afforded, it was never as easy as live and let live or simply be yourself. There were always obstacles in life. Even so, over a decade in America had shown Jay a life he'd never dreamed possible; he was thankful for it every day.

Shady Place was alive with its usual buzz that morning. Passersby greeted Mike and Jay with the zeal so common to the natives. Like the rest, Mike and Jay had taken note of Jim's neglected newspapers as they chatted in front of Mike's house.

"Whatcha make of this?" Mike pointed to Jim's driveway.

Jay shrugged. "I do not know. I suppose something could have happened to him. He was quite rude to me when I tried to give him his tour."

"Someone should probably check on him, maybe call Stern or something," Mike said, chewing on a Twizzler.

Jay said, "I am sure Linda will find her way to him soon enough."

"I bet; that one's like a dog with a bone. She's wound so tight; I bet she's got a hidden wild streak," he said, winking at Jay. "Know what I mean?"

Jay nodded uncomfortably, "I do know what you mean. I do not know what kind of sexual predilections she may or may not have, however."

"It's like those ultra-conservative Republicans or super uptight churchies. Real polished and prim-like on the outside, then you get 'em alone at home, and bam," he slapped his fist into his palm, "out come the whips and chains!"

Mike laughed at himself. Jay did his best to mimic the excitement Mike had built up, but this really wasn't his sort of conversation, and Mike could tell. "How long you say Tommy's gonna be at that convention?"

Jay appreciated the change of subject matter. "He should be home tomorrow…" He paused and backtracked. "That is what he said, I think. Yes, tomorrow."

"Did you think anymore about what we talked about the other day? You know, people dyin' and all?" Mike asked.

Jay shook his head. "I did not think you were serious."

"Right, of course not," Mike said. "I'm goin' for a walk; I'll see you later."

Jay looked at his watch. "Yes, it is for the best I go. I have a pickleball match in thirty minutes."

All of the booze was gone. Jim had decided against the rubbing alcohol. Instead, he sobered up and cleared his mind with a nice hot shower. Jim watched Jay and Mike part ways. Mike was leaving on foot; a new behavior. The perfect opportunity to stalk his prey.

Mike walked at a brisk pace through the streets of Shady Place. It was the same everywhere you went, the inhabitants waving and smiling whether they knew you or not. Jim trailed at a safe distance, ducking behind a tree or parked car when he thought Mike might look back.

But Mike never looked back. He stayed true to his course, oblivious to the fact he was being observed. He moved forward with aplomb, certain no one knew or cared what he was up to. A For Sale sign marked his destination. It was already sold, Sam made sure nothing stayed available for long in Shady Place.

For the first time on his journey, Mike was uneasy; he warily glanced around before creeping around the side of the house.

Jim watched from a safe distance, snapping photos with his phone; a gentle clicking sounded with each shot. He quickly worked his way to the edge of the property for a better view. He paused before he got too close and used an oak tree for cover.

An old man hunched forward on a Rascal motorized scooter slid up next to Jim. "Whatcha lookin' at, son?" he asked.

A startled Jim whipped around, on guard, but there was nothing there, not until he diverted his eyeline down to find the old man. "I'm bird watching. Now beat it, or you'll scare them away!"

"Well, that's not very nice," the old man said as he scooted away.

Jim looked back in time to see Mike try to open various windows around the house. The third try was the charm; he took one last look around to make sure no one was watching before climbing through the window. Jim caught the whole thing, snapping a string of photos, including several action shots of Mike falling face first through the window. Those would stay in Jim's personal collection long after he took Mike down.

Mike poked around a small bathroom, looking inside the medicine cabinet, examining the bottles, and rummaging through drawers. Jim held his phone up to the open window and snapped a photo. *Click.* Mike jerked up at the sound, but there was nothing there. He stuck his head out of the window, but Jim had managed to dive behind some bushes. Mike waited an extended moment, scanning the area, but no one was there; he dipped back inside.

Jim flipped through the photos in his phone. Another nail in Mike's coffin. This was going to be easier than he thought.

He was labeling photos of Mike with notes like "breaking and entering?" and "extortion?" Click, print, label with a Post-it.

Heather's voice emanated from the speaker on Jim's phone. "Are you fitting in? Are you making any friends at all?"

"Huh? Yeah, it's just like old times, lots of friends," he said.

Heather replied, "Don't do that, Daddy. Don't be sarcastic."

"You promised to make an effort," Jenny joined in. "It's been a week; are you at least trying?"

"You need to get out and socialize. Go golf! Do something, anything!" Heather pleaded with her father.

He wasn't listening, though. He was tacking photos to his wall, building a case against O'Flaherty. But something outside caught his eye. It was a woman in his yard with a small dog...and it was shitting.

"Bitch!" Jim yelled as he banged on the window.

The girls were confused, offering a combination of "Excuse me?" And "Daddy!"

Jim grabbed the phone and darted for the door, "Not you, hold on."

He burst through his front door as the woman was leading her pooch away, "Hey! Hey, you! Lady!"

She spun around to meet him, stone-faced.

"You think it's OK for your dog to shit in my yard? Come pick this up!" He shouted, his face reddening.

She gave him a once-over, then flipped him the bird and continued on her way, leaving a stunned Jim in her wake.

Still on speakerphone, Heather asked, "What's happening?"

Jim recovered from his shock and took a step forward. "Get back here! You forgot your—" He looked down, realizing he had stepped in it. "Shit!"

The girls blared through the speaker in unison, "Daddy!"

Jim looked down at the phone in his hand, but it was the laughter coming from next door that drew his attention. Beverly was standing in her driveway trying to subdue her amusement. The crimson on Jim's face was for a different reason now.

"Those mutts are out of control; they just go wherever they like," she said.

"Who's that?" Jenny asked.

Heather chimed in, "She sounds pretty!"

"Girls, I'll call you back," Jim said into the phone. He disconnected the call and turned his attention to Beverly. "I must look ridiculous."

"You do," she said.

He extended a hand to her. "Jim, Jim Phillips."

"Beverly Stanton," she said. "You're the new old man everyone's been talking about."

Jim was confused. "Old man? I've got to be one of the youngest—"

She cut him off. "Age-wise, sure, but young or old is more of an attitude."

He huffed his disapproval.

"See? You have to be careful, or they'll start calling you Old Man Phillips!" she laughed.

"Maybe I am Old Man Phillips. Practically a step away from the grave as it is," he said.

She touched his arm. "Someone who is a step away from the grave wouldn't be out here yelling at old women to clean shite off their lawn. There's something left in there; you're fiery."

"Fiery? I like that," he said.

Beverly pointed to the newspapers in his driveway. "You should probably pick those up. People were starting to wonder if you were dead."

He looked at the pile of papers. "Oh, yeah. I've been...*busy*."

"Right, busy. Well, it will certainly be nice to have a big strong man next door, James."

He smiled at her; he was beaming. She returned a wink before turning to leave. She gyrated her hips, just for him, as she walked away, saying, "Don't forget to clean off your shoe!"

He rubbed his shoe into the ground vigorously.

Mike watched the whole exchange next door slack-jawed, his licorice slipping further and further from his mouth. Jay and Tommy were bickering at his side, arguing the merits of brand-name versus generic pharmaceuticals. Mike interrupted, "What did you say his name was?"

"Who?" Tommy asked.

Mike pointed next door.

Jay said, "Jim."

"Jim what?"

Jay responded, "Phillips."

Mike stared at Jim as he disappeared inside his house. He backed away from Jay and Tommy toward his garage, never averting his eyes, "I...will...uhh, see youse later."

He was backing away so quickly he nearly fell over a lawn chair in his garage. Before Jay or Tommy could respond, the garage door was closing. Soon afterward, all of the blinds around his house quickly slammed shut one after another.

Total lockdown.

Jay said, "That was strange."

"Ain't nothin' bout this place surprises me," Tommy said. "Hungry?"

Jay replied, "I could eat."

SHADY PLACE

Mike found the best vantage point he could inside his house. He stood in front of a set of closed blinds and took a deep breath, then separated the blinds with two fingers and peered out to the street.

How did he find me?

TEN

Jim and Mike didn't see much sunlight over the next few days.

Great care and diligence went into a vigilant watch from Jim's house. If Mike made a move, he would see it. But it had been days with no movement. Jim didn't know Mike had seen him, but he stayed the course. He had stocked up on groceries and booze, canceled his newspaper service, and created a new Spotify playlist. Maybe Mike had made a break for it in the middle of the night? Maybe he was onto Jim. But how? Regardless, Jim was prepared to hunker down.

Mike was ill prepared for a standoff, but that's where he found himself. He paced the house constantly, barely sleeping. His food supplies were dwindling rapidly. Tommy and Jay tried to visit him, but he refused to answer the door. The second time they visited, they could see him looking at them through the blinds, but he quickly disappeared.

"It has been two days, Mike. What is going on? Are you ill?" Jay asked.

"Go away," was his only response.

"The hell you doin' in there, man?" Tommy questioned.

The front door cracked a little, and Mike spoke to them through the opening. "Could youse get me some stuff from the store? I'll give you a hundred bucks each."

"Get it yourself, fool!" Tommy said.

"This is highly unusual, Mike. I think you should come outside," Jay said. "Perhaps we can all go to the store together?"

"Forget it." Mike closed and locked the door.

Tommy and Jay shrugged and left.

Jim watched with great interest from his holdfast. He found the scene peculiar. There was definitely something going on with Mike.

Mike slumped down at his dining room table. He was a mess. He hadn't slept, shaved, or bathed. His toupee lay discarded on the floor; even it was feeling the effects of the disruption to the normally scheduled programming.

When his phone rang, it startled Mike. *Beverly*. He'd forgotten about their date that night. The conversation was brief; he faked a cough and told her he was sick. They would have to go out another time.

When the call was over, he lost it. Tossing the phone aside, he screamed, "Shit!"

It would have pleased Jim to know the psychological damage he was causing Mike *O'Flaherty*, his nemesis. But he didn't know. He was just doing what he was trained to do: observe, collect data, and derive conclusions. Even while he prepared coffee in his kitchen, he could still see Mike's house. His resolve was unwavering; he could outlast any man, especially Michael O'Flaherty.

A knock at the door distracted him. He definitely wasn't expecting anyone. When he opened the door, he found Beverly standing there with a glowing smile.

"Old Man Phillips!" she said.

"Oh, come on, that's not fair."

She smiled. "I had dinner plans for this evening, but they fell through. I thought maybe you might want to join me instead?"

"Dinner?" he said. "With you?"

She made a show of how offended she was. "Wow, certainly not the reaction I was hoping for!"

"Sorry, sorry. That wasn't how I…" he fumbled for the right words. "Of course I'll go to dinner with you. When?"

"Now?" She pointed to his shirt. "Actually, you should clean yourself up a little first."

He looked at his filthy shirt. He hadn't changed it in two days. "Right, five minutes."

"Take ten!" she snarked.

*

Mike's head tracked Jim's car as he drove away with Beverly. He'd done it to himself. He smashed his fist against the wall and screamed in frustration, "Fuck!"

*

Dinner was awkward. Jim hadn't been on a date in over forty years, and it showed. He let Beverly do all the talking. A little about the weather, how good she was at tennis, how much she was looking forward to the next social, how much she absolutely loved the calamari at this restaurant but that was just the appetizer, she'd have to try something new for an entrée. He heard every word but wasn't really listening. There was only one thing on his mind.

"So, that guy, Johnson, on the other side of me, you know him well?"

Beverly was confused. She had only asked him if he was enjoying his time in Shady Place so far, but that was what he offered in return. "I've known him a few years."

"What do you know about him?" he asked.

"What do you mean?" she questioned.

"Where did he come from? What is he into?" He needled away further, "Have you seen him doing anything, you know, out of the ordinary?"

She shook her head at him. "Mike? You're asking about Mike?" She waved her hand in front of his face. "Right here." She pointed to herself.

"Sorry, I'm being rude," he admitted.

She asked, "Do you know him?"

"What? No, of course not!" He searched for an excuse. "How could I? I mean, I just like knowing who my neighbors are is all."

"I'm your neighbor," she said.

"You're right," he replied. "What do you know about Beverly? Where did she come from? What is she into?"

She rolled her eyes.

"Better?"

"Better," she said.

When they got back to the neighborhood, Jim walked Beverly to her door.

"Thanks," he said. "I needed that."

Beverly batted her eyelashes at him and unlocked her door. "Would you care to come inside for a nightcap?"

He was in. But Jim hadn't gotten the memo. "I'm actually going to turn in; I'm really tired."

He extended a hand to her, expecting a shake. In return, he received a blank stare and silence for an inordinately long time before laughter filled the night air.

"You're a strange duck, James," she said in disbelief.

He still didn't have a clue what he was passing up. She kissed him on the cheek and went inside.

*

Mike watched Jim and Beverly the best he could through the window in the side door of his garage. He squeezed a bottle of scotch with one hand and clenched his other fist tightly until he saw Jim walk away. Mike smiled and took a long swig of his scotch. Small victories.

*

Jim's first date in more than half his life was over, and he had survived, but the guilt kicked in as soon as he arrived home. He picked up the picture of Karen he kept on his desk and stared at it in silence. His eyes lowered away from the photo. It was taken on the last day everything was right.

*

They had to climb over a thicket of saw palmettos to get down to the beach, but it was worth it. The area was less traveled than most, and the dunes offered privacy from the street above. The sand was almost orange, shellier here than the other areas they had visited on their trip down the Florida coastline. Karen took her shoes off and left them at the edge of the palmettos.

"Come on; let's walk through the water!" she said, running to the sudsy shoreline.

Jim took off his shoes and followed, then turned back to their belongings. "You think our stuff is safe here?"

"Get over here; no one wants your ratty old shoes," she replied.

They held hands as they quietly strolled down the seaside. They were on the wrong coast for a glorious sunset over the water, but the waves were peaceful, and the salt air felt good on their skin.

"I really like that neighborhood," she said. "Shady Place. We could live there."

"Maybe, but I'd really like to shoot that idiot Realtor," he said. "You don't think I'm old, do you?"

She stopped and grabbed hold of his cheeks, then kissed his forehead. "I look at you, and I still see the same dumb kid I fell in love with all those years ago. Did you like it?"

"I actually did like it," he said, smiling a little. "You really think we could do this?"

"I know we can," she said. A tear began to roll down her cheek. "I want you to promise me that if something happens and I can't make it, you'll still come." She looked away after she said the words; she couldn't stand to see his face.

"What? Why wouldn't you?" he asked, then it hit him. "That phone call earlier; it was your doctor, wasn't it? What did he say?"

The words were soft, but poignant, and seemed to hang in the air forever. "Malignant brain tumor."

The last time Jim cried was when his mother had died. Before that, it was some schoolyard scrape, but that day, he couldn't stop the waterworks. He mumbled, pleading with Karen, the heavens, God, anyone who would listen. "There's a treatment. We'll beat it! Chemo, surgery, whatever is necessary..."

She turned back to him; he was on his knees now. He leaned his head against her stomach as he wept. She rubbed his head, trying to console him. She was going to have to be the strong one that day.

"We will see what can be done when we get home. We'll sit down with Dr. Young and figure it all out," she said. "But right now, I want you to stand up and look me in the eye." She forced him to his feet and wiped the tears from his eyes. "Promise me, no matter what happens, you will follow through and come back to this place, this paradise."

"But I can't," he said.

Unacceptable. She wasn't going to take less than affirmative; he had to say it for her. "No buts. Promise me."

"Not without you."

"Jim, you can always carry me with you, but you're going to have to let me go and move on with your life." She failed to reassure him but was insistent. "Now promise."

He frowned at her, but wouldn't speak. She didn't press any further, just asked him silently with her eyes to grant her this one small offering: *please.*

"I promise."

She buried her head in his chest, and they sobbed together. It might have been a minute. Maybe it was an hour. It could have been days. It didn't really matter at that point.

"Now what?" he whispered.

"I don't know," she said.

The answer was completely unsatisfactory for Jim. It was never an acceptable answer for the man who always had a plan. *I don't know.* It left too much uncertainty, but sometimes it was all you could say.

"I know," she said, pulling away from him to retrieve a digital camera from her pocket. "Take my picture."

His hand shook as he tried to hold the camera and focus on

his bride. She looked the same to him as she always had. She might as well have had a flower in her hair, like the day they met. Beautiful young lady, mother, bride, career woman, his everything. All at the same time.

He quivered as his finger depressed the shutter button.

Click.

🌴

He put the photo down and sighed, then poured himself a drink and tried not to feel guilty, or worse, sorry for himself, but that was out of the question.

ELEVEN

"A nightcap!" Jim slammed his hand down on his desk when it dawned on him.

He tilted his head back in disgust at his own ignorance. All he could do was laugh at himself. The thought of what he'd missed out on caused his mind to wander.

He sat down at his computer and typed in the search bar. He turned his picture of Karen away, then unbuttoned his pants. It was either that or a cold shower, and Jim didn't much care for cold showers.

The act was not one Jim was ever proud of, but he was still alive and still a man. He meandered his way through a sea of depravity until he settled on something somewhere between shameful and inappropriate.

As he clicked on images, several soft thuds sounded above his head. He tried to press through, but the sound persisted. The distraction was disrupting his rhythm, but he kept going.

⁂

Rolls of toilet paper soared through the darkness toward Jim's roof.

They were dressed in black. Hunched and twisted, there were two masculine and one slender feminine apparitions dancing like shadows in the moonlight. They didn't move very quickly, but they steadily tossed roll after roll until they were out. The leader nodded to one of the others. The subordinate retrieved a small paper bag from a nearby golf cart.

Jim's porch light revealed the figure of a man. Easily in his eighties, he placed the bag on Jim's doorstep. Looking back to his compatriots for encouragement, he lit the bag on fire, rang the doorbell, then ran to the golf cart. "Go, go, go!" he shouted.

The trio peeled out as much as an electric golf cart could, but only far enough away to be able to see what happened next.

Jim opened the front door to a flaming bag, "What the…"

The ghosts had failed to realize who they were dealing with. This wasn't the first flaming bag Jim had encountered on his doorstep. Within thirty seconds of opening his door, he had retreated inside, returned with a glass of water, and extinguished the flame.

"I know you're out there," he shouted into the darkness. "Show yourselves, punks!"

A strained voice shouted back from the darkness, "You shouldn't have yelled at Ruthie! The shitting isn't going to stop until you apologize!"

I knew it was on purpose, Jim thought, before addressing the shadows. "Apologize? Who the hell is Ruthie?"

"You yelled at her on the street!" the female apparition called to him, then hesitated and continued, trying to sound tough, "Asshole!"

The third figure chimed in. "And zip up your fly!"

Jim looked down; the constant thuds had interrupted his activity. In his haste to discover the source, he'd failed to batten down the hatches. Unashamed, he zipped up. "I'll show you an asshole! Stay here; I'm getting my gun."

He was gone again.

The figures whispered to each other, questioning how serious he was. He was bluffing for sure; he had to be, they agreed. When he returned brandishing a Glock 9mm, they changed their minds and turned tail. If they had been cartoons, a dust cloud resembling their shapes would have lingered in the space the trio vacated.

Jim stepped into his yard, holding a few lit firecrackers behind his back, and waved his gun in the air. "You know, Florida has a stand your ground law, and I'm feeling mighty threatened at the moment!"

He lobbed the fireworks toward the vandals and shouted, "That's what I thought! You better run!"

The fireworks exploded in the street, reflecting brightly in Jim's maniacal eyes.

Summer days in Florida are hot. During these hot days, water evaporates from the ground into the air. This is called water vapor. When the night comes and the air cools, the ground radiates heat into the air, but as the ground cools, the moisture in the air begins to fall back to the earth. The temperature at which this occurs is called the dew point. It's the phenomenon that leads to the wet look we are so accustomed to when waking up and stepping outside on a summer morning.

When Jim stepped outside for the first time the next morning, he witnessed firsthand the effects of the dew point. The toilet paper that so innocently covered the eaves and much of his roof had turned from a fine paper to a total gooey mess.

He stood atop a ladder, cursing under his breath as he scraped the sloppy globs into a bucket at his feet. He felt a slight burning sensation on the back his neck, but it wasn't until she spoke that he realized it was the rigid glare of Linda Stern below him, surveying the mess.

"Mr. Phillips," she said. "Unapproved decorations are a fineable offense in Shady Place."

The slow pace with which Jim turned to meet her gaze was only a minuscule indication of the rage boiling over inside him. He dropped a handful of slop to the ground and descended the ladder in full defense mode. "Oh, no, no, no. This was vandalism!"

"Vandalism? This is a respectable community. I assure you nothing of that sort occurs in Shady Place, Mr. Phillips. But you," she said, shaking her head at him in disapproval. "Firing a gun in the middle of the night? You are lucky no one was hurt."

Jim said, "They were only fireworks!"

"Nevertheless, Mr. Phillips, they are not allowed. Make sure you pay this on time, or the interest will accrue daily," she said, attempting to hand him a fine.

"Seriously? You're fining me?" he said incredulously.

She pointed to the date and the amount. "Yes, make sure to deliver it to the address listed below by the prescribed date. You can mail it or—"

He snatched the fine from her hand. "Yeah, yeah; give it to me. I can use it to wipe my ass since I seem to have used all of my toilet paper to decorate my house."

"Do as you must, Mr. Phillips," she said. "Good day."

She left him holding the fine. He was steaming, but his anger dissipated as his gaze followed her to her golf cart. He hadn't noticed before, but beneath the iron façade, she was actually quite fetching. Jim shook his head, recovering from the meandering thoughts, *Get hold of yourself, Phillips.*

A few extra bucks for overnight shipping meant the cameras Jim ordered got there quickly. He wasn't going to be caught off guard again. Wireless, night vision, motion sensors, all the bells and whistles. Jim went top of the line. He mounted cameras in every direction, eight of them in all; and of course, one pointed right at Mike's house.

Just like everything Jim did, the installation process caught the attention of his neighbors. Mostly, they watched from the street, whispering to each other. Only Beverly made a concerted effort to come check out what was going on.

"Beefing up security?" she asked.

Jim stopped turning a screwdriver and looked down from his perch. "Too much uninvited redecoration of my home. I'm sure Stern'll fine me for this, too."

"Redecorating? That's one way to look at it."

"Apparently, I yelled at someone named Ruthie," he said, turning back to his screw tightening. "Hey, look, I'm sorry. I didn't mean to cut our night short like that. I haven't, you know, dated in… well, a long time."

"It's OK; I get it," she said. "You just need to ease back into it; we'll try again soon."

He was glad she couldn't see how wide his grin was. "I'd like that."

"Looks like that one is pointed at my house," she observed.

"Well, yeah, I mean…"

"Don't worry; it's nice to know you're keeping an eye on me," she said before leaving.

He did have his eye on her. He watched her the entire way back to her door.

Mike hadn't ventured further than a few feet from his front door in days. He sat in a lawn chair in his garage nursing what was left of a bottle of scotch. He was finished feeling sorry for himself; enough was enough. He put down the scotch and rose to his feet.

"I can't live like this," he said out loud.

He went inside, showered, shaved, and generally cleaned up, all the while giving himself an internal pep talk. He gathered all the papers from his dining room table and placed them neatly in a folder.

Hiding in the dark for days had rendered his eyes no match for the bright Florida sun. His pupils needed a moment to adjust. When they did, he spotted Jim installing a camera on the front of his house. *What's next, a moat?*

He considered turning back before Jim saw him. The distance between them was less than thirty feet, but it felt like a cavernous divide. He played out a number of scenarios in his head:

Jim will respect him for coming over. *No, probably not.*

It's been so long, he probably forgot all about him. *Unlikely.*

He'll shoot him on sight. *He wouldn't. Would he?*

His instincts as a police officer will force him to help with investigating the murders. *Yeah, that's it; that's the one.*

That's what it took to get Mike to make the thousand-mile journey over thirty feet of grass, but when Jim turned around and spotted him halfway through the trek, time stood still.

Maybe he's over it, Mike said to himself.

It felt like the dolly zoom shot in *Vertigo*, when the camera dollied closer and zoomed back all at once. Jim dropped down from his ladder quickly, locked in on Mike. It was enough to stop Mike dead in his tracks.

The recognition was instantaneous. Jim calmly placed the screwdriver he was holding on the ladder and clenched his fist. Mike resumed his approach, slowly, but steadily toward Jim.

"Hey, Phillips," Mike said, hoping a friendly greeting would calm the beast.

It didn't.

"Hey, O'Flaherty. Nice hair!" Jim said. He then punched Mike squarely in the jaw, sending the papers scattering across the yard and his hairpiece off-kilter.

"Not over it," he mumbled to himself as he barely managed to stay on his feet. He rubbed his jaw. "It's Johnson now. Can we talk?"

"You know it would only take one call to the marshals, and you're gone," Jim said.

"I know; please don't! I'm begging you. Shady Place is my home! I don't want to leave!" Mike pleaded. "That's why I came to you."

Jim shrugged. "Maybe I already called them. Maybe they're on their way now. Or maybe I would rather have you right here, where I can keep an eye on you. That way, when you slip up, I can be the one to bring you down for good!"

Mike was surprised. "What? You already knew I was here?"

"Of course! I'm not an idiot; I have eyes," Jim said. "I'm going to bring you down. Leopards don't change their spots, and neither does scum like you."

"Is this still about Peterson?" Mike asked.

"Don't you say his name!" Jim clenched his fists tighter. "Mark my words, I will take you down for what you did. One way or another."

Mike was at a loss for words. He wanted to run, but all he

could do was hold his throbbing jaw and wait. He was convinced Jim would strike him again, flinching when Jim motioned to the ground.

"Get your shit off my lawn before I get another fine," Jim said, then turned and walked to his front door.

Mike gathered up the papers. "Wait, that's why I'm here, I need your help! I wanted to show you something; people are dying—"

"You're out of your damn mind if you think I'm helping you with anything," Jim cut him off, heading back to the house. He turned back for one last jab. "Oh, and fix your hair; you look like an idiot."

Mike gently touched his toupee as Jim slammed the door and was gone. Mike finished gathering his papers from the lawn and muttered to himself again, "Definitely not over it."

TWELVE

Jim calibrated his new cameras through a program on his computer, with nearly 360 degrees of monitoring around his castle. He even set it up to alert his phone if there was activity detected by one of his eyes in the sky.

This made it easier for Jim to try to create some semblance of a routine. His first step was to start running. It had been years since he'd even thought about working out, but after spending time with Beverly and examining his unattended gut in the mirror, he decided it might be time to lose a few pounds, get back into fighting shape.

He kept an eye on the street for a lull in the traffic, but it never seemed to come. Then around four o'clock in the afternoon, it seemed as though everyone had vanished. He threw on an old pair of sneakers, grabbed some headphones, and made his way outside.

You have to get loose, so Jim stretched. He made a pathetic attempt to touch his toes, but his hamstrings were too tight. He took turns pulling his feet up to his butt, grimacing with each pull. That was as good as it was going to get.

It was hot, and Jim was already starting to sweat, but he wanted to run when no one was around; now was that time. He plugged his headphones into his cell phone and hit play. Really loud. His playlist began blaring through the earbuds, and Jim nodded his head with the rhythm.

He was ready. *I'll start off slow*, he thought walking away from his house. He got about ten feet before Beverly pulled into her driveway and flagged him down. He pulled his headphones out, the music was still blaring, and causing Beverly to raise an eyebrow.

"What on earth are you listening to?" she asked.

He looked at his phone. "It's a random playlist; I think this one is Avenged Sevenfold."

"It's very loud, dear," she said.

"Gotta get pumped for my run," Jim explained.

She shook her head and replied, "You may want to wait a bit for a run; it's about to rain."

"Looks like blue skies to me," he said.

She smiled at him knowingly. "Don't say I didn't warn you, darling."

He shrugged and put his headphones back in before jogging off. He wasn't really ready to move that fast, but he wanted to impress Beverly, so he took up a quick pace. When he was sure she couldn't see him anymore, he slowed down and caught his breath.

The streets were empty. It was heaven. Jim was alone, enjoying a nice, peaceful jog. This was his time. After a few blocks, he found Sam putting the finishing touches on a new for sale sign. A For Sale by Owner sign was discarded in the yard nearby. Sam waved Jim over. "Hey, Mr. Phillips!"

Jim shook hands with Sam and greeted him. "So, this one was a for sale by owner?"

"It was, then I converted and got it sold. Only took three days to find a buyer. People should know better than to not use me!" he said.

"Seems like you're the only game in town," Jim noted.

"Only one that matters," Sam said, then he pointed to the sky. "You should start heading back home; it's going to rain soon."

"That's what people keep saying," Jim said. "All I see is clear skies."

"Florida in the summer," Sam observed. "Every day, mark it down. Haven't you noticed?"

Jim shrugged. "I'll be fine."

He started jogging away, and Sam called out to him from behind, "Call me when you're ready to sell. People would kill to get a house in here."

Jim gave him a thumbs-up over his shoulder and put his headphones back in. He was feeling the music. It was almost operatic, but with electric guitars and drums. If he hadn't been so preoccupied with watching Mike's house, he would have noticed that the rain did come every day like clockwork. So, when a loud thunderclap rang out, he was genuinely surprised.

Dark clouds rolled in quickly and the heavens opened up, unleashing a deluge Jim was certain would lead to a flash flood that would sweep him away. He stood there thinking about his next step. Luckily, no one was around to say I told you so.

A horn honked behind Jim; it was Sam. He rolled down a window and offered the wet rat a lifeline. Jim reluctantly climbed aboard.

"You should probably run in the morning," Sam remarked. "Or maybe a few hours after it rains so it can cool down. It gets really humid after one of these."

"I'll probably just get a treadmill," Jim said.

"You can always take advantage of the world-class gym," Sam offered.

Jim hoped not responding would allow them to ride in silence. Jim's favorite topic for discussion was nothing. But it wasn't Sam's; silence didn't suit him.

"You fitting in OK here?" he asked.

Jim sniggered. "Not exactly. People don't seem to like me much."

"I've heard the rumblings," Sam said. "I'm not sure why. You seem like a swell guy to me. I mean it, really; I think you're a neat fella."

Jim assumed Sam was making a weak attempt at humor, but let it slide. When they arrived at Jim's house, sheets of rain persisted in barraging the car.

"I think you just need to get out there and do things. Meet some new people. Join a club or maybe a sports league. Show them who Jim Phillips really is," Sam said.

Jim shook his head. "You sound like my daughters."

"Jim, I want to share a little something with you," he said. Jim was about to resist, but Sam just pressed on, shutting down any objections he might have had. "I had a really hard time a few years ago when the economy basically took a dump on this whole country. I got really low. I mean really low. You know who pulled me out?"

Jim opened his mouth to speak, but Sam cut him off again.

"The people of Shady Place. They helped me out, gave me odd jobs, cooked me meals, and one even became a silent partner in my business. If you open up to this neighborhood, it will take you in. It'll feel like…like your home. That's what we all want, isn't it?"

Jim dropped the resistance and took in what Sam said. He thought about it for a second, then resumed being Jim. "You sound like an advertisement."

Thane laughed. "Guess I just can't turn it off."

The rain slowed, then ceased as quickly as it had arrived.

"That's it?" Jim asked.

"That's it," Thane said.

Jim opened his door to get out. He turned back to Sam, wanting to thank him for the encouragement, but all that came out was, "Thanks for the ride." He closed the door and walked away.

"If you ever need anything, even to talk, just give me a call," Sam called to him from his car. "Especially if you decide to sell your house! Listings are getting so rare in here, people practically have to die for something to come on the market!"

Jim just waved a hand back over his shoulder. Sage words from such a young guy. Was he wiser than Jim at half his age? He shook it off in time for the humidity to hit him. It was like an elephant standing on his chest. He could barely breathe, so he retreated inside.

🌴

Before he showered, Jim took another peek through his blinds. Like a morning glory stretching its petals to the first light, Shady Place stretched its legs, shook off the storm, and returned to the bustling hive of activity that had disappeared such a short time ago.

THIRTEEN

Mike gave up on hiding from Jim. It was too much effort and too much of a headache, so he went about living his life. If Jim called the marshals, he called the marshals. They would probably just come get him and make him go live somewhere else. That was the worst-case scenario he told himself. So, life went on.

It was another glorious morning in Shady Place when Mike got up and inhaled a renewed breath. He rose from his bed, showered, shaved, and had a relaxed cup of coffee. Then he puttered around the house for a little while, waiting, until he got a brief phone call. He agreed to meet the caller in ten minutes on the golf course, by the bathroom between the ninth and tenth holes. He grabbed the envelope Jim had watched him receive from the black SUV only a few days before. He mounted and positioned his hairpiece, then headed out.

Mike fired up his golf cart and clicked for his garage door to open. The motor of a golf cart is more kitten than lion, closer to a lawn mower than a muscle car, but it got the job done in a neighborhood like Shady Place. As he backed it out of his garage, the obnoxious beeping of the E-Z-GO Backup Buzzer should have sounded, but Mike had followed the instructions of a YouTube video and disabled the vexing device.

Mike cruised through the neighborhood with a gentle breeze blowing through his toupee; he was always careful not to go too fast so it didn't jostle askew. He was happy to wave and greet everyone he passed; he really did love it there. Screw Jim Phillips, this was his neighborhood.

Jim's Shelby sat idling for hours that morning.

He had to turn the motion sensors off on his cameras; there was just too much activity. His phone never stopped buzzing from the automatic text updates he received. He could have sat inside his house staring at the screen, waiting, hoping for Mike to do something, but he wanted to go old school. A stakeout was in order.

He tried to leave the car off so as not to draw attention, but even in the morning, the heat was too unbearable, so he fired her up. Jim's car sounded more like a lion than a kitten.

He ducked down in the driver's seat and peeked over the steering wheel. He watched the morning walkers meander past his house, paying particular attention to anyone with a dog. It wasn't boring; he was observing.

He noticed the walkers came in waves. Often packs of two or three. The ones with dogs seemed to travel alone, but greeted everyone. Everyone was always greeting each other. Occasionally, a scooter or Rascal would whiz by, some granny and her geriatric pup squeezed into a too small basket on the front whipping past pedestrians with the meep meep of what passed for a horn as their only warning. But no one seemed to mind; everyone was friendly here.

It was just like Sam had told him. Open up to it, and it'll feel like your home.

It made Jim sick.

Every once in a while, a golf cart would zoom by, a bag of clubs attached firmly to the back. Jim considered the idea of calling for a tee time, maybe hitting the links, or even just going to the range to hit a bucket of balls. He used to love golf, it helped calm and distract him. His clubs were just sitting there in the garage, idle, unused for the better part of a decade. It was decided; once he ridded this place of his nemesis, the shithead, he would get back into golfing.

He was pretty deep into his train of thought when Mike's garage door opened and his golf cart backed out to the street. He hadn't considered the fact that Mike might have a golf cart, but he would make it work. He let the cart get a good head start; then he began his pursuit.

It had been a while, but Jim hadn't forgotten his training. Mike rode along peacefully in his golf cart a few hundred feet ahead, hugging the curb so cars could pass, completely unaware he was being tailed. Jim kept a perfect distance, slowing when Mike slowed, speeding up as he sped up. Synchronicity.

Behind him, cars were beginning to line up. He was doing fifteen in a thirty-five mile per hour zone. The drivers behind him were getting restless. Yes, they were older, and they drove slower, but this was too much for even them. They began to honk, so Jim waved them on, *just go around!*

He was worried the honking would grab Mike's attention, but it didn't. He just kept moving forward, completely oblivious of Jim's pursuit. A '75 metallic brown Lincoln Continental crept up next to Jim. The driver, a man in his late eighties, was pressed up against the steering wheel. He was barely able to see in front of him, probably why the car was in pristine condition except for the front and rear bumpers, which had obviously been used to gauge how close he was to other objects. He turned his head slowly to make eye contact with Jim, then shook his head in disappointment before continuing on ahead.

Jim couldn't help but laugh. Just ahead, Jim noticed Mike turn off on a cart path, somewhere he definitely couldn't follow. He got as close to the path as he could, parked his car on the street, and got out. Another horn sounded as a car passed Jim, the driver shouting out the window that he couldn't park there.

The path was lined with trees to separate houses and the different holes of the course from one another. This allowed Jim's clandestine activities to continue. He wove in and out of trees, trying to keep pace with Mike. He was in the shade, but it was hot. Really hot. The sweat began to pour as he maneuvered his way. He probably should have begun his new exercise regimen a little sooner, but he wouldn't be deterred.

Mike enjoyed the ride along the cart path; it was peaceful under the canopy of live oaks. They were old trees and protected in Florida. Everyone thought of palm trees, the sabal palm is the state tree, but the live oak, that was the one, big, strong, and best of all, it provided shade. Palm trees? Not so much.

The road ahead was forked; he veered to his right without hesitation and traveled a few more feet before parking in front of the sanctuary to those who traveled the greens of Shady Place. The ninth and a half hole as they called it. When he got there, another man was waiting for him. The man was hulking, easily six and a half feet, but he had a bum knee, so he hobbled slightly as he approached Mike. This was Ted.

Jim caught up and positioned himself just out of sight among the trees. He made sure the audio was off on his phone this time before he snapped a few photos of Mike and Ted shaking hands and exchanging pleasantries.

"I think you'll find this is what you were looking for," Mike said as he handed over the envelope.

Ted handed him a small wad of cash and said, "Thanks; sorry we couldn't meet at the house."

As soon as Mike accepted the cash, Jim sprang into action, "A-ha! I got you, you son of a bitch!"

Ted stumbled backward, clutching his chest.

"What the hell?" Mike said. "What are you doing, Phillips?"

"I got you!" Jim proclaimed. "What's in the envelope?" He looked to Ted, "Is he blackmailing you? Is he your bookie? Whatever it is, we'll get the police; don't worry!"

Ted dropped to his knees, breathing heavily, still holding his chest.

Mike rushed to Ted's side. "I think he's having a heart attack."

"Oh, get up; you're fine," Jim directed Ted before snatching the envelope.

"You're making a mistake," Mike said.

Jim examined the contents of the envelope. "Hamilton?"

"Theater tickets," Mike said.

Ted implored them for help. "Ambulance, please!"

"Surprise for his wife's birthday," Mike continued. He pulled out his cell phone and dialed.

All Jim could muster was, "Oh."

"You either need to back off," Mike said. "Or give me a hand here."

Realizing what he had done, Jim began to retreat, "Ummm, I uhhh, I was just…leaving." He began to walk down the cart path nonchalantly, then broke into a sprint as Mike spoke to the 911 dispatcher.

"This isn't over, O'Flaherty!" Jim shouted back over his shoulder. "I know you're up to something!"

When Jim reached his car, he was out of breath and sopping with sweat. He tried to play it cool, calmly sliding up to his driver's side door and casually dropping into the vehicle. When he started the engine, he noticed a piece of paper under one of his wipers.

Shady Place Security, Parking Violation, $125.

FOURTEEN

Once he was sure Ted was all right, Mike gathered the information he had put together about the deaths in Shady Place and headed straight for Jim's house.

He banged furiously on Jim's door, but there was no answer.

Jim was watching his computer monitor as Mike incessantly pounded. Even through the black and white image, he could tell the intruder was turning red. He reached into his desk drawer and put his hand on his Glock, but decided it wouldn't be necessary.

When Jim finally opened the door, he chomped into an apple to appear as nonchalant and disinterested as possible. Just another day, as though nothing had transpired a mere thirty minutes ago. "Yeah," he said. "What do you want?"

"What do I want?" Mike nearly forgot why he was so frustrated, "You almost killed my friend!"

Jim took another bite of his apple. "Did he die?"

Mike took a second to soak in Jim's utter disregard. "You can't just go around scaring people in here; don't you know where you are?"

"Got a point? Or you come here just to lecture me?" Jim asked.

"It's time for you to shut up and listen to me," Mike said, pointing a finger in Jim's face. "I know you hate me. I know you think I'm a criminal, but people are dyin' in here, and I need your help figurin' out why!"

Jim wasn't impressed; he simply took another bite of his apple and let Mike keep screaming.

"You do what you gotta, but I ain't hidin' anymore," Mike continued. "This is important; you need to look into it." He tried to hand Jim the folder, "It's all in there. Take it!"

Jim chewed his apple slowly for a moment, then snickered derisively and went back inside, closing the door behind him.

"Asshole!" Mike shouted at the closed door. He propped the folder against the door and turned to leave.

"Everything OK?" Beverly asked from her driveway.

Mike shook his head and shrugged. "Just peachy. Got plans tonight?"

"I do now."

Jim watched from his window as Mike and Beverly climbed into Mike's Cadillac. Seeing them together left him concerned. Beverly had just been on a date with him, one that ended with her inviting him in for a nightcap. Was she still seeing Mike? She must be; there they were climbing into his car, headed who knows where. Mike must have assumed Jim was watching because he offered him a one-fingered salute as he dipped into his Cadillac.

Jim wasn't sure why, but it wasn't sitting right. He and Beverly had only been on one date, but he felt possessive. How could she be going out with *him*. Jim liked to play scenarios out in his head; it had always helped in solving cases, but this time, he was considering the outcomes of Mike and Beverly's date. None of them ended in a manner he found acceptable. He decided in the end he really didn't care. Not at all. Why should he? She was an adult and could do what she wanted.

He didn't want to be here to begin with. What did he care what other people did? No, he didn't care one bit. *Keep your head down, Phillips.* He repeated his mantra and poured himself a glass of scotch.

Then he sat at his desk chair and stared at his security monitors.

It was the same restaurant she had just been to with Jim. She liked the salmon crab cakes there. A panko-crusted mixture of crab and salmon, with green onions, diced red peppers, wasabi dipping sauce, and a sprig of fresh cilantro. She had thought about it all day and probably would have gone even if Mike hadn't asked her out. But it was always better when someone else was willing to pay.

They sat at the same table and even had the same server, who asked her about being back again so soon, which she shook off with a smile and little giggle. That was usually enough to get any man to move on from a subject.

"Did you come here with Phillips?" Mike asked.

She changed the subject. "The salmon stuffed crab cakes are delicious here; I haven't been able to get them out of my head."

"What do you make of that guy? Did he say anything about me?" he asked her. "Somethin' don't seem right about him, you know?"

Déjà vu. She narrowed her eyes and stared him down for a second before responding, "Are you being serious? This is getting ridiculous; why don't you two just date each other?"

"What?" He was confused, "Why would we—"

She cut him off. "You know we aren't exclusive. Jealous is not a good color on you, Michael."

"You're right, as usual," he said. "One hundred percent right."

"Besides," she said as the server returned, "a little competition never hurt anyone."

The server was ready for drink orders, and Mike was quick to oblige. "Scotch, double."

Of course, Jim wasn't concerned at all. He didn't care enough to drink half a bottle of scotch or check his watch every ten minutes for the last two hours. He wasn't interested in what was going on outside the glow of his security monitors.

He hadn't actually moved from that spot since they left. His back felt it, too. He got up, stretched, and went to his front door for some fresh air. As he opened the door, Mike's folder slid down on top of his foot. The street was empty; most of the natives were no doubt nestled in their beds, recharging for their morning activities. The air was still and filled with blaring cicada songs that are prevalent on Florida summer nights. He breathed in the air, appreciating the calm. Maybe it wasn't so bad here.

He leaned down to pick up the folder but was quickly distracted by a small scattering of dog crap in the middle of his lawn. He couldn't believe he had somehow missed another assault. Before he could think too hard, the gleam of headlights approached. He snatched the folder and retreated inside, where he watched Beverly and Mike move the party inside her house.

He slapped the folder down on his desk. He sifted through a few pieces of paper on his desk until he found Jay's card. He punched the numbers in his cell and waited. "Patel, it's Phillips. I will take that tour of the neighborhood after all."

FIFTEEN

Jim spent a long time staring at a fresh pile of crap on his lawn. It was evident that it was intentional. The video evidence was inconclusive. It was almost as if someone was bringing fresh piles and tossing them on the lawn without even bringing a dog. His consternation grew with each new pile, but he had more pressing concerns.

"James," Beverly said as she sidled up next to him. She cocked her head at the feces and shook her head.

"Beverly," he returned.

"Dinner tomorrow night?" she asked.

He pointed to Mike, who was making his way to the end of his driveway to retrieve his newspaper. "What about shithead?"

"We're all adults here. I'm asking you to dinner; would you like to go or not?"

Mike stood in his driveway staring at the two of them. He was holding his newspaper sheepishly, desperate to know what their conversation was about.

"Sure," Jim said, raising his voice as he continued. "Dinner sounds wonderful. It's a date!"

He was nearly shouting by the time he finished the sentence. Beverly rolled her eyes, but she enjoyed pitting them against each other. Mike huffed and grumbled to himself as he headed inside.

"I'm off to tennis. I'll talk to you later," Beverly said, walking away. She turned back. "You really should go apologize to Ted; maybe you and Michael could go see him together?"

Jim prepared a rebuke, but Jay cruised up on his golf cart, allowing him to skirt the issue. Jay was pleading into his cell phone, but the person on the other end was not giving in. When he reached Jim, he rushed off the phone and tried to mask his frustration with a half-smile. "Hello, Jim, Beverly. Are you ready to go, Jim?"

He was, but Beverly wasn't going to let him go without one more poke. "Think about it, James."

Jay had a long canned speech about all the wondrous amenities Shady Place had to offer. It was as if someone had fitted the brochure with a speaker and it was regurgitating the details verbatim. Jim was half listening as Jay drove the cart and rambled on.

He hadn't said a word for ten minutes before he interrupted Jay. "What do you know about my neighbor, Johnson?" The emphasis on Johnson was somewhere between contempt and resentment. He loathed calling him that.

The question threw Jay off his routine. He spit out the last word on his mind, something about the fitness centers he was sure Jim would love to take advantage of. Then he asked, "Mike? Why do you ask about him?"

"He's my neighbor; just trying to find out what I can about him," Jim said. "How long have you known him?"

"A few years now. He is a very good guy. Very nice and helpful," Jay said. "I am certain he could get you anything you need. He is very resourceful. Not very good at pickleball. Speaking of pickleball, did you know we have a national pickleball tournament coming up soon in Shady Place? I am to compete; I am quite good."

"What? Pickleball? I don't even know what that is. Has O—" he caught himself on Mike's name and continued. "Johnson, Mike, ever done anything you find suspicious?"

Jay shrugged off the question. "Suspicious? Mike? No way." He then continued to pelt Jim with more than he ever wanted to know about pickleball.

Jim zoned back out, staring off into the distance toward the tennis courts they were approaching.

Shady Place had both men's and women's tennis leagues, divided generationally to maintain fair competition. Beverly was in a doubles league with a few of her "friends" from the neighborhood. They were more acquaintances than friends. Probably not even that. They didn't like Beverly. They felt like she hoarded men. She wasn't the only one who was single. Why couldn't she share?

The matches were usually relatively tame, more gossip than real competition, but it was good cardio and good to get out of the house. Sometimes, the verbal jabs sailed across the court faster than the balls. Beverly and her partner Tina squared off against Anne and Jeanette. Tina was a comely woman in her late fifties who would never pose a threat to Beverly on the dating front, but was in good enough shape that they always had a chance to win.

Anne was Filipina who had immigrated to this strange new land as a teenager in the seventies, with her American husband. She had quickly assimilated and excelled as a business owner. She moved to Shady Place when her husband died in 2009 and never looked back. Jeanette was married, but she hated her husband. She wished someone, anyone would whisk her off her feet and away from that useless sack of crap at her house. Maybe someday.

Beverly served. "Fifteen-love!"

She lobbed the ball gently and batted it softly enough for a return. They batted the ball around calmly a few times, and eventually, it dropped in for a point to Anne and Jeanette.

"So, Bev," Anne said, preparing for another serve from Beverly. "I heard you got a new hottie next door. Real live one. Maybe I go pay him a visit."

Beverly fired off another serve, this one with a bit more zip. Anne returned it, and the pairs began to smack the ball back and forth with more ferocity. Eventually, Beverly smacked the ball too hard, and it went out. She was visibly frustrated.

"Maybe I show him a good time; he like that, I think," Anne prodded.

Beverly tried to ignore her and prepared to serve, but Anne called out again while the ball was in midair, "Don't forget to call out score; you losing fifteen-thirty, Bev!"

Beverly let the ball fall to the ground, prompting more taunting from Anne. "That's a fault, Bev!"

Jeanette turned to Anne and said, "You're going to piss her off."

"I know," Anne replied.

Tina said, "Come on, Bev, we should be killing them."

"I know, Tina," Beverly said. "Get off my back."

"Maybe if you spent less time on your back and more on your game, you'd have a better chance," Jeanette added.

Tina laughed until Beverly shot her a death stare, and then she turned around sheepishly.

Beverly called out the score and served again. They batted the ball around a few times, Anne poking and prodding at Beverly with little digs until Beverly slammed home a point and let out a triumphant roar.

"That's thirty-thirty!" Beverly shouted.

"Hey, isn't that your new neighbor now?" Jeanette said, pointing to Jay and Jim approaching. Beverly and Jim made eye contact, and he waved. The whole group watched, with Beverly smirking and waving back.

Tina said, "Oh, he looks nice. Maybe I should ask him out! Is he married?"

"Don't waste your time," Beverly said. "He's mine."

"Hey Mr. New Guy, you come see me sometime, OK?" Anne called to Jim, but he didn't hear her as they zoomed by the tennis courts.

Beverly shrugged it off. "Why would he want chow mein when he can have London broil."

"She's not Chinese," Tina said. "She's Filipina. And why wouldn't he be interested in me? You're not the only single woman in Shady Place, you know."

Beverly ignored Tina, preparing to serve again, "Thirty-thirty."

Tina mumbled under her breath, but just loud enough for Beverly to hear, "Bitch."

With the ball still in the air, Beverly decided to redirect the trajectory on her serve. The result was a line drive right into the middle of Tina's back that sent her crumbling to the ground.

"Maybe you should spend less time on your back," Beverly said.

Tina rubbed her back. "I didn't even say it!"

"Oops," Beverly shrugged.

🌴

Jim looked back to the tennis court; the girls were gathering around Tina on the ground. He could see Beverly standing over her, reveling in the triumph.

"Pickleball is a cross between tennis and badminton," Jay said. "Perhaps a little like ping-pong. Do you have any questions?"

Jim hadn't been listening. "Huh?"

"You asked me about pickleball, and now I have told you all about it," Jay said. "It is quite exciting, no? Do you have any other questions about the game?"

"I didn't ask..." Jim shook his head. "I do have a question. Have you noticed anything strange going on in here?"

"How do you mean?" Jay asked.

"In Shady Place," Jim said. "Anything unusual, crime, maybe unexplained deaths?"

"You sound like Mike. You should definitely talk to him."

"Let's head back," Jim said.

Jay was confused. "But the tour is not complete."

"The tour is complete," Jim informed. "Take me home."

They rode in silence. Jim contemplated what he would do with his unseemly neighbor; then his mind drifted to his date with Beverly. His second chance for a first impression. Jay fidgeted, obviously wanting to say something to Jim, who tried to ignore Jay's squirming but it was filling his peripheral vision.

"You gotta piss or something?" Jim asked.

"Oh, funny. No, I...actually," Jay hesitated but decided to push on. "May I ask your opinion on something?"

Jay probably didn't want Jim's honest opinion, but Jim decided to be nice. "OK."

"What would you do if you loved someone and they definitely loved you, but they were too ashamed to tell anyone?" Jay asked.

"What are you going on about?" Jim asked.

They reached Jim's house, and he jumped off the cart before it even stopped. Jay was still speaking, but Jim was gone.

"Right, thanks for the tour," Jim said, halfway to his front door.

A dejected Jay cursed under his breath as he drove away.

SIXTEEN

A quick trip to the closest big box home improvement store for supplies was all Jim needed. A piece of plywood, a small pine post, and some paint. The tools: a circular saw, a hammer and nails, he already had. It would be a crude design, but it would serve its purpose.

As he worked away, Heather began to text him.

Hi, Daddy, what r u up 2?

He continued to work, stopping only to respond.

Hello, I am bludgeoning a singer.

What!?! R they that bad?

His fingers always seemed to mess up on the keypad of his phone; autocorrected messages were the norm.

Building a sign. I hate texting.

LOL. So, no singers are being harmed?

Not today, but I may go to the local theater later; I hear they are pretty bad.

They'd never admit it, but his daughters had inherited their sense of humor from their father. He knew he could joke with them and they would get it. Some people just didn't understand Jim's wit.

Oh, Daddy, u never change. Made u a tee time tomorrow at 10.

Shouldn't have.

Please go; have fun!

OK, for you.

Great. You need to come over soon. We have horse sex in the backyard.

It took Jim a moment to internalize the message. It was obviously another autocorrect. He hoped it was an autocorrect. Maybe their sense of humor wasn't the same? He thought about it, then did the only logical thing he could think of, and played along.

Just send a pic.

LOLOLOLOL, we got horseshoes! Damn autocorrect.

Wait, u want a pic of horse sex?

He laughed out loud this time.

He put the finishing touches on his project and slid his phone into his pocket. With the gentle push of a button, his garage door squealed open. He emerged holding his creation and a mallet.

Mike watched from a lawn chair in his driveway, Twizzler dangling from his lips, as Jim drove the sign into the grass in his front yard.

Jim stepped back to admire his handiwork, inspired by decades of no smoking signs sinking into his brain, or maybe because he fell asleep to *Ghostbusters* the night before. It was a crude cutout of a dog pooping nestled inside a red circle with a line diagonally bisecting the image.

Mike stepped over to get a better look. He chuckled so hard, his Twizzler fell out of his mouth. "You're going to get a fine," he said.

"Mind your own business," Jim replied.

Jim went out of his way to brush past Mike on his way back inside.

Jim cleaned up his workspace in the garage. It took less than five

103

minutes before the knock came at his front door. When he opened it, he found Linda Stern standing before him holding a piece of paper.

"You're kidding me," he said.

"Then you know why I'm here."

"Dog shit."

"Mr. Phillips, you cannot simply place a sign in your yard," she said. "There are forms. For an unapproved sign, you must request a variance at a homeowner's meeting."

She handed him the paper and he promptly crumbled it. "I'll be sure to fill this out."

"That, Mr. Phillips, is a fine," she continued. "Have you read any of the documents I gave you?"

The quietness was agonizing, but there was no way Jim was going to give in first this time. Who did this woman think she was. The silence remained so long, he considered giving in.

"It is a privilege to live in Shady Place, not a right," she said. "We have a three strikes policy, and that's two. Faster than anyone who has ever lived here, I might add."

He had already won the standoff, but he wanted to show his resolve. He gave her no response, only an empty gaze.

"Good day, Mr. Phillips. Be sure to pay those fines."

Mike stood by smugly watching Jim from next door. He couldn't wait for his chance to chime in, "Told you!"

Stern returned to her golf cart to leave just as Beverly emerged from inside her house. The two shared dirty looks while exchanging counterfeit salutations.

Beverly waved to Mike and Jim. "Hi, boys!"

They both smiled and waved back, then gave each other dirty looks.

Beverly timed backing her car out perfectly to narrowly avoid hitting Stern. It sent her careening off course, naturally, but not enough to do any damage. She cursed Beverly's name under her breath in a rare moment of lost composure.

As the two women made eye contact, Beverly lifted a knowing eyebrow at Stern. "Sorry, Linda."

Jim sat at his desk perusing the file Mike had left with him. A collection of newspaper clippings mostly, obituaries of fallen Shady Place residents. They were all men who had died in their sixties or seventies, but nothing seemed out of the ordinary. No shootings or stabbings, just natural causes. He wasn't seeing the connection or why O'Flaherty...Johnson was so worked up.

The day had been one gut check after another, but tomorrow would surely be better. A round of golf and dinner with Beverly. Beverly, just the thought of her made him smile. Yes, tomorrow would be a good day. He would forget about Mike, relax, play some golf, and go on a date.

But first, he would have to deal with whoever just knocked on his door. *It never stops*, he thought.

Jim was pleasantly surprised to find Beverly standing on his doorstep, but his smile quickly evaporated when Mike poked his head around the corner. He obviously didn't want to be there. This was Beverly's doing.

"What's this?" Jim asked.

Beverly took Mike's hand and reached for Jim's. "We are all going to see Ted."

"We?" Jim asked, refusing to give his hand.

"Yes, all three of us," she said. "We are going to see how he's doing, and you are going to apologize for giving that poor man a heart attack."

"I'm not going anywhere with him," Jim said.

"I told you," Mike crowed.

"Both of you shut up and come with me." She grabbed their hands and pulled them both to her golf cart. Any resistance and she was sure to have dragged them by something much more sensitive.

The ride wasn't long, but it seemed to last forever. The quiet wasn't so much awkward as it was excruciating. Beverly rode alone up front, having forced the boys to sit next to each other in the back. As children tend to do, they wrestled for leg room, each pushing the other silently back and forth with their knees in an attempt to gain just the slightest territorial advantage. Beverly watched in the rearview mirror but didn't interfere. Either she enjoyed stoking the embers of their rivalry or had some plan for them to work out their differences. Safe money was on the former.

It wasn't long after they reached Ted's house that his wife, Lisa, found herself squarely in front of Jim. "You think it's OK to just go around yelling at people?"

She was little in stature, but that was the only thing small about her. She boomed at Jim like a voice from the heavens laying a reckoning upon him. It took him by surprise. He struggled to get a word in, but this was his come to Jesus talk, and it was going to be a one-sided conversation. The words came at him like bullets from a machine gun, each one aimed right at his very core.

Do you know where we are? Half the people here have heart conditions! What do you have to say for yourself? Do you know how lucky you are he's OK? If anything had happened to him…

After every line she spoke, she paused as if she wanted a

response, but as soon as he opened his mouth to speak she'd fire off another round. Beverly and Mike tried to hide their amusement but were about to lose their shit over the torture Jim was enduring.

Finally, Lisa stopped. "Well, what do you have to say for yourself?" she asked.

"I…"

She waited as he mumbled his reply.

"I'm sorry."

"You damn well better be," she yelled, pointing down the hall. "But I don't know why you're telling me. Ted's down the hall. March!"

He lowered his head. "Yes, ma'am."

Beverly and Mike couldn't hold in their laughter anymore, but when Lisa turned her attention to them, eyes still burning with fiery hatred, they were muzzled immediately. She smiled gently and took on the demeanor one might expect from a pocket-sized woman of seventy.

"I'll get lemonade for everyone!" she chirped and fluttered away.

Jim slunk his way slowly into Ted's den. Ted was reclined in an old BarcaLounger, enjoying a World War II special on the History Channel. Jim hadn't yet made a sound when Beverly and Mike came in the room behind him. Mike cleared his throat loudly, causing Ted to spin his chair around.

"Mike! Beverly! What brings you by?" he said jovially. When he noticed Jim, his tone shifted to serious. "Phillips."

Beverly and Mike offered sentiments of concern over Ted's condition, but Jim was still hanging back guiltily. Beverly pulled him forward by his arm and nodded him toward Ted.

"Hey, so, Ted, I just wanted to…you know," he did the best aww, shucks, rub your foot in the ground, contrite act he could muster, "apologize for what happened the other day." He extended a hand to Ted.

Ted returned an unflinching narrow-eyed stare before smiling and shaking Jim's hand with vim and vigor. "It's OK," he shrugged it off. "It was actually just a panic attack. Doc says the ticker is strong; just a couple of days R and R, and I'll be good as new!"

"I think Jim's yelling days are behind him," Mike said, slapping Jim on the shoulder. Jim's sharp look told Mike it might be too early for such familiarity.

Ted nodded knowingly. "Got an earful of Lisa for your trouble; that should be enough to put anyone in line."

Lisa joined them with a tray full of lemonades. Four to be exact. "Lemonade!" she proclaimed. She passed out glasses. First to Ted, then Beverly, then Mike. Then she put the tray down and took a long swig of the fourth glass before turning to Jim. She released a loud, exaggerated ahhhhh before declaring, "None for you."

The group laughed, but Jim took it in stride and let them have their moment at his expense. He turned his attention to the television behind Ted.

"W W two," he said. "I love this one!"

Ted smiled. "Third time I've seen it; did you see the one on Iwo Jima last week?"

"One of my favorites!" Jim said with excitement. "I had it TiVoed, but I lost everything when I moved down here."

"Well, I have it recorded still if you want to watch," Ted offered.

"I'd love to!"

Beverly, Lisa, and Mike watched in awe at the blossoming bromance. Jim plopped down on a sofa near Ted.

"Jim, I think we should let Ted rest," Beverly said, trying to move Jim along.

Ted waved her off. "Really, I'm fine."

"Go ahead; I can walk home," Jim said.

"Did you know the US was the only country Germany officially declared war on?" Ted asked Jim, ignoring the rest of the group.

"Hell yeah," Jim agreed. "They're still regretting that one!"

"Bye?" Beverly said, positing more of a question than statement.

Jim nodded without turning back. "See ya."

Beverly and Mike weren't sure what to make of the situation, so they left in silence.

Jim and Ted immediately bonded. They were both former cops and obsessed with US military history. Ted told Jim about his time in the Army. He was a member of the 23rd Infantry Division, serving in Vietnam. Jim told him he was jealous that he'd actually missed the cutoff to serve during the war, so he went to the police academy instead. Ted assured him he was better off fighting the war on crime than spending time in actual war.

They talked, laughed, and enjoyed military documentaries until the sun went down. They never would have stopped if Lisa hadn't asked if Jim was going to join them for dinner. Jim politely declined, but the two agreed to hit the links when Ted was cleared by his doctor. Lisa took the opportunity to mock the two for making a play date and told them to kiss good-night.

"A real firecracker you've got there," Jim said. "No wonder you've got anxiety!"

In Ted, Jim had found something he hadn't had in a long time. A friend.

SEVENTEEN

It had been a long time since Jim last golfed. So long, in fact, he had to wipe a layer of dust from his clubs. He was looking forward to a quiet round. By himself. A few hacks and deep thought. A calm serenity.

When the course attendant told him he would be attached to a threesome of golfers that was awaiting his arrival at the first tee, it set Jim on the verge of throwing a tantrum.

It seems they were full. This was common, single golfers being placed into a group to move things along faster. Jim knew it, but it didn't stop him from wanting to cause a scene. He considered a snide remark, but a little voice inside his head that sounded eerily similar to Jenny's told him to be nice.

*

When Jim reached the first tee, he found a few familiar faces milling around, waiting for the rest of their foursome.

"Jim! Are you our fourth?" Jay asked.

"I only see three of us," Jim said, then he got his first good look at Tommy since reaching Shady Place. "You're Tommy Griffin!"

"I am," Tommy said.

"World champion boxer," Jim said.

Tommy nodded. "I was."

"What the hell are you doing here?" Jim asked.

Tommy responded, "Golfin', or at least tryin' to."

"Your fight in '74 against Haynesworth. That fourth round knockout; I was there, man," Jim said, faking a swing at Tommy. "Bam!"

"Hey, Phillips," Mike shouted as he approached on his golf cart. "Don't give the champ a flashback!"

The voice caused the hairs on the back of Jim's neck to shoot straight up. "You've gotta be kidding me!"

"You're late, Mike, as always," Tommy said. "Let's roll! Gotta move so we don't slow down play for everyone else. New guy first."

Jim shook his head. "I'm not playing with him."

"Come on, Jimbo; no need to be like that," Mike said. "He's just sore Beverly likes me better than him."

Jay and Tommy rolled their eyes knowingly at each other. Jay said, "Beverly has a way of turning men against one another. Please, let us play golf and not think about her."

Jim wanted to tell them exactly who Mike really was. *What* he really was. They wouldn't want to spend time with that low-grade thug. That *criminal.* He could tell them; he could ostracize Mike, even have him removed by the marshals, but that would be too easy. Too unsatisfying. He was lost in thought until Tommy tapped him on the shoulder.

"Whattaya say, Jim? Tee it up?"

Jim nodded and fetched a ball from his bag. He teed it up and lined up to swing.

"So, Jim," Tommy asked. "What's with that getup? Long pants? It's gotta be ninety-five out here."

Jim was the only man in the foursome wearing pants. The others were adorned in nice shorts. A course rule allowed them to, but not Jim; he wouldn't disrespect the game with shorts. Never mind the fact it originated in Scotland and was often played in a kilt. His misguided sense of purity simply wouldn't allow him to parade around the course with exposed legs.

"I'll be fine," Jim said.

"Maybe a hat, or some block," Tommy offered.

Jay added, "I've got an extra hat in my bag."

Jim stepped back from the tee. "I appreciate the doting mother act, fellas, but I'm good."

"Yeah, fellas," Mike stepped in. "He can make his own bed. Go on, buddy; let 'er rip."

And that was that. The group all teed off in succession. Jim's ball went the furthest and truest, but he was still disappointed; the shot was a good ten yards short of where he felt it should have landed.

Tommy and Jay rode together, and Mike patted the seat next to him in his cart for Jim to join.

"No way," Jim said.

"Come on; it'll be suspicious if you don't ride with me," Mike said.

"You're suspicious."

Mike grew frustrated with Jim's inflexibility. "Just put your shit aside for a few hours and golf. Do you really wanna walk in this heat?"

Jim sighed and climbed aboard. "We ride in silence."

"Whatever you say, boss."

⁂

It was like riding a bike. Over the first two holes, Jim demonstrated his prowess on the links, while the others showed why they had handicaps over fifteen.

By the time they reached the third hole, Jim was melting, sweat soaking his cotton shirt and pants.

"You hangin' in there, Jim?" Tommy asked.

Jim wiped away the moisture. "Two strokes up on you clowns. Worry about your own score."

Tommy shrugged. "I just try to shoot between my age and my weight. I ain't missed yet."

"That is why you remain so robust," Jay said.

"Robust?" Tommy asked.

Mike chimed in, "He's calling you fat."

"Look at the balls on the little Indian man," Jim said.

Jay patted Tommy on the belly. "He is a large pussycat. No balls necessary."

"You're lucky I don't hit girls," Tommy replied.

It went on like that at every hole, gentle jabs passed around the group. Jim appreciated the camaraderie but abstained for the most part.

Between holes, Mike and Jim generally rode in silence. It suited Jim, but Mike occasionally made an observation about something on the course or one of their shots the previous hole. The efforts were futile, though. Jim refused to engage. He simply trained his gaze forward, pining for the next stop to arrive.

It worked well for Jim until Mike found a way to draw him out.

"I'll make a deal with you," Mike said.

Jim snapped, "I don't make deals with criminals."

"So, you are listening," Mike crowed. "Just hear me out. You win, I'll never bother you again. I'll even leave the neighborhood if you tell me to. Hand to God. Call the marshals myself."

"Go on," Jim said.

"I win, you help me investigate the murders," Mike said.

Jim considered the offer. "What's the bet?"

"Simple; lowest score today," Mike said.

"I'm already up three on you," Jim replied, understandably skeptical. "What's the catch?"

"No catch."

They caught up to Jay and Tommy just in time for them to overhear Jim accept the bet. They shook on it. It was official, but they weren't going to get away with making a bet and not letting the group in on it.

"Y'all make a bet?" Tommy asked. "What's the stakes, boys?"

Jim wasn't sure how to respond, but it didn't matter, Mike was on top of it. "Worst score today's gotta streak at the next social. You in?"

Jim shot Mike an apprehensive look. All it earned him in return was a confident wink.

"Hell, no," Tommy said.

"I will not be participating in such a ridiculous display," Jay said. "I wish the best of luck to you both."

At the end of the fifth hole, Jim was already up five strokes. He was quick to announce the score after each hole and taunt Mike at every turn, but the humidity and the sheer intensity of the sun were beginning to show their effects on him. He leaked sweat from every pore in his body and began to show visible signs of physically breaking down.

By the eighth hole, he was ragged.

"You OK, Jim?" Tommy asked. "Startin' to look a little…red."

Jim waved him off. "Quit asking me that. A little heat never hurt anyone." He wiped his brow, preparing to swing.

"Your statement is fundamentally incorrect," Jay said as Jim drove the ball.

He shanked it miserably to the right of the fairway. Throwing his club down, he turned to Jay, barking, "Damn it, Patel! Don't you know not to talk during someone's backswing?"

"Easy, killer," Tommy stepped in.

Mike patted Jim on the back. "I believe that is called a hook."

Actually, it was a slice, but Jim wasn't about to acknowledge Mike. Doesn't matter what you call it, it was a bad shot.

By the time they reached the eleventh hole, Jim was glowing red from sun exposure. Sweat was pouring down his arms as he prepared to putt, and he wobbled a bit as he hit the ball. It should have been a layup, but the shot fell a foot short of the hole. He lined up another putt, this time pushing it past the hole. He huffed in disgust at himself.

"I think we're even," Mike said. He turned to Tommy and Jay. "Are we even?"

They nodded in agreement.

Jim tapped his ball in and brushed past Mike. "Seven more holes."

"You may want to call it a day, Jim," Jay said. "Your face is redder than a baboon's buttocks."

Tommy and Mike laughed.

But Jim? Jim was still not amused. "Very funny. Let's go."

"That was not a joke," Jay continued. "Both a baboon's buttocks and your face are very red."

Jim found no solace at the thirteenth hole. His breathing had slowed as he watched Mike drive a ball straight down the middle of the fairway. It wasn't a long or powerful shot, but it was all he needed. He turned to Jim to make sure he'd been looking. "We can call it if you want, Jimmy boy. You're down three and fading fast."

Mike had poked the bear. Jim pushed past him with a renewed vigor, a man on a mission. "Get out of my way," he commanded.

He didn't waste an ounce of the momentum he'd built moving from the cart to the tee box. He plopped his ball down quickly, lined up his shot, and drove the ball.

THWACK! A long, straight drive flew down the center of the fairway thirty yards past Mike's ball. Mike nodded to Jim in approval. Maybe the game wasn't over after all.

Jim headed straight back to the cart, but his knees buckled. He dropped like a sack of potatoes into Tommy's unsuspecting arms.

"Whoa, there. I got ya!" Tommy lowered him gently to the ground onto his back.

"I'm dying," Jim muttered weakly.

"You're overheated," Mike said.

"Pretty sure I'm dying," Jim countered.

"Jim, you must take a moment. Here is some water," Jay said, trying to hand him a bottle of liquid salvation. "You must have some fluids and cool down."

Jim tried to sit up and slapped the bottle out of Jay's hand. "I don't need any..."

He tried to stand, but the world went dark.

When Jim came to, he was in his bed with his shirt off. His arms, neck, and head glowed bright red. He found the foursome had moved to his bedroom, his fellow golfers surrounding his bedside.

"What the hell are you idiots doing in my house?" he asked.

Mike took charge. "You passed out on the course, tough guy."

"You probably drugged me," Jim said. "Had to cheat to win."

"You're ridiculous, Phillips," Tommy said.

Jay and Tommy were finished with Jim's irrational behavior. They weren't sure why Mike was trying so hard with this guy. With or without Mike, they were out of there.

"Are you coming, Mike?" Jay asked.

Mike let them go. "In a minute."

Jim could hear Jay trying to calm Tommy down as they exited his house. It turned out a doctor was in the group immediately behind theirs. He assured them that if they got Jim home and made him drink some water, he'd be fine. Tommy wanted to leave Jim on the course to fend for himself after his attitude all day, but Jay and Mike insisted on taking him home.

Once he was sure they were gone, Mike turned his attention to claiming his prize. "Looks like I won."

"We didn't finish," Jim said.

Mike was disappointed. "You gonna welsh on a bet?"

No. No, he wasn't. "I'm still going to find out what you are up to and put you where you belong. Behind bars."

Mike smiled. "Right; get some rest, buddy. I'll stop by tomorrow, and we can talk about starting our investigation."

Jim feigned a smile, but it disappeared the second Mike patted him on the arm. It was only a gentle pat, but the outline of his hand lingered for a second, creating a white space surrounded by fiery red flesh. For the first time, Jim realized how incredibly sunburned he was, and he failed to hold in a squeal of pain.

Satisfaction was plastered across Mike's face in the form of a smug smile. He left Jim alone to inspect the havoc the sun had wreaked on his body.

Mike called back from the front door, "You might want to pick up some aloe for that."

EIGHTEEN

Jim stood in his bathroom gawking at his shower. His torso was a most pristine alabaster next to the glowing burgundy of his arms and head. The thought of a cold shower was appealing and terrifying all at once. On one hand, he'd never been a fan; on the other, his skin was on fire.

The sensation of the frigid water soothed his burns but caused the rest of his body to retract. It was the oddest shower he'd ever taken. *Maybe a bath next time*, he thought, but he wasn't a bath person, always thought it was like marinating in your own juices.

A quick search on the Internet told Jim that lotion with aloe vera, some ibuprofen, and lots of water would be the simplest remedies for his first-degree burns. And rest, of course. But in Shady Place, rest never seemed to be an option for Jim. No sooner had he lay down on his sofa than there was a knock at the door.

This time, it was Beverly. She had her back to him when he opened the door and began speaking before turning to looking at him. "I wasn't sure you were home; your car's not—" She stopped speaking when she turned to Jim and saw his skin. She put her hand to her mouth in shock, then smirked a little. "What the hell happened to you?"

"Apparently, I should have worn sunscreen," he said.

"Apparently?" She gently touched his forehead. "You should be smarter than that, James. Do you still want to go on our date?"

His face told her he'd forgotten all about it.

Jim noticed Mike watching them from his driveway. Refusal would surely feel like a victory to his neighbor, and Jim couldn't have that, even if he did feel like someone had poured a vat of acid over his head. He assured Beverly he hadn't forgotten, he just needed to change clothes, and he'd be ready.

By the time Jim was ready, Sam had pulled his car over and was speaking with Mike and Beverly. As Jim approached, Sam stopped talking and turned his attention to Jim's radiant skin. "Holy shit, Jim, you have got to invest in a bottle of sunscreen, or I'll definitely be selling your house next!"

"Yeah, real funny," Jim groused. "Jim's got a sunburn, let's all laugh at Jim! How 'bout a little sympathy; these are first-degree burns, you know!"

Mike pulled out a cigar and held it close to Jim. "Think I could light this off you?"

Beverly playfully pushed Mike's arm. "Behave."

Jim pointed to a woman walking a dog across the street. The resemblance between the dog and Mike's hairpiece was striking. "Hey look, Johnson, isn't that your hair? It's trying to escape!"

Beverly and Sam shared a chuckle at Mike's expense, but Mike's toupee was a touchy subject for him. "I'll see you all later," he said, retreating with his tail between his legs.

Jim wasn't finished with him, however. "You're going to have to move faster than that; it's getting away!"

Mike flipped him off over his shoulder, then disappeared inside his house.

"You kids be good," Sam said. "I'm off to see how Ted's doing. Oh, and Jim, a little cornstarch will do wonders for that burn!"

Beverly picked the restaurant again, which was fine with Jim. He really didn't know anywhere in the area yet and didn't want to be the reason they had a bad date. Ever the gentleman, he pulled her chair out for her before taking his own.

They were quickly joined by an overly excited server.

"Good evening; my name is Matthew, and I'll be taking care of you tonight," he went into a finely rehearsed spiel but changed course as soon as he beheld Jim's burn. "Whoa, I was about to tell you about our lobster thermidor special tonight, but probably don't want to eat your own kind! Unless you're into cannibalism. You're not into cannibalism, are you?"

Beverly laughed.

Jim flushed, not that anyone could tell through his burns. "You little…"

"Jim, he's just teasing," Beverly chided, touching his arm gently.

"Sorry, I couldn't resist," Matthew continued. "But seriously, you're a little young to be practicing for your cremation already. OK, so you aren't really young…at all."

Jim was thoroughly confused. "Guess you don't really want a tip tonight?"

"Tip? You can have just the tip," Matthew said. "Want any more and you'll have to pay."

Jim tried to stand up, but Beverly motioned with her hands for him to stay put. "Please bring us a nice bottle of champagne. I'll talk to him," she instructed Matthew.

"OK, remember my name is Matthew," he said slowly. He

wrote it on a piece of paper and laid it on the table. "There, I wrote it down in case your sundowners start to flare up."

Jim's jaw dangled as Matthew left. "I want to see a manager; this is unacceptable."

"Relax. It's a theme restaurant; the waiters make fun of you the whole time," Beverly explained. "I thought it would be a hoot to see how you reacted."

"We're going to pay good money to be ridiculed?" he asked.

She pointed to the other tables, where the patrons were all laughing and joking with their servers. "It's fun, James! Lighten up!"

"We have drastically different ideas of fun," he said.

She nodded in Matthew's direction. "You should try to give it right back to him; they like it when you interact."

Matthew returned carrying a bottle of champagne. He made a scene of popping the cork. It was loud and fired across the restaurant as the foam ran over the edges and down the side of the bottle.

"Oops, a little premature," he said. "But I don't need to tell this guy about premature."

Beverly laughed, covering her mouth with her hand. Light caught a brilliantly glistening diamond bracelet on her wrist.

"Wow, nice bling," he said. "I'm not saying she's a gold digger, but...wait, yes I am."

Beverly was actually offended by the accusation; maybe it hit a little too close to home, "I bought this myself, young man." She turned to Jim and reassured him, "An investment paid off."

"Got her own money," Matthew nodded. "Make sure you put out for your sugar mama, pops."

Jim wanted to make a snappy comeback, but the whole thing had him caught so off guard, he couldn't formulate a coherent sentence.

"All kidding aside, I do have a special tonight," Matthew continued. "It's a pesto over pappardelle, or tongue pasta."

He winked at Jim on the word "tongue."

"Pesto is made with nuts, isn't it?" Beverly remarked.

Matthew confirmed, "Why, yes, it is…"

"What? You don't want nuts in your mouth?" Jim interrupted.

Matthew smirked at Jim, appreciating the attempt at humor.

Beverly did not, especially not at her expense. The look she shot him made his sunburn seem like a gentle tickle.

"It certainly looks like she doesn't want yours in there," Matthew noted.

"I'm allergic to nuts," Beverly said. "You were supposed to get him, not me!"

Matthew laughed at them.

"Oh, right," Jim said. He took an exaggerated look up and down the server's lanky body. "I'm assuming you don't want my nuts in your mouth, either?"

Too far. The table was silent and uneasy until Beverly decided it was time to move on. "I'll take the most expensive item on the menu, and he gets the check."

"But no nuts?" Matthew brought it back around.

"No nuts," she said.

Matthew turned to Jim. "And for you?"

"Bread is free, right?"

The rest of dinner went surprisingly well. Jim lightened up and took the gentle ribbing the server was dishing out. He was actually beginning to socialize with other human beings in an acceptable manner.

After dinner, Beverly helped Jim pick out a suitable lotion, with aloe, for his burns. When they got back to Jim's house, Mike was waiting for them in his driveway.

"That's one way to make sure nothing happens between us," Jim observed.

But that's not why he was there. Jim got out and opened Beverly's door for her. He tried to ignore Mike's presence, but he was bursting with something to tell them.

"Youse guys, I gotta tell you something!" Mike said.

"It can wait until tomorrow," Jim said.

Beverly agreed. "You'll have your turn, Michael."

Beverly's last comment didn't sit well with Jim, but she had made it perfectly clear where everyone stood. He tried to lead her to her door, but Mike persisted.

"Ted's dead!" he shouted.

Beverly and Jim stopped abruptly and turned back to him. It was clear from his face that he wasn't trying to shock them into paying attention to him.

"What?" Jim asked. "He was fine!"

"Oh, that's a shame," Beverly added. "He was such a dear man. What happened?"

"A heart attack," Mike said.

No one spoke. They stood in somber reflection until Mike broke the silence. "Jim, you got a minute? I got something I need to run by—"

Jim interrupted him. "We can talk tomorrow."

Whatever mood had been created by a pleasant evening was crushed by the weight of the revelation they'd been handed. Beverly's night was finished; she handed Jim over gracefully, "You boys go

commiserate over your fallen comrade. I'll talk to you two tomorrow."
She kissed Jim on the cheek. "Make sure you put that aloe on your
burns; it'll help."

They both watched her walk away; it was a sight they could
never get enough of, even in such a dour time. She turned back and left
them with a single, calculated comment. "I'll talk to *you* tomorrow."

They answered her in unison, both assuming she was talking
to them.

A moment of contemplation was in order. For once, Jim
didn't want to punch Mike. There were heavier concerns weighing on
his mind. He needed a drink, a scotch to wash away the preceding
moments that had destroyed an otherwise wonderful night.

"Sorry about your date," Mike said. *Not.* In his mind, he was
doing cartwheels. It wasn't the circumstances he would have chosen,
but he couldn't argue with the results. "Think you could come to my
house for a minute to talk?"

"Can it wait until tomorrow?" Jim asked.

Mike said, "Just come over; got a Macallan twenty-five I've
been saving."

A twenty-five-year-old scotch would do the trick.

"Let me take this inside; I'll be over in a few minutes," he
replied.

🌴

Jim gently rubbed lotion on his skin in front of his bathroom mirror.
The burn was tender to the touch and beginning to throb. He popped
a few ibuprofens in hopes of dulling the pain. He was closing his
medicine cabinet when an old prescription bottle caught his eye.

He took the pills to the kitchen and looked out of the window
toward Mike's house. The light in his garage was on, but he was out

of sight. He quickly ground the pills into a powder and neatly swept the resulting pile into a small Ziploc bag.

Jim was slowly nursing the healthy portion of the Macallan twenty-five Mike had poured him. It was delicious. He could have guzzled the whole bottle, but it wasn't meant for that. It was meant to be savored. Woody and smoky, with a citrusy fruit flavor; he swirled it slightly in his mouth before swallowing it down. A hint of cinnamon, too, he thought. *Delightful.*

Mike had been prattling on while Jim took in the flavors of the best scotch he'd ever tasted. It tickled his esophagus all the way down.

"Isn't this stuff like a thousand bucks a bottle?" he asked.

Mike threw his hands up. "What? Yeah, something like that. You been listenin' to me at all?"

"Honestly, no," Jim laughed. "Sorry, this is just…this is some scotch."

"Well, if you want any more, you're gonna have to talk to me here," Mike said.

Jim conceded. "OK, OK. Thought we were drinking to Ted."

"Exactly," Mike said in an aha moment. "Why we drinkin' to Ted? Because Ted's dead. And why's Ted dead?"

"Heart attack?"

"Heart attack! Now you see? It's what I was sayin' to you!" Mike was pacing. "Whoever killed him, they didn't know! They thought he had a heart attack the other day, but he didn't. You heard him; it was a panic attack!"

Jim shook his head in disbelief. "Hold on, you think someone killed Ted? He was in his seventies; maybe he did have a heart attack. I think you're connecting dots that aren't there."

"You said you would help me! I bet you haven't even looked at the stuff I gave you," Mike complained. "We made a deal, and now it's time to keep up your end. This was murder, and you gotta help me do somethin' about it!"

It pained him to do it, but Jim pounded the rest of his scotch. Still delicious. He pointed the glass at Mike. "Tomorrow. I'll take a look tomorrow."

"Tommy and Jay are coming over," Mike said. "You should hang around and have a drink to Ted's memory with us."

Jim pointed to the Macallan, enough of that might help the throbbing from the burn subside. He needed to hydrate. Scotch is a liquid. *Close enough.*

"Pour me another one of those?"

"Yeah, but I gotta put it away before they get here," Mike said. "Like you said, shit's expensive."

It wasn't long before Tommy arrived; he was just as surprised as Jim and Mike that Ted was gone, but didn't seem to think anything nefarious had occurred. At least he wasn't letting on if he did. He was, however, more than willing to join them for a drink in Ted's honor. The trio was about to toast Ted when Jay showed his face and, more importantly, his fancy footwear.

He arrived as he always did, on his golf cart, but this time, he was in a bathrobe. His feet were adorned with oversized fluffy, pink bunnies. They lit up with each step he took.

Tommy looked away as if he couldn't believe Jay had actually worn them out of the house. He was half asleep, zombie-walking his way to the others, each step accented by bunny eyes lighting up.

"What the hell is on your feet?" Mike asked.

Jay looked down and shrugged at his fuzzy slippers. "Oh, they are my Bright Bunnies." That was all he offered. They were his Bright Bunnies. No big deal.

"More please," Mike pressed for further explanation.

"There was a late-night commercial on TV Land. I was to send them to my family back in India, but when they arrived, I decided to keep them. They are perfect for the nighttime. I find I must urinate quite frequently after bedtime."

A sentiment they could all agree upon. His explanation was reasonable, but whether or not it was true, only Jay knew.

"Pink, though?" Jim asked.

The question elicited another shrug from Jay. They let it die and returned to the task at hand: drinking to Ted's memory. Mike poured everyone a shot from a less expensive bottle of scotch. They said a few thoughtful words, clinked glasses, and threw back a shot.

Jay scrunched his nose at the brown liquid. "Do you have anything that is not so harsh?"

Jim rolled his eyes; first, the pink bunnies, and now this.

"We're drinkin' to a real man; we're drinkin' a man's drink!" Mike said.

Tommy said, "It'll put hair on your chest!"

The comment hurt and confused Jay. Sometimes, he felt like he didn't quite get American humor, even after all these years. In his drowsy state, he wasn't sure how to take the gibe. He chose literal. "I have hair on my chest."

The group laughed at him, but he still wasn't sure if they were serious or not. Mike decided that deserved another shot. The others tried to wave him off and head out, but he wouldn't have it.

So they drank.

A lot.

Jay had relinquished his Bright Bunnies to Mike, who stomped around his garage in them playfully. Jay would have to buy another pair to guide any future late-night bathroom trips. He drank a lot more than he should have that night. Tommy was trying to slow him down and get him to go home, but Jay was in a form no one in Shady Place had ever seen him before.

"No, I do not want to go home!" he shouted at Tommy. "I am drinking a man's drink to a real man! I am fitting in! I will grow more hair on my chest!" He lifted his shirt, exposing a patchy clump of graying chest hair. "Is this not what you want of me?"

"OK, little man, you're drunk," Tommy said, wrangling Jay. "Time to go." He led a belligerent Jay toward his golf cart. "Goodnight, fellas. Say good-night, Jay."

"Good-night Jay," he said to the group, or maybe it was to himself. He had no idea how hackneyed the joke he'd just tried to land actually was.

Mike raised his glass to Tommy. "Be safe; don't forget you can still get a DUI on a golf cart!"

Jim and Mike were alone again. They stood in silence for a long moment before Jim said, "Look, O'Flaherty, sorry, Johnson, Mike. Maybe I've been a little hard on you."

Mike choked on the sip of scotch he had just taken. "Jim Phillips? No, can't be, who is this guy?"

Jim took his glass. "Yeah, yeah, I know, I'm a hard ass, unsympathetic whatever. One more drink, and then we'll call it a night." He turned his back on Mike to refill their glasses. "Tomorrow, we'll start our investigation." He dumped the contents of his Ziploc into Mike's drink and handed it to him.

"To Ted."

Mike eyed Jim suspiciously, then raised his glass. "Ted."

Clink. Drink.

NINETEEN

Being awakened by a bucket full of freezing cold water was a shock to Mike's system. Realizing he was tied to a chair and blindfolded was an entirely different kind of shock. His mouth was gagged, but that didn't stop him from trying to speak. All that came out was a muffled gurgle.

Maybe it's a drunken dream? A nightmare.

He thought about where he could be. The last thing he could remember. What was it? Drinking to Ted in the garage. Had they caught up to him? Was he about to get whacked? Not before a good torture; he was sure of it at this point. He struggled to loosen himself but to no avail.

"You're awake, good," Jim said from behind. "Now we can talk."

Mike again tried to speak, but the gag made it impossible. Jim removed the gag but left the blindfold intact.

"Phillips? What is this? Have you lost your mind?" Mike asked. He managed to maintain his cool but was visibly concerned. He couldn't see what Jim was doing but could hear him fiddling with something behind him.

"Interesting question," Jim snickered, spinning around with a syringe. He held it a few inches from Mike's face and lowered the blindfold.

Mike squinted, "What is that? What are you going to do?"

"Sodium thiopental," Jim said, flicking the needle in true super-villain fashion, complete with tiny discharge from the tip.

What the hell is he doing?!

Mike's eyes went wide. "You can't kill me!"

Jim smirked at him, leaned in, and whispered, "It's truth serum."

He rolled up Mike's sleeve and stabbed him in the arm, then depressed the plunger.

"You don't need that," Mike pled. "I'll tell you anything!"

"In a few minutes, you will…" Jim cocked his head, a shit-eating grin plastered on his face. He backed away and picked up a set of jumper cables connected to a car battery. They crackled and sparked every time he rubbed the ends together.

Mike was certain Jim had gone off the deep end. He was clearly crazy and going to do something they would both regret. He could scream, but it wouldn't do him any good. These homes were built too well. He knew they were in Jim's garage, and there was no clear path to escape.

He was completely at Jim's mercy.

It felt like the "truth serum" was kicking in. He didn't have anything to hide, but for some reason, Jim thought there was. It could have been the drugs, or the booze, or the whole icy bucket of water to the face, but he was woozy, and Jim was circling him like a shark.

Jim attempted to employ his tried and true interrogation method. Tried and failed. He was too amped up to wait in silence.

Instead, he pounced, firing questions at Mike in rapid succession. Mike did his best to keep up.

"How long have you been here?"

A little over two years.

"Why did they move you?"

I couldn't take the other places.

"Other places? How many?"

Three.

"What's going on with you and Beverly?"

We're dating, but she won't get serious.

"What makes you think people are dying in here?"

They are too young. I knew them; they were healthy!

"Why did you kill Frank Peterson?"

I didn't! I swear! Why don't you understand, it was Spitzer!

"Spitzer?"

Walter Spitzer, a loan shark. It was in my testimony...

Jim stepped back and turned away from Mike. He never thought about what the testimony may have revealed, what information Mike might have had to wrangle himself into witness protection. Up until he moved to Shady Place, he hadn't thought about any of it. He'd been too busy with Karen's illness and the subsequent self-pity.

"You never even looked at the testimony, did you?" Mike asked.

"Shut up." He didn't turn around.

Mike sensed an opening. "I'm not a killer, I was nowhere near clean, but I never killed no one."

Jim was fuming; he was at a loss for words as the thoughts flooded his mind.

"You ruined my life!" Mike continued. "I had a good, no, I had a great thing goin' back in Philly, and you took it away from me!"

"You were a criminal," Jim said softly, still looking away.

"Yeah, so what, I was," Mike said. "You were a cop. You took everything away from me. If I was gonna kill someone, it woulda been you. Pain in my ass then; pain in my ass now."

"Maybe I'll cut you loose, and we can see what happens," Jim offered, turning around to face Mike.

Mike shook his head. "I didn't want to kill you then, and I don't now."

"Could have fooled me that night in the warehouse."

Mike nodded in agreement. "That was not a good night for me, but listen to me, Jim. I hated you, you and your goddamned vendetta against me over some misunderstanding about your partner. You cost me my wife, my children...I ain't seen my grandkids since they were babies."

"Where's your wife?" Jim asked.

Mike wriggled his hands. "Maybe you could, you know, cut me loose, and we can talk like normal people."

"Just keep talking," Jim said. "What happened to your wife?"

"Gone. She split after our second stop, the one right before here. She didn't love me as much as the old lifestyle I guess." He wasn't guessing, actually. She told him as much. This life wasn't what she signed up for. The divorce papers were served before he even knew Shady Place existed. Her current whereabouts are the intellectual property of the US Marshal service. "What about yours? Couldn't handle retired Jim Phillips? You drive her away?"

"Don't you talk about her!"

He realized the only reason Jim would react that way is if the worst had happened. "Oh, I'm sorry, I didn't—"

"It's not fair, you here living as a free man!" Jim clenched his jaw and shook his head. "You don't deserve it..."

"You think I'm free?" Mike had nothing to hide. "I look over my shoulder every day of my life. I love Shady Place, but it's worse than prison." Jim's presence had reminded him of that fact more than ever. "I envy you, Phillips."

"You envy me?" Jim balked. "I must have given you too much."

"I do," Mike said. "You say and do what you want; you always have. You're unwavering. You got no idea how good you got it. I don't just envy you; I think I resent you. You could go back home anytime you want. Something I can't do."

"Home's not what it used to be," Jim conceded. He looked hard into Mike's eyes. They were pleading with him. If he was lying, he was the best liar Jim had ever met. "You killed Ted, didn't you?"

"Seriously?" Mike asked.

"Then who?"

Mike shook his head. "I don't know, but we can find out."

Jim cut Mike loose and ensured he understood what his fate would be if he told anyone what had just happened in Jim's garage. Then he said, "Come back tomorrow, and we'll get to work."

T WENTY

Jim never went to sleep the night before. He stayed up making notes on Post-its and placing them on various surfaces around his house. He didn't realize how long exactly he'd been at it, but when he realized daylight was beginning to sneak through his windows, he dialed his old captain.

When the voice mail picked up, he left a typical Jim Phillips message. "Cap, it's Phillips. Call me back."

He had called to verify Mike's claims, more to catch him in a lie and stick it in his face, but the answers to his questions would have to wait. He spent the previous night drinking with, then interrogating his neighbor. Completely rational and sane behavior.

He was sitting on his toilet. Not using it. Just sitting on it. He stared at a note he had just written, but it was gibberish. He had been awake so long, his own writing was starting to seem foreign. He looked around the room at the walls, the shower curtain; they were covered in Post-its with little fragments of information. Mostly disjointed thoughts. He was tired, starting to space out a bit, but his doorbell snapped him back to reality. He slapped the last scribbled note just below the light switch.

His walk to the front door reminded him how "productive" he'd been the night before. Notes lined the walls along the way from the bedroom to the front door. Everywhere he looked, he'd left some precious nugget of info.

When he opened his front door, he found Mike wide-eyed and bushy-tailed. He was looking around rapidly and fidgeting when Jim let him inside.

Jim pointed to the names of each of the "victims" Mike had identified. Each one had their own Post-it with their name, date, and address. They were in chronological order, wrapping around the room.

Mike was having a hard time standing still. He ran his fingers over each of the names. Every word he spoke came out rapid-fire; it was like he had to get them out quickly or he might lose them forever.

"What's with the Post-its?" Mike asked, pulling one off. "They're everywhere, man. Note, note, note." He pointed each time he said "note."

Jim seized the note from Mike. "It's my process. Don't touch." He placed it back where it belonged.

"Must work; you got me." Mike's mind was blown. "Oh, man, that's how youse caught me! No one ever caught me before you. You're so good!"

Jim chuckled to himself at Mike's behavior. "Tell me why you think these guys were murdered?"

"Oh, so many reasons." Mike kept up his breakneck pace. "They were healthy, active, so full of life! I knew them all! There's no way they all died so close together. It's suspicious, highly suspicious. It's suspicious, right? Don't ya think?"

Jim contemplated and shook his head. "I need more than that."

"OK, OK, OK. How 'bout four heart attacks?" He tapped six different notes on the wall. "Two slip and falls. A wrong medication? Insulin overdoses? Two of them! Who does that?" *Tap, tap, tap, tap.*

"These guys weren't clumsy mooks; they weren't careless. This is murder!"

Jim nodded along. "All men."

"Yes!" Mike shouted. "All men! All lived alone! Like us! Oh man, we could be next! You think we could be next? Oh god…"

Jim covered his eyes and rubbed his forehead. "Relax. They lived alone—that's opportunity. What's the motive?"

"Exactly! That's your job! You're the super-duper detective! The pit-bull, that's what we called you, you know?" He shook his head; he didn't know why he couldn't calm down. His heart was racing, and he couldn't stay still. "Sorry, I'm rambling, I don't know what's goin' on. I…I just got so much energy…"

Jim laughed. "Probably the shot I gave you."

"The sodium pe—truth serum?" Mike asked, twitching. "But why do I got so much energy?"

"Because it was B12. You were probably low. And I did give you a lot."

Mike scratched his head. "Huh? B12?!"

Jim wrote Ted's name on a Post-it and slapped it on the wall. "We should go see Lisa."

"That's a great idea!" Mike was still pumped up. "See this; this is why I came to you! I bet she will help bust the case wide open! When do you want to go? I'm ready now if you are!"

"Now is good." Jim looked Mike over. He had morphed into a flibbertigibbet overnight.

Jim had devised a perfect plan to help relieve some of Mike's extra energy. As Jim drove Mike's golf cart toward Ted and Lisa's house, Mike walked briskly alongside the cart, greeting everyone they passed along the way excitedly.

"She may not want to talk to us, but we need to see what she remembers while it's fresh in her mind," Jim said.

Mike was a little out of breath from trying to keep up with the pace Jim had gradually increased as they moved ahead. "OK... sounds...good..."

"One thing doesn't really connect, though," Jim said. "Ted doesn't fit the MO. He was married and lived with his wife. We may just be grasping at straws..."

Mike was jogging and gasping for air. He may have had more energy, but he was incredibly out of shape.

When they reached Ted and Lisa's, Sam was already planting a For Sale sign in the yard as movers emptied the house.

"Thane," Jim said. "What are you doing here?"

"Lisa didn't want to wait to list the house. Attorney called me this morning," Thane responded. He was more concerned about Mike, who was doubled over trying to catch his breath. "You don't look so good, Mike."

Jim waved off any concern for Mike. "He's fine. Is she in there?"

"Nope, attorney said she's not coming back, to just to send him the paperwork," Thane said. He pointed to Mike. "You sure he's OK?"

Mike was heaving, but managed a shaky thumbs-up. "I'm good!"

"Weren't you just here last night?" Jim asked Thane.

"It's really crazy. One minute I'm here, and Ted seems fine," Thane said. "The next, I'm getting a call from an attorney. They won't even give me a forwarding number or address for Lisa."

Mike leaned against the golf cart, beginning to catch his breath. "Crazy."

Jim considered Sam's words carefully before speaking. "I thought you were doing well. Don't you have someone to help you put up those signs?"

"Don't mind getting my hands a little dirty," Sam smirked. "I remember what it was like when times were lean. Wasn't so long ago."

O'Flaherty began to formulate ideas. He mumbled to himself under his breath, "Hands dirty…"

Jim was on the same page but didn't want to tip their hand to Sam. He stepped on Mike's foot to shut him up.

"Sign's just for show, anyway," Sam said proudly. "Got a contract coming in this afternoon."

Mike rubbed his foot. Jim had stomped on it a bit harder than he'd meant to. He wished Sam luck with the sale and drove the cart away. Mike looked back at Sam, while Jim eyed him in the rearview mirror.

"It's him; it has to be him," Mike exclaimed. "You see it too, right? I know you do. 'Hands dirty.' He practically confessed."

"He told me twice that people had to die in here for listings to come on the market," Jim said coldly.

"Boom! There ya go; we got him!"

Jim rubbed his neck as he contemplated. He forgot about his sunburn, and the touch stung. He tapped the steering wheel instead. "It makes sense, but—"

Mike interrupted him. "We gotta go to the cops; that's the next step, right?"

Jim shook his head. "We don't even have circumstantial evidence at this point. It seems too easy. I need to do some digging."

140

"Why don't we rough him up a little, make him talk?" Mike was frustrated.

"That's the kind of shit that got you here in the first place, *Johnson*," Jim pointed out. "We should see the coroner. Maybe he can tell us what happened to Ted."

They had reached Mike's house. He was still full of energy and ready to go. "Great, let's go!"

"Calm down, Skippy," Jim said. "I need to shower and eat something."

"Want some company?" Mike asked.

They both realized how it sounded as soon as the words came out. Neither said a word for a moment. They just looked around awkwardly, waiting for the other to say something.

"So, later then?" Mike said.

"Yeah, later," Jim concurred.

They never looked at each other. They simply parted ways. As quickly as humanly possible.

TWENTY-ONE

Jim once again found himself staring at a pile of excrement on his lawn. It was getting old. Really old.

"Hey, Jimbo." Mike strolled up to him, a fresh Twizzler hanging from his mouth. "Ready to go see Doctor Death?"

"Doctor Death?" Jim asked.

Mike shrugged, "Thought it sounded like a coroner."

"Canoe-maker," Jim said. "That's what we called them."

They took Jim's car to the medical examiner's office. Jim's hatred for Mike had dissipated over the past few days but was still eating at the back of his mind. He put on his best game face, deciding to keep it on a civil level. No more, no less. This made for an awkward car ride.

"So, why canoe-maker?" Mike asked.

Jim had already moved on, so the question took him by surprise. "Huh?"

Mike continued, "Said youse called them canoe-makers."

Jim nodded, *Oh, yeah*. He shrugged. "When they do an autopsy, they crack open the ribs, then remove the organs from inside the body one by one, examine them, weigh them, whatever they need to do."

He could tell Mike was disgusted. The big bad gangster was

squeamish? Jim found it amusing, so he continued, "What's left is a hollowed-out cavity. Just a body with a big, open space. You could climb right in, ride it down the creek if you wanted." He paused while Mike digested the image. "Canoe-maker."

"I'll stick to Doctor Death," Mike said.

Jim pointed at his Twizzler. "Intestines look a little like that licorice whip you got there."

Mike took the Twizzler out of his mouth and looked at it in disgust. He put it in Jim's cup holder and shuddered.

"What's with that, anyway?" Jim asked.

Mike pointed to the cigar resting in his shirt pocket. "Doc said no more stogies. Said they was killin' me. Heart attack, cancer, all that shit."

"Oh yeah?" Jim asked. "Want a light?"

"Ha, ha," Mike said, assuming Jim was joking. He knew he probably wasn't. He wasn't going to give up, though. When Jim made a joke like that, it showed him a crack. He'd wheedle him down until they were friends. All he needed was for Jim to buy in; then he'd be free to live in Shady Place forever.

All he needed was Jim to buy in—easier said than done.

They rode in silence the rest of the way to the coroner's office.

The office was a mess. The place looked like a bomb had gone off inside a filing cabinet. There were open files strewn about, empty food and beverage containers, and even surgical utensils. Jim insisted Mike let him do the talking.

So, Mike lay back and watched Jim work his magic.

The coroner presented as sloppily as his desk. He was halfway through a bag of Cheetos and a big gulp of Mountain Dew when Jim began questioning him. Even though it had been out for over five years, he was only part way through *A Dance with Dragons*, the most recent novel in the *Song of Fire and Ice* series on which his favorite show *Game of Thrones* was based.

"I need the report on Ted…" Jim stopped, realizing he didn't even know Ted's last name. "Theodore?" He turned to Mike for help.

"Williams."

"Ted Williams?" Jim said. "You sure?"

Mike nodded. The coroner cocked an eyebrow at Jim.

"The ballplayer?" he asked. "Isn't his head frozen somewhere or something?"

Jim didn't appreciate what he perceived to be a joke at his expense. "Don't mess with me. He died yesterday. Early seventies, white male. Supposedly a heart attack. Have you done the autopsy yet?"

"I'm not messing with you," the coroner responded. "I don't have to tell you anything, but I don't have anyone back there like that."

Jim pushed around some papers on the desk. "How would you know with all this shit everywhere?"

"Excuse me, sir, but I do know which dead people I have on my slab," he said, growing annoyed with Jim's brusqueness.

Mike whispered to Jim, "Maybe they took him somewhere else."

Jim had done his research; this was the only medical examiner in a fifty-mile radius. He should be here. Even if his body hadn't made it there yet, they had other names, names that had to have come through this office. Jim pulled out the list of names Mike had given him and slapped it down on the desk. "How about these people? They been on your slab?"

The coroner sighed. He looked at Jim and Mike standing

before him. This lobster-faced man was pestering him on his lunch break when all he wanted to do was read his book. "I can't give out any information if you aren't family or law enforcement."

Maybe he was a little rusty, but Jim was usually able to get information out of people a little easier than this. He pulled out his badge and dropped it on the desk.

The coroner leaned forward and examined it. "We aren't in Philadelphia. What else you got?"

Mike stepped in and took over the negotiation. "Can we talk for a minute? Just me and you."

The coroner closed his book. "I'm not going to get any more reading done, am I?"

Mike nodded for Jim to step away. He was confused and agitated, so stepping away probably was the best thing for Jim at that moment. He watched Mike and the coroner speak in hushed whispers. Occasionally, they motioned toward Jim, but the conversation seemed to mostly revolve around something on the desk.

Jim told himself it was the list, that Mike was pleading with him to look over the list, but would inevitably fail. Of course he would fail; there's no way Mike would succeed where Jim had flopped. Then something in the coroner's demeanor changed. Jim could see him mouth the word "really" multiple times, with Mike assuring him, "Yes, really."

And that was it. They called Jim back over, and the coroner took the list over to a file cabinet in the corner. He started pulling files and setting them aside.

Jim was an amalgamation of emotions in no particular order: confused, anxious, angry, and jealous. All that came out when he opened his mouth was, "What the hell?"

"We're good," Mike said, then winked at Jim.

We're good? Jim thought. *That's it? We're good!?* He needed more, "What did you promise him?"

Surely it was something illegal; that's why he wouldn't let Jim hear their conversation. He appreciated the plausible deniability of not being privy to the conversation, but it proved the theory he was the same old Mike.

Mike pointed at the desk. "See that book?" Jim nodded, and he continued, "Game of Thrones...I told him I could get him the sword from the TV show signed by the author of the books."

"You have that?" Jim asked.

Mike shook his head no; it was an empty promise, but it got the job done. Jim didn't agree with the practice, but the results were there, so he went with it.

The coroner returned to them with a stack of files. "You can look through them over there," he said, pointing at another desk covered in random office debris. He held out the files briefly but retracted them when Jim tried to take them. "You swear you've got it?"

"Of course," Mike said calmly.

The contents of the files were unsatisfactory. Jim flipped through each of the reports quickly, with Mike watching intently. He ran his finger across the information contained inside each file, setting them aside as he finished. After the fourth, he looked across the room at the coroner. He was oblivious, consumed by the tales of Westeros, but he could feel Jim's eyes on him.

Jim continued reviewing the files, showing an increasing amount of concern and frustration with each folder he set aside.

"Well?" Mike asked.

Jim just shook his head, then gathered the folders into a neat pile. He headed back to the coroner's desk and dropped them in the trash can at his feet.

"Hey, what are you doing, those are official records!" The coroner quickly retrieved the files.

"Who is your licensing body?" Jim asked.

"What?" The coroner was confused.

"Who is your licensing body? I'm assuming the Florida Board of Medicine?" Jim said.

Mike whispered to Jim again, "What are you doing?"

"What are you talking about? Why would you go to them?" The coroner asked. "I'm not sure what you think—"

Jim pointed at the files. "Did you even perform the autopsies? Did you even look the bodies over? Run toxicology? Anything?"

"What? Of course, I do them all the same." He stopped and opened a few of the files, then realized he'd been caught.

Jim tapped his finger on the files. "Every single one of these files was filled out exactly the same. Boxes are checked quickly and consecutively. There's no hesitation or passage of time in the checks on the boxes. Tell me you dictate and fill out later. Then we can go listen to the tape. You've got it, right?"

The coroner was embarrassed but tried to cover himself. "There was nothing suspicious about any of them, why should I have…Sometimes, maybe I'm not as thorough…" He hesitated, then continued, "What do you want from me? They were all old."

It was a bluff on Jim's part. He'd had a suspicion, and it was right.

"So what?" Jim asked. "You're a professional. You do your job; it's that simple. You're lucky I don't report you." He turned to Mike. "Let's get out of here."

Mike shook his head in disappointment at the coroner as he and Jim left.

"Hey wait, what about my sword?" The coroner called after them.

Mike spun around and wagged a finger at him. "No sword for you!" Then he immediately spun back around, and they were gone.

In the hallway, Jim asked, "Soup Nazi?"

Mike just smiled widely and pulled a new Twizzler out of his pocket.

TWENTY-TWO

Jim hoped they'd forgotten, that maybe the recent "bonding" he and Mike had done would get him off the hook. That wasn't the case. Not even close.

He wasn't surprised when the knock came, but he still tried to ignore it. Then his phone rang. Then text messages flooded the screen. Then there was a knock at his den window. The party had come to him, and it wasn't leaving until he opened the door.

When he did finally open the door, his stoop was packed. All his new friends were there waiting.

Mike was in his best tropical print shirt, but he wasn't chewing on a Twizzler. Tonight, it was a cigar. Still unlit, of course.

Jay was happy to let his body breathe more, donning white linen pants, a white linen shirt, and a pair of flip-flops.

Tommy kept it cool. He threw on the first clean collared shirt he could find and paired it with an old pair of blue jeans. Blue jeans weren't actually allowed at the clubhouse in Shady Place, but no one, not even Linda Stern, had ever said anything to Tommy, and they probably never would.

Then there was Beverly; when Jim let the group in, she was all he really noticed. She had squeezed herself into a tiny black dress, the kind that women had been using to get noticed for decades. The kind that kept the boys' jaws slacking away from their faces. The kind that had Jim speechless for once.

They had all been speaking for a while to each other and at Jim, but he wasn't responding.

"Well, James, are you going to just stand there?" Beverly asked jubilantly. "Or are you ready to go be social?"

"I believe your attire has rendered him unable to speak, Bev," Jay said. The group laughed at Jim's expense.

He snapped to, realizing he'd been staring. "Huh? What social? Is that tonight?" He faked a cough. "I think I'm coming down with something. Probably best if I wait until the next one."

"Oh no, you don't," Tommy said, grabbing Jim and pulling him out of the doorway. "Tonight's the night, sunshine. Throw on your party pants and let the good times roll."

"OK, OK!" Jim pulled away. "At least let me put some shoes on. Damn, what's the big deal…"

He continued muttering to himself as he turned back inside. He tried to close the door, but they wouldn't let him. He resigned himself to his fate; he would have to pay up on his bet with Mike.

The quintet crammed themselves onto Tommy's golf cart and headed off to the clubhouse. They had only made it a few feet before Tommy observed, "Kinda messed up, the black guy driving around all you honkies."

The group let out a sarcastic groan of disapproval.

"Just sayin' maybe y'all should buy me a few rounds," Tommy smirked.

They reminded him he was the one who insisted on driving, though they couldn't blame him for trying to garner some white guilt, but Jay wasn't in on the joke.

"What is a honky? I am not a honky?" he said genuinely confused. "Am I?"

"Close enough, little man," Tommy said, patting Jay on the back. "Close enough."

※

The clubhouse was packed. It felt like the whole neighborhood had turned out. He was convinced Mike had told everyone in Shady Place about their bet, and they all wanted their peek at the goods.

"Drink?" Mike asked Jim, patting him on the back.

Jim knew he couldn't get out of the bet, but he didn't have to fulfill his obligation sober. There was a sign posted by the bar:

One tequila, two tequila, three tequila, floor. Half off tequila shots.

It featured a graphic of a shot glass on its side. Tequila always did the trick for Jim, and it was half off.

"Tequila. Make it a double."

"Good man," Mike said.

Jay wrung his hands in anticipation. "I cannot wait to see this!"

Jim raised an eyebrow at Jay's excitement but quickly forgot about it when Mike handed him a tequila. Before Mike could take a sip of his drink, Jim had thrown his back and was sucking air through his teeth at the sting of the alcohol on his throat. Should have gotten a lime.

"Who's ready for some dancing?" Beverly asked.

Jim shook his head. "I don't dance."

"I do!" Mike said as he slapped Jim on the back then led Beverly to the crowded dance floor.

"Don't start the show without us!" Tommy said to Jim as he and Jay followed Mike and Beverly.

Jim made his way to the bar but trained his attention on the bustling crowd getting their groove on. The night's host was a live one-man band. He was set up with a laptop, a guitar, and an amp, playing all the best oldies the locals had grown up with. The songs that invoked memories of where they were when they'd first heard them. He strummed the melody while his laptop provided the percussion. As the night progressed and he had a few more drinks, the words changed; some would become mumbles and incoherent babble, but the crowd would always be into it, and the self-proclaimed Jazzman of Shady Place would definitely be taking home one of the lovely ladies in the crowd.

Jim soaked it all in, paying particular attention to Beverly and Mike swaying to the music. He'd never admit it out loud, but they looked good together. He surveyed the whole room; it just wasn't his scene, but he could see the appeal. The camaraderie, the excitement, the pure elation. He got it. It just wasn't him.

"Want another?" A voice conjured Jim's attention away from the dance floor.

When he turned around, he found a bartender waiting expectantly. He wasn't young, but mid-forties wasn't old for Shady Place, either. Jim looked at his empty glass and nodded, plopping it down on the counter. "Keep 'em coming. Heavy pours."

"Troubles?" The bartender asked, never worried about extending the cliché of drink-slinger as therapist. It usually led to better tips.

"Liquid courage," Jim said. "Something I have to do tonight."

The bartender handed him another tequila, more than half full. This time, he got a lime. The bartender offered to start a tab, to which Jim offered a quip about his HOA fees covering booze.

The music stopped, and the Jazzman made an announcement while Jim drained his libation. "Remember, everyone, there are free condoms at the bar." Jim's eyes widened as he continued to drink. The Jazzman continued, "The only way to stop the spread of STDs is to be careful!"

The crowd cheered, and the music began again.

To stop himself from spitting all over the bartender, Jim gagged on the tequila. It burned his throat as he coughed uncontrollably for a moment. The bartender offered him a glass of water, but Jim held up a hand to indicate he would be OK. Instead, he bit the lime. *Smooth.*

"Was he serious?" Jim asked.

The bartender pointed to an oversized fishbowl next to Jim's elbow. There was a sign that read: Take one, take two, just be safe whatever you do! This place was loaded with clever little signs.

An attractive Shady Placer brushed up against Jim as he read the sign. She grabbed a handful of condoms and winked at him before goosing his butt. She disappeared into the crowd before Jim even knew what happened.

"They're frisky here," the bartender said. "No one's getting pregnant, but they forget about VD."

Jim stood in bewilderment before slamming the rest of his tequila back. He wasn't sure he'd ever understand this place. It was like they had looped back around to high school. A bunch of horny teenagers. No, that wasn't it. It was more like a coed summer camp.

Jim placed his glass on the bar and nodded; it was all that was necessary to bring another round. He reached in his pocket and produced a folded piece of paper.

"You work a lot of these things?" Jim asked.

The bartender nodded. "Every one of them for the last few

years. Great money. Some other benefits."

"You too?"

The bartender smiled, "I said they're frisky."

Jim took a long swig of his new tequila. *This place*, he thought.

"You know any of these guys?" Jim asked, sliding the paper to the bartender.

Jim killed what was left of the tequila and bit into another lime.

The bartender slid the list back. "I knew them all. They're all dead, though."

"One more," Jim said, sliding his glass back again. "Anything stand out about them?"

The bartender poured and nodded. "They all dated your friend Beverly." He paused. "A few of them actually had run-ins with Mike over there. Jealousy, I'd say."

Jim looked across the dance floor at Mike and Beverly dancing close to each other. The new information was of great interest. Had he been looking the wrong direction? Was Mike so clever as to turn him on to the murders and point him to a suspect, but all the while, he was the killer himself?

Was he so drunk he'd heard the bartender wrong?

Was he drunk enough for what he needed to do next?

Jim tossed a few twenties on the counter. "Is that enough?"

"More than."

"I have to get out there before this place turns into an orgy," Jim said, half joking, half convinced he'd slipped through a portal in time to Caligula's palace. "Sorry about this…"

The bartender gave Jim a confused shrug and watched him throw back what was left of his final courage booster.

"I never welsh on a bet."

With that, his pants were around his ankles, and his shirt was on the floor. It only lasted a few seconds, but time slowed down for Jim.

He was drunk enough he didn't care that he was as naked as the day he was born in a room full of strangers. He shuffled his way toward the dance floor and awaited the embarrassment that was to follow.

The Jazzman saw him first and immediately changed his tune. "Disco Inferno" gave way to Ray Stevens's "The Streak," and the sea of dancers parted.

The embarrassment didn't come, though. There was no self-consciousness, no fear or anxiety. He actually didn't care. In fact, he was beginning to enjoy himself.

His slow shuffle turned into a confident strut.

He was feeling it.

Jay nodded and smiled with a double thumbs-up.

Beverly's jaw was approaching the floor.

Mike was grinning from ear to ear until he looked down at Jim's considerable manhood and frowned.

Tommy held up his cell phone, videoing the whole ordeal, even telling Jim to smile, but the sound was lost among the catcalls from the excited ladies in the crowd.

A few dollar bills even flew across the room to Jim's feet.

It was liberating. Naked, free, the shackles of conformity tossed aside.

When he reached the middle of the crowd, he did a triumphant spin. Then it happened. If it had been a record, the needle would have raked the grooves as the music came to a screeching halt.

The room fell silent, and Jim found Linda Stern standing in

front of him with her hands on her hips and the disdain she held for Jim Phillips pouring from her eyes.

"Are you high, Mr. Phillips?" she asked.

He smiled. "Only on life, Stern. Only on life!"

"Let's go; you're out of here!"

"But the night is young. Let's dance!"

She led him away to a barrage of boos and hisses, but none to her face. Everyone she passed was silent. If she turned in the direction of a dissenter, they immediately shut up.

They all feared her.

All of them but Jim. When they reached the door, he broke loose and ran back to the middle of the dance floor and shouted, "Do the hustle!"

The crowd cheered for him; it was a last stand William Wallace would have been proud of. It was short-lived, of course, as Stern had Shady Place security escort Jim to the parking lot.

In the end, only one thing really mattered that night.

Jim Phillips never welshes on a bet.

It was a clear night, with more stars in the sky than Jim could count. He never learned the constellations, so he connected the dots on his own, creating images that meant something to him.

"Baseball. A bat. A police badge. Handcuffs." He mumbled what he saw out loud.

He had tried closing his eyes, but the spinning was too much to handle. He continued to stare at the sparkling blanket above him, wishing he could pull it up to his chin and sleep.

When they finally made their way outside to Jim, that's where the group found him, lying on the ground staring upward. He continued to recite the images he saw, "A Tommy. A Jay. A Beverly. An O'Flaherty."

The group looked at Mike, who shrugged his shoulders and threw up his hands. "He's drunk." He followed up by shooting Jim a look that could have ignited the sunburn on his face.

"I am definitely drunk," Jim said.

"Come on," Tommy said, pulling Jim to his feet.

"Too fast, too fast," Jim protested, staggering as he rose, but eventually, he balanced himself with Tommy and Jay's help. "OK, I'm good."

"We should get you home," Jay said.

The group piled back onto Tommy's golf cart and started for home. Jim was in the back with Beverly and Mike, staring at the street behind them.

Jim's face showed a man who was not in a good place. The feeling in his stomach and head confirmed as much. The saliva was building in his mouth and the strong urge to belch was growing. As logic would dictate, the moment the cart lurched forward, the contents of Jim's stomach projected toward the street behind them.

"I'm good!" Jim said, holding a hand in the air. "Puke and rally. Let's get another drink!"

Beverly hopped off the cart and took Jim's hand. "I think we should probably walk, James."

"OK," Jim said. "You know, you're really pretty."

She smiled and put his arm around her shoulder. "Aren't you sweet."

Mike immediately jumped off the cart and joined them. "I'll help make sure he gets home OK."

"Are you positive?" Jay asked. "It is a long walk."

Beverly tapped the side of the cart. "The fresh air will do him good."

"Don't forget," Mike said, leaning over to Tommy. "You can get—"

"Yeah, yeah," Tommy interrupted. "I'm not gettin' a damn DUI on a golf cart, fool."

With that, Jay and Tommy were off, leaving Mike and Beverly to babysit.

"I have to say, I never expected that tonight, James," Beverly said.

Jim shrugged. "I lost a bet."

"To me," Mike chimed in.

The expulsion did Jim good; he was starting to rebound and sober up a little, but not enough to restrain his thoughts. He turned to Mike. "I got a little information out of the bartender about our victims."

"Victims?" Beverly asked.

Mike furrowed his brow and pursed his lips at Jim. *What is he doing?* "I don't think we should talk about this—"

"No, it's OK," Jim cut him off. "She should know. They were all guys she dated."

Beverly stopped walking. "What? What are you talking about?"

"Mike thinks they were murdered," Jim said, very matter of fact. He had sobered up enough to know exactly what he was doing.

Beverly was incredulous. "Murdered? Who was murdered? I know a few of the men I...oh, my. Do you really think?"

Mike was so upset with Jim he couldn't muster a single word, so Jim proceeded to lay it on. "It seems *Johnson* over here had run-ins with a few of them, too. What's up with that, Mike?"

Beverly and Jim turned their attention to Mike, who stood before them smiling. The cigar he'd been chewing hung loosely from his lips. "Come on, now; you know I could never—"

"No, of course not. Right, Jim?" Beverly cut in.

Jim began walking away slowly. "It's just a theory, anyway."

The group walked most of the way back to their houses in silence. With just a few words, Jim had created a palpable tension. He knew what he was doing. Would he have done the same if he was sober? Probably not, but he was still drunk, so he really didn't care. Jim figured the move put him a step ahead of Mike for Beverly's affections.

Jim was satisfied with himself. The night had been a success. Well, it had been something. What, he wasn't so sure of. He closed his eyes and realized just how drunk he still was; when he opened them, Beverly and Mike were staring at him. They were in front of his house, and he wasn't quite sure how long they'd been standing there.

"I'm going to go inside," Mike said. "Care to join me for a nightcap, Bev?"

Beverly kissed Mike on the cheek and said, "Too much excitement for me tonight. I'm going to make sure this one gets tucked in OK."

He knew what she really wanted to do. Jim was going to get his nightcap. It was impossible for Mike to hide his disdain for Jim. He lingered for a moment, with Jim and Beverly's attention trained on him. "Good-night, then."

Jim swayed back and forth. He had no idea what Beverly intended for him, but in his drunken state, still found the courtesy to wish his old friend a pleasant evening. "Night night, Mikey. Sleep tight!" He gave a gentle wave, jiggling his fingers in Mike's direction.

"Shall we?" Beverly asked Jim with a coy smile, offering her hand.

Jim nodded. "Yes, we shall. I just need, my, ummm, keys…yes, my keys, that's it."

They walked through his grass toward the front door as Jim fumbled for his keys. As he attempted to pull them loose from his pocket, they turned sideways, and his hand caught.

He went down hard; face first.

At least the grass is soft.

The last thing he heard was Beverly calling for Mike to wait for her.

One tequila, two tequila, three tequila…

He was out.

🌴

Beverly didn't like it when they went to Mike's house. She found it depressing. It was so sparsely decorated, like those transitional apartments men stayed in right after their marriages fell apart. The two of them sat in his kitchen sipping coffee and exchanging reserved pleasantries.

While Jim wouldn't be sure how much of that night's conversation actually happened, Beverly and Mike would remember it all.

They laughed a bit about Jim's streaking and the way he handled Stern, the old battle-ax. And of course, there was the projectile vomiting off the back of the golf cart. Such a crazy night, even by their usual Shady Place standards. However slurred his words may have been, Jim had put something out there that was hanging over their heads like a dark cloud in Mike's kitchen.

"What was Jim going on about tonight?" she asked him, adding a spoonful of sugar to her coffee.

Mike tried to assuage her concerns. "Just drunk talk. Who knows what's goin' on in that head of his."

Beverly knew as well as anyone that drunk ramblings are usually the truest, but Mike obviously didn't want to talk about it. "OK, Michael; I think I'm going to turn in. Should we help Jim get inside?"

"He's a big boy," Mike said. "He can take care of himself. Why don't you and me step into the other room." It was a nightcap, after all.

She slowly pushed her coffee cup away. It wasn't particularly good coffee; some dehydrated crystals she'd managed to choke down a few sips of to be polite. It brought her back to the reason she generally liked to host her dalliances instead of making house calls. Her palate was far more refined than the tastes of most of the men in Shady Place. She would have much rather been sipping on a nice cup of Earl Grey.

"Thank you for the coffee," she said politely. "But I think I'll actually be on my way for the evening. I've got tennis with girls in the morning, and I'm a bit knackered."

He was going to ask what knackered meant, but from the context, he figured she was going to bed and not with him. She kissed his cheek as he walked her out, and the night was over.

Mike dumped out the coffee he'd made just a few moments before and poured himself a scotch. He contemplated if he'd done something wrong that evening, but chalked it up to Beverly's being knackered, a term he learned from a quick Google search did in fact mean she was tired, but not from sex as the site he read indicated, a usage that had fallen out of favor in recent years, or in his case, minutes.

He was still keyed up, and having Beverly in the house without getting to enjoy the pleasure of her company left him with only one option before bed. It was natural, and everyone did it, he always told himself, but it didn't stop him from feeling guilty afterward. Growing up Catholic will do that to a man.

*

Jim was still lying in his yard when Beverly left Mike's. She checked to make sure he was still breathing before she wandered back to her sanctuary.

"Silly man," she whispered, kissing him on the forehead before leaving him to sleep it off on his lawn. She still wasn't sure whether he was playing hard to get, wasn't interested, or simply had no clue how to date.

The moment she got inside, she picked up the phone and dialed. "Are you free, my dear?"

*

After they left, Beverly and Mike to escort the tipsy Jim back to Shady Oak Way, Tommy and Jay found themselves embroiled in a heated argument. Jim wasn't the only one who'd had too much to drink that night. The duo had been bickering since they left the others near the clubhouse moments before.

It began simply as a dispute about Tommy posting Jim's streaking video on YouTube, but had quickly careened out of control.

Why do you care?

Didn't think you even liked him?

I don't understand you.

They were barking at each other, the lines blurred between who was upset about what. The argument had nothing to do with that night. There was something that had been brewing for a while and was reaching a tipping point. Tommy was in the middle of making a fervent point that would have turned the tide in his favor when flashing lights behind urged them to pull over.

It seems that during their discourse, Tommy's golf cart had been swerving unchecked as he spoke with his hands in lieu of minding the wheel. Shady Place security had the power to write citations and even involve local police if they felt it was necessary. In this instance, they found the grounds necessary to issue a sobriety test to Tommy. Mike would be pointing and laughing if he could see them now, but he couldn't, and he would never even know this had happened. Tommy wouldn't give him that satisfaction.

Luckily, Tommy's celebrity and affable personality afforded him certain liberties common folks weren't able to capitalize on. Shady Place security didn't call the police or even issue him a citation. Instead, he signed a few autographs and posed for a few selfies. Just another day in the life.

All Jay could do was watch from the sidelines. It's all he could ever do.

TWENTY-THREE

Nothing interrupts a deep sleep like the full strength of a sprinkler blasting you in the face.

That was Jim's most vivid memory of the night of the social. Waking up to what felt like a fireman's hose trying to peel the flesh from his skull. It was powerful enough to force him to his feet, if only briefly. The wet ground caused him to slip and tumble to his knees. He scrambled, trying to crawl away from the assault of the water cannon that seemed to be trained directly on him.

He managed to drag himself to his front door, where he sat for a moment trying to regain his bearings. He was soaked and dirty; a little drunk still, to boot. His watch told him it was three thirty and the fact that it was still dark out told him it was a.m. He covered his face with his hands, trying to pull it together, then shook off the funk the best he could.

He would get up, go inside, shower, and go to bed. Easy enough. Except that his keys were sinking into the sod right next to his new nemesis: the sprinkler. If you were to ask Jim Phillips what happened that night between him and his sprinkler head, he would never tell you. He'd swear one of the landscapers must have hit it with their mower or maybe one of those damn dogs that wouldn't stop shitting in his yard had dug it up and run off with it.

What really happened was far more pathetic and, to an outside observer, entertaining. The sprinklers in Jim's yard featured rotating heads. They covered an arc of 180 degrees. Each rotation took twenty seconds, ten clockwise, ten counterclockwise. Jim followed the path of the sprinkler head, guarding his keys. His head moved back and forth with the rotation.

Clockwise. Counterclockwise. Back. Forth.

He trained his attention singularly on the movement. When he thought he had it timed right, he made his move. He stepped down onto the yard and moved toward his keys. He had to retrieve them before they sank further into the depths of the lake that he was convinced was growing in his yard.

As soon as he stepped off the porch, Jim was reminded of what happens when you focus on one aspect of the problem so intently you forget about the others. He was immediately blindsided by another sprinkler on his right. He tried to move quickly to dodge the newest barrage but found himself immediately sprayed from his left side.

He was drenched. His clothes, his shoes, his face. Every inch was covered. His only option was to retreat from the aquatic assault being unleashed on him from every angle. He sought refuge on the front porch once more to regroup and reassess his options. Admittedly, the deluge of cool water was soothing on his sunburn, but he needed to focus.

Jim studied the pattern of rotation for all the sprinkler heads. He plotted his course and made a second attempt, a third, and even a fourth. Each time, he was hit from a new and unexpected source. Each surprise hit sent him reeling, a blow from a heavyweight knocking an underprepared opponent around the ring.

He dropped down on his porch step and stared at the

minefield. He was disappointed in himself. Dejected and defeated by a sprinkler system. *You're better than this, Phillips! Pick yourself up! You can do this!*

He had himself psyched up and ready to go. He calculated in his head the perfect route. He stood at the edge of the lawn and was ready to make his move when it dawned on him.

Without hesitation, Jim walked straight across the lawn. Water pelted him from every angle, but he was undeterred. He reached the original perpetrator and stood over it. It continued rotating 180 degrees, ten seconds clockwise, ten seconds counterclockwise, until Jim reached down and ripped the sprinkler head from the ground and threw it in his driveway.

He threw his arms in the air in triumph and stood over his fallen adversary.

A small trickle of water gushed from the pipe that had previously been connected to the sprinkler head. *Glug, glug, glug.* A death knell.

That was the moment he decided he would never tell anyone what really happened that night.

He picked up his keys and led his own personal victory parade to the front door, sprinklers firing in all directions around him. They were weepy for their fallen mate. He was the victor. He had won. His prize was before him.

As soon as he put the key in the door, the sprinkler system reached the end of its timed cycle, and all the heads ceased spraying. Jim looked back over his shoulder.

"That's right," he said, convinced they had surrendered in defeat.

As the sprinkler cycle continued its progression, the next zone on the side of the house kicked into full effect.

They're regrouping! Jim thought, then rushed inside.

🌴

The scene sent waves of terror through Jenny's body. Muddy footprints covered Jim's front porch, and the front door was slightly ajar, keys still dangling from the lock. The footprints continued inside, leading deeper into the house.

"Daddy?" she called inside softly, to no response.

She followed the muddy prints through the foyer, then living room, and toward Jim's bedroom. She called to him again, but there was still no response. Her heart was starting to race; something must have happened to her father. Was there a home invasion? Worse even? She wasn't sure what she was about to walk in on, so she tried her father's cell phone for the dozenth time.

Straight to voice mail: "It's Jim, you know what to do."

She needn't leave a message, it would have been the sixth of the morning, and he obviously wasn't listening to them. She was sure he must have forgotten to charge it. That had to be it. But her father never forgot anything so simple. But he *was* getting older; maybe he was changing. Maybe he needed to see a neurologist.

Jenny was like Jim in her inability to control overthinking, so her imagination was running wild. This time, her mind was going to the worst place, leaving her hesitant to enter her father's bedroom.

The door was half open, a dirty handprint near the middle panel of a six-panel door. She knocked gently and called softly once more, "Daddy?"

The silence persisted.

Maybe he's not even home.

She cautiously pushed the door open and found what she was looking for. Her first instinct was to call the police or an ambulance—

until Jim let out a little grunt of a snore, more of a snort really, and moaned.

Jenny was relieved her father was alive. This was good. Now she could kill him. She quickly discerned the source of the filth leading to his bedroom was Jim himself. He was lying face down in bed, his shoes and all his clothing still on, caked in dirt and grass. His comforter and pillow were equally contaminated, but he was so deep in slumber he didn't even notice.

Once she was able to soak it all in and confirmed he was indeed OK, she got pissed.

"Hey!" she shouted. "Wake up, old man!"

Jim gave her nothing more than a soft moan, so she shook his foot and yelled at him again. When she got closer, she could smell the booze on him.

"Oh, Daddy! What did you do last night?" she whispered to herself, shaking her head, before retreating to the kitchen.

She returned carrying a glass of ice water. She rubbed Jim's back and tried to wake him once more, to no avail. She connected to Heather via FaceTime on her iPhone and caught her up. She felt her sister deserved the opportunity to witness what she was about to do.

When they were growing up, if she or Heather were still sleeping one off at almost noon on a weekday, they would never hear the end of it and be treated to merciless torment from their father. So, when she was given the opportunity to return the favor, she didn't feel bad. Instead, she reveled in it.

"What the shit!" Jim flipped over with a start as soon as the water hit the back of his head. He spun so violently, he fell off the bed, flopping onto the floor like a fish out of water. He let out a loud groan and grabbed his head with both hands. "Owwwww, my head."

Jenny stood next to Jim pointing her phone in his direction to allow Heather's smirking face to take in the scene. Jenny's face was considerably more dour and judgmental.

He pulled his hands away from his face and looked up at his daughters. "Your mother used to make that face at me."

Jenny huffed and rolled her eyes. "What the hell happened to you? Why aren't you answering your phone? Make me drive all the way over here to check on you. You know, I thought you were dead…"

Heather was more amused than upset at this point, but she wasn't the one who drove all the way over to check on him. Jenny ended the call then laid into her father. She kept berating him, but he stopped listening. The throbbing in his head was exacerbated by every shrill word that spewed from her lips until he finally threw his hands up in surrender. "I'm sorry! Can you please, for the love of god, stop yelling at me for two seconds?"

She did, and he refocused. His mouth was dry, his head was pounding, and his stomach was twisting in knots.

"Daddy, what the hell did you do last night?" Jenny asked calmly.

His sunburn felt secondary to the effects of the hangover. "Last night? Last night was a battle; an honest to god battle."

"Care to elaborate?" she asked. "And what the hell happened to your skin?"

He smacked his lips together. "Sunburn. I need water and an aspirin. And coffee, I need coffee."

"I'll put on a pot of coffee and get you some aspirin and water, but you need to go shower. You're filthy," she said. "And you stink."

After smelling himself, he was willing to concede that fact and did as he was commanded.

The coffee smell almost had Jim floating across the house like an old Saturday morning cartoon. The aroma drew him out of his bedroom into the living room. The prospects of coffee and an aspirin were the solace his body and head needed.

"That coffee smells delicious. Get a little of that in me, and I'll tell you about my night." He was actually smiling when he came out of his bedroom until he saw Jenny wasn't alone.

"Don't worry, I'm already catching her up on last night," Mike said grinning smugly at Jim. He took a sip from his mug. "Coffee's delicious; come join us, Jimmy boy."

Jim stood staring, his jaw clenched tight. Suddenly, the pain was a lot stronger than before, but it had moved to his ass.

"Streaking, Daddy? Really, what has gotten into you?" Jenny asked. She plopped some aspirin on the counter with a glass of water. "Take these."

"I lost a bet," Jim said, before turning his attention to Mike. "What are you doing here?"

Mike took another sip of coffee. "Came to check on you; you were pretty wasted last night. I found this in your driveway…"

He pulled something out of his pocket and waved it back and forth. It was Jim's decapitated sprinkler head.

Jenny looked at the little black piece of plastic. "Is that a sprinkler head?"

"Hmmm, weird, I'll have to look into that," Jim said, snatching his felled foe from Mike's hand and burying it in his pocket.

"Wouldn't have anything to do with all the mud, would it?" Jenny asked.

Jim filled a coffee cup with his back to them. He decided if he simply didn't answer, maybe they'd drop it. They did, but the silence was filled by a voice that Jim was in no mood to hear.

"Anyway, where was I?" Mike said. "Right, so we're there with all our friends, and your dad, your dad just drops his pants and trots his happy ass right across the dance floor. Jazzman, that's what the music guy's called, starts playing "The Streak!" You know that song from the seventies. Classic! Then—"

"Wait, wait, wait," Jenny interrupted. "Did you say our friends?" She turned to Jim. "You made friends? Mike, are you friends with my dad?"

Mike laughed. "I guess you could say that. Yeah, we're friends."

Jim wouldn't say that. He stared at Mike hard. So hard, Mike could feel it. The day was already going terribly for Jim. He loved his daughter but didn't appreciate unannounced pop-ins. Mike had no business being there. His head was still throbbing, and his bowels were screaming at him. At that point, his most logical option was to start drinking, but he thought it to be in bad taste.

Before Jim could respond, Jenny was calling her sister again. "He made a friend!"

She held the phone up for Heather to see Mike. Visual confirmation. She was as blown away as Jenny was. Mike enjoyed the spectacle and waved to Heather.

Jim continued staring at Jenny and Mike in silence, stewing in his own misery. He walked over to the sofa and parked himself in front of the television and turned it on without a word.

"What are you doing, Daddy?" Jenny asked.

Jim waved a hand at them without turning around. "Mike can finish telling you about *my* night. I'm going to watch *SportsCenter*."

"He always like this?" Mike asked Jenny, who nodded silently in the affirmative before ending the call with her sister.

"Yes," Jim said. "I'm always like this. If you don't like it, you know where the door is."

It occurred to Jim that his prime objective of solitude had been put under severe duress. It took years to build up the kind of walls that made people anxious to avoid him and leave him alone, and here they were, crumbling at his feet. He was miserable but didn't love company. If they insisted on being in his house, it was going to be under his terms.

"Let him sulk; finish your story, Mr. Johnson," Jenny said.

Jim cringed at his daughter calling notorious criminal Michael O'Flaherty "Mr. Johnson." He considered throwing Mike out on his ear or calling the marshals right then and there. He checked his pockets for his phone but found only the cold dead remnants of his sprinkler head. His phone must be in his bedroom somewhere. Yesterday's pants, most likely.

"Please, it's Mike," Mike said, smiling at Jenny. "I really think I should leave; let Mr. Cranky-Pants over there recover alone. It was a pleasure, young lady."

"You know what, I think you're right," Jenny said. "I'll walk you out. Daddy, I'm leaving."

"OK," Jim said gruffly.

Jenny walked Mike out but didn't leave. Instead, she parked herself in front of the television, blocking Jim's view. She firmly placed her hands on her hips and cocked her head at him. It was the second time she'd reminded him of Karen that day. "Are you just trying to be an ass or are you really this bad?"

"Is he gone?" Jim asked.

"What?" Jenny threw her hands in the air. "Mr. Johnson? Is Mr. Johnson gone? Yeah, he didn't want to be around a sour old man, and neither do I. I thought maybe we could get some lunch, but I don't think I could stand sitting across the table from you."

Jim rubbed his face in frustration. His skin still hurt when he touched it, but not as much now that the healing had begun. "You're right; I'm sorry."

She relaxed a little. "You know, I was really worried about you and finding you like that…" She shook her head. "Then Mr. Johnson tells me this story about you streaking through a party. What's going on with you?"

What's going on with you? He thought about the question. He didn't really have an answer, at least not a satisfactory one. He could have told her the truth. Mike was, in fact, a criminal. He was sort of dating his neighbor Beverly, who was also sort of dating Mike, the criminal. Did that mean he was dating Mike? No, but that was one to file away for later consideration. He could have told her he was working an angle on a potential murder case.

Or he could just say, "I'm trying to fit in. Isn't that what you and your sister told me to do?"

"Well, I guess…" Jenny hadn't expected the answer she received. He never did what he was told to do. "Yes, so you're really trying?"

"I said I would," he said.

"OK, I'll take it. Lunch?"

"Sure, let me find my phone. You can call your sister and tell her I'm trying."

She did, and he found his phone, but it was dead. Completely dead, actually. It had taken damage from Jim's watery adventure the night before. He made a note to order a new one when they got home from lunch. He wrote it on a Post-it and slapped it on the inside of the front door.

"I see you're back to Post-it notes," Jenny said. "I thought you only did that when you had a case."

He looked at her out of the side of his eyes. "Just a tool to help an old man remember."

TWENTY-FOUR

It was like she was waiting for them. When Jenny dropped Jim off from lunch, they found Beverly quickly scooting across her lawn to greet them. Jenny wasn't planning on getting out of the car, but Beverly's presence piqued her interest. It wasn't so much that she was curious what Beverly wanted but rather to see how her father interacted with such an attractive woman.

"Who's that, Daddy?" Jenny asked coyly.

Jim didn't say a word; he just opened the door and got out of the car.

"Oh, good, you're alive!" Beverly said. "I knocked on your door a little while ago, but you didn't answer. The way we left you last night, I feared the worst, James."

Jim shrugged. "I'm fine."

Jenny recognized the voice immediately. "You didn't tell me your neighbor was so pretty, Daddy."

"Oh, thank you, darling," Beverly beamed. "I'm Beverly. You must be one of this old codger's daughters."

Jenny offered her a hand. "Yes, I'm Jenny."

The two chitter chattered away while Jim stood idly by. He allowed his gaze to wander until his eyes landed on Mike standing in his driveway staring at them. The two locked eyes, neither wavering until Jenny shook Jim's arm.

Jenny and Beverly were both staring at him, waiting for an answer. To what, he had no idea. So, he gave the best answer he could muster. "Huh?"

"My toilet? It's leaking. I asked if you could take a look at it for me," Beverly said.

Jim hemmed and hawed. "Well, I'm not sure if I can—"

"Of course he can!" Jenny interjected. "He used to fix everything around our house back home."

It seemed so far away. So long ago. Another lifetime.

"Yeah, OK," Jim said. He looked over to Mike, who was still leering at them, then raised his voice. "Sure, I'd love to come check your plumbing!"

Jenny and Beverly shared a look while Jim sent a smug half-grin in Mike's direction.

"Jenny, it was a pleasure," Beverly said, hugging her this time. "James, I'll see you in a few minutes."

Beverly left them alone, Jenny observing her father's lascivious ogling as Beverly slunk her way home.

"You can retract your tongue," Jenny said. "She's gone."

⁂

After last night's preview, Beverly was disappointed when Jim arrived carrying a toolbox. She was hoping he'd being wearing a tool belt—and nothing else. Fully clothed with a toolbox would have to suffice; she led him to the bathroom and pointed out the culprit.

"I'll see what I can do," Jim said.

She smiled and ran a skilled hand across his shoulders before slipping out of the room. "I'll be back in a few minutes."

She went to her dresser drawer and retrieved something black and lacy, then peeked around the bathroom door to make sure Jim wasn't looking. His attention was trained on his toolbox as he searched for the best utensil to tackle the task at hand.

She squeezed into a tiny black negligee. It was form-fitting and a bit too small, but that was by design. She made sure all her different parts were where they needed to be, concealed, but not entirely. Perfect. She sucked in her tummy and measured her curves in a full-length mirror. A tuck here, a little pull there, and she was good to go.

"Hey, Bev," Jim called from the bathroom.

She threw a bathrobe on to conceal Jim's surprise.

"What is it, dear?" she asked, leaning against the doorframe.

Jim spoke without looking up; he was tightening a nut connecting the toilet tank and bowl. "It's just a loose nut. Weird, though; they don't usually come loose on their own."

"Maybe I just needed an excuse to get you inside my house," she said, letting the robe fall to the floor. She looked good, she knew it, and she knew that Jim would appreciate it. And of course, show his appreciation.

He was speaking as he slid out from behind the toilet. "Why would you need an excuse?" His face turned a new shade of red, a blush deeper than the remains of his sunburn. His jaw fell slack, but he couldn't assemble any sound. He sat up and put his wrench in his toolbox. He was very slow and very deliberate in his actions.

"I guess I didn't," Beverly said, taking a step closer.

Jim stood up and washed his hands in the sink. He made no eye contact, instead staring down at his hands. "So, was there anything else you needed?"

Beverly stared at him in the mirror. *What the hell is wrong with this guy?* She was confused and dismayed. Offended? A little bit, yeah, she was offended. It seemed Jim Phillips was going to be more of a challenge than she ever imagined.

"Do you, by chance, play poker, James?"

He looked up from his hand-wringing. "I do."

"Then you'll join us for poker night tonight," she said, pulling her robe back over her body.

Jim couldn't help but stare. She must have been cold because her high beams were on. He averted his eyes, feeling he'd been caught looking, like his hand was in the cookie jar.

But Beverly was more than all right with Jim looking. She hesitated, even considered dropping her robe again. They held in a silent pause for an agonizing eternity until he stretched a hand toward her. *This is it,* she thought. But it wasn't, he reached past her for a towel and patted his hands dry.

"Great, then I'll see you tonight."

He left, clumsily brushing past Beverly in the doorway. She didn't make any effort to get out of his way. She'd never been so overtly rejected. Was she rejected? She wasn't quite sure what had just happened.

She stood there for a moment, occasionally blinking and tapping her fingers on the counter. *Is he gay? No, just an idiot,* she thought.

She nodded to herself in silence. *Challenge accepted.*

Jim knew what he'd passed up when he left Beverly's house that afternoon. He wasn't an idiot or coy. Every fiber of his being wanted to rip what little clothing she was wearing off her body and throw her on the bed so he could ravage her.

So, what was stopping him? He knew what he wanted as a man; biologically, his body craved what Beverly was offering, but his *heart*, his heart was still stuck.

It actually surprised him that she was even interested. It was flattering, but he couldn't see why someone who could have her pick of any man in Shady Place wanted him. Nevertheless, it felt good. No, it felt great. Now if only he could get past his problem and reap the rewards.

When he got home, he found himself staring at Karen's picture again. To see her face always made him smile, he figured it always would, but he was feeling other emotions now that betrayed what he felt was his duty to a memory that faded more every day.

Karen would have punched him in the arm and told him to snap out of it. She would have told him to quit feeling sorry for himself; she was the one who was dead, not him. She was always so pragmatic like that. He put her photo down and decided a nap was in order if he was going to spend another night out.

T WENTY-FIVE

Toward the end, they were allowed to bring Karen home from the hospital. There was nothing more to be done inside institutional walls, and she wanted to be home, in her own bed, or at least a bed that belonged to her. It was still a hospital bed, but at least she was home. Jim had turned the living room into the closest semblance to their bedroom he could so she would be comfortable.

She was a shell of herself, gaunt and frail. Her eyes had sunk, and her face had become long and weary. But to Jim, she still looked the same. He still saw that spry young thing he'd met so long ago. Surgery didn't work. Neither did chemo. Radiation wasn't an option. None of the drugs were doing anything, except attacking the very core of who Karen was. So, she stopped taking them; she would rather live with the pain for what time she had left and be herself, experience what she could with her daughters, her grandchildren, her Jim.

She had a stack of unread books next to her, the titles she'd always meant to get to. She watched TV, but it seemed more like she was just staring in its direction instead of actually watching. She slept a lot, often without realizing she'd fallen asleep, but Jim was always there when she woke up.

He always had a smile for her. The nurse was there frequently. A doctor on occasion. But Jim? He was always there. If not in the room, he was close by. You could see it on his face, though. He was tired. It was three years that felt like a lifetime, and it had taken its toll on his health. He'd lost weight, nothing like Karen, but enough to prompt questions about whether he was eating.

She knew it was the end. The girls knew it was the end. Even the young grandchildren could sense something wasn't right.

What's wrong with Grammy? Why is Grammy so quiet? Why won't Grammy play with us?

Jenny and Heather took it hard. That woman wasn't their mother anymore. It was just a husk that shared a vague resemblance to the woman who'd raised them. Jim had summoned them home from Florida because he thought they should be with her. He would never say it was because she was close to the "time." She needed them to be there. In reality, though, *he* needed them there.

The moments of clarity came and went for Karen at the end, but on a Tuesday, in the fall, with a crisp wind blowing and the threat of snowflakes earlier than usual, she had a moment that let Jim know she was still in there. Heather was holding her mother's right hand as Jenny rubbed her shoulder softly. They had sent their husbands and kids out for dinner at Karen's request.

She was weak, but her voice was at its strongest in months. "Girls, I want you to take care of your father."

They listened to her but didn't want to accept the connotation of her words.

"You know Daddy doesn't need any taking care of," Heather said.

Karen strained a smile and squeezed Heather's hand in response. "Please; he won't listen to me. You girls are all he's going to have left…" She stopped to cough. "Please make sure he keeps going…"

181

Jenny burst into tears. "I can't do this!"

She was out of the room before Karen could blink. She found herself alone in the kitchen, staring out back to the tree house her father had built for them when they were little.

Karen asked Heather to lean in closer so she could kiss her, then sent her away to comfort her baby sister. It was Jim's turn.

It was obvious what was happening, but Jim had yet to accept the fact that Karen might not be there next year, let alone next month or week. It couldn't be time yet. He was just happy she was so lucid in that moment. She was actually there.

"Do you remember what we talked about?" she asked him.

He shook his head, kissing her hand. "I don't want to talk—"

"Listen to me, my love," she cut him off. "You have to do it! Go on with your life. There's so much still in front of you."

He often let his mind wander when he was disinterested or didn't want to hear something. This time, it was the latter. If he checked out, she couldn't break his heart. That wasn't going to happen. Karen squeezed his hand with a force that shouldn't have been possible from a woman in her state.

"Don't do that; do not disappear on me, James Phillips," she barked. "This is important, so you give me all your focus."

"But—"

"Just stop and listen to me," she commanded, her voice clear and strong and a sparkle in her eyes he hadn't seen in years. "I fought as hard as I could, but I'm finished. I don't have many words left, so you need to hear me now."

She squeezed his hand again, but this time tenderly. A reminder she's still here, so listen up. His eyes were beginning to water, but he quickly wiped them. He didn't want anything to take away from the angel before him.

"You go to Florida and live the rest of your life. Always keep me with you, but move on. I'll be waiting for you wherever we end up."

She was smiling up at him. He could hardly see it through the tears that were clouding his vision. No matter how much he tried to wipe them away, they wouldn't dissipate.

"I haven't seen you cry since Heather was born," she said, beaming at her partner for all those years.

The lump in his throat made it hard for him to talk. "I don't think I can."

She grabbed him by the ears and pulled him close, whispering in his ear, "You have to promise me."

He stuttered the words, barely getting them out. But he did; he gave her his promise.

She pulled him closer and kissed him. Like the first time. The flutters, the twist in the stomach, the rush of it right down to their cores.

Then she let go.

It was over.

She was fifty-eight.

TWENTY-SIX

Jim's catnap left him in a worse place than when he dozed off. It left him in bed staring at the ceiling for a while. The memory of losing Karen still weighed heavy on every fiber of his being. He didn't believe in signs, never had, but his own subconscious was another story. A memory pushed to the forefront in the guise of a timely dream.

Karen was right. She was gone; there was no reason he should feel beholden to a ghost. But he did. The torment he put himself through over two women tugging at his heartstrings was agonizing but unnecessary. He knew it; it was ridiculous, and it was time to focus on himself.

Starting tonight.

Attempts to use rice to soak the water out of his phone were hopeless. It took him an hour and a half on the phone with his cell phone provider to get a new phone ordered. They promised him free overnight shipping for his troubles. Troubles that were created by his own doing, but he somehow convinced the company they owed him that compromise. If it wasn't there tomorrow, he'd have another round of troubles for Kamal from Oklahoma, who conveniently couldn't tell him the capital of the state he was in.

He was still without his lifeline, though, at least for another night. That night, he was supposed to play poker but had no clue when or where. When a knock came at his front door, he had a feeling it was now.

Jim was expecting Beverly, she was the one who invited him, after all, but when he opened his door, it was Mike who greeted him. Why should he be surprised? Mike seemed omnipresent in Shady Place. Jim couldn't escape him, so why wouldn't he be his escort to poker that evening?

"Phone dead?" Mike asked.

Jim simply nodded and offered a one-word response. "Yep."

"Ready to throw some darts?" Mike smiled, his trademark Twizzler flopping around from the side of his mouth as he led Jim to his car.

"Darts? I thought we were playing poker."

Mike laughed. "Always so serious; just messin' with you. Come on."

This was a new day for Jim. He still didn't trust Mike, but he was turning over a new leaf. He forced an awkward cockeyed smile that showed a little too much tooth and paired it with an obviously fake laugh. "Funny."

His look was disturbing, almost deranged. So much so that Mike recoiled, cringing with concern. "Are you having a stroke?"

"What? I'm smiling," Jim said.

"I can call someone. What's it they say? FAST, right?" Mike said. "For a stroke, it starts with the face thing. Droopin' or some shit."

"It was a smile, damn it!"

"Raise your arm, that's the A," Mike joked. "Come on, Jimbo, raise your arms for me!"

Jim stopped and clenched his jaw. Mike turned when he noticed he'd lost his travel mate. Jim stared at him in silence, trying to decide whether or not to turn around and go back inside.

"Jim? Talk to me, buddy," Mike said. "The S is for speech; you don't talk to me, I'm really gonna think you're strokin' out here!"

Mike wasn't serious. Every word came with a snide curl of his lips that told Jim as much. It was annoying. Everything about Mike annoyed him. The fact that he was roaming around free still ate at Jim. He knew he could change that, but all it would do is send Mike somewhere else in the world to roam around free, grinning like the jackass he was. He could have gone back inside, but they were going to see Beverly, and he'd be damned if he'd let Mike put in the face time while he sat at home by himself.

Who are you? he thought. This was his new reality.

Engage. Interact. Fit in.

"You know…" Jim stopped, he was going to call him childish, worse than his idiot sons-in-law, but he reconsidered. New Jim wouldn't say that. Instead, he went somewhere he never thought he would. "My wife died from a stroke."

Mike's mouth fell open. The blood drained from his face, and he rubbed the back of his head nervously. "Shit, man, I'm sorry! I didn't…"

Jim didn't have to fake a smile this time; it just came naturally. "Wouldn't that be some shit?"

"Nice one," Mike chuckled softly with relief, "dick."

They had to park on the street when they arrived at Lynn and Bonnie's house. Every turn at Shady Place had been something new for Jim. He didn't know what to expect when he got inside. He hadn't played poker in years, but he figured it was like riding a bike.

Mike and Jim were the last ones there. Jim already knew Beverly, Tommy, and Jay, but he didn't know their hosts, Lynn and

Bonnie, or that they lived here together. When they got to the table, the game was already in full swing.

Beverly was at the head of the table with an empty seat to her left and Tommy to her right. Jay was at Tommy's side, as usual, with an empty seat between him and Bonnie. Lynn was to her right, with an empty seat between her and Beverly.

Mike and Jim looked at each other, then to the empty seat at Beverly's side. They both casually began to make their way toward the vacant seat; they were in a dead heat until they reached the chair. At that point, the music stopped, and they were left standing with one chair between them.

They both grabbed an arm of the chair. It was on wheels and became the rope in a violent game of tug of war. They both pulled, then both tried to sit at the same time until one finally found himself planted firmly in the seat, the victor.

The loser found himself in Lynn's lap, looking up at her with a forced smile. "Hi, I'm Jim."

"I'm Lynn," she said with reservations. She was naturally blonde, and it blended seamlessly into the silver that had crept in with the years. In her mid-sixties, she was frail, with pale-blue eyes that were fierce, but kind.

Bonnie leaned over, squaring her eyes with Jim's. "Hi, Jim. I'm Bonnie. Do you think you could get your head out of my wife's lap?"

"Right, of course," Jim said.

Bonnie was on The List. Right behind Beverly. She was half-Korean, but one hundred percent striking. Beverly actually counted her as a friend, most likely because they weren't in competition for any of the men in Shady Place.

Beverly sat by with a sly half-smile as her suitors puffed their chests for attention. She knew exactly what she had done with the seating arrangements, but wasn't sure if Jim would take the bait. Mike was easy, he was already wrapped securely around her little finger, but she had two little fingers, leaving plenty of room for Jim. Now he just needed to cooperate.

Jim took his seat at the opposite end of the table from Beverly and Mike, a fact that didn't sit well with him. Now that he'd decided to actually go for it with Beverly, Mike was more than just an annoyance; he was an obstacle.

They made proper introductions of Lynn and Bonnie, or All-in Lynn and Bon-Bons, as they were affectionately known in the poker group. A pile of plastic chips sat in front of Jim, organized by color and denomination.

"The buy-in is one hundred dollars," Jay informed Jim.

Jim cocked his head a little. "This isn't just for fun?"

"Fun when I take your money!" Tommy boasted.

Jay poked Tommy's arm. "When was the last time you took money from anyone at this table?"

Tommy took the ribbing in stride as Jim retrieved some cash from his pocket.

"So, you the guy who killed Ted?" Lynn asked. "You could have just asked if you wanted to join the group, eight works just as well as seven, you know."

Jim bumbled with the accusation, torn between going on the defensive and possibly cracking a joke, because she was obviously joking. *Right?* She didn't really think Jim killed Ted. No one could think that.

"I'll take your silence as an admission of guilt," Lynn said, rolling her eyes.

To Jim's surprise, Mike stepped in to his defense. "He didn't mean anything with Ted; he was just excited to see an old friend. Classic Phillips."

Jim was surprised Mike made such a blatant reference to the fact that they knew each other before Shady Place. He wondered if anyone else at the table had caught the implications of such a callous statement.

The cards were dealt as they spoke. Texas Hold 'Em. Jim was familiar with the game but had mostly played five card stud and draw. What he considered classic poker. Hold 'Em was more of a gimmick if you asked him, but he would concede to house rules. He was the new guy, after all.

"I was unaware you two already knew each other," Jay said, tossing his cards aside.

Mike seemed to be taunting Jim with the line of discussion. "We ran into each other a few times back home. Fifteen." Mike tossed a handful of chips to the center of the table.

"Not sure this is somewhere you really want to go," Jim said, matching Mike's bet. "Call."

The rest of the table quickly bowed out of the hand, leaving Mike and Jim to duke it out mano y mano, a proposition that Jim was more than happy to oblige.

Three cards were turned over, the ace and eight of spades and the nine of clubs. Jim liked what he saw. So did Mike. It really didn't matter what the cards on the table were, though—they were going to have it out.

"You never talk about your past, Mike," Tommy noted.

Mike shrugged. "We used to call him the pit-bull. Pit-Bull Phillips." He threw more chips in the pot. "Twenty-five."

"Keep it up, *Johnson*," Jim said before calling the bet.

Another card, this time the seven of diamonds. Neither man blinked. The table sat silent, watching the battle unfold.

"Yeah, old Pit-Bull was just like a dog with a bone," Mike said. "I check."

Jim tapped a finger to indicate a check. Their eyes were locked across the table.

Last card, the two of spades.

Jim and Mike sized each other up.

"I'll check to you," Mike said, tapping the table. "Whattaya say Pit-Bull?"

"I'm not getting into this with you right now," Jim said. He pushed all his chips into the pot. "I'm all-in."

Bonnie leaned over to Lynn and softly muttered, "You're usually the first one to do that."

"Call." Mike didn't hesitate, calling Jim instantly with a satisfied smile. "Show me your straight, Pit-Bull."

Jim had his cards ready to turn over, but hesitated when Mike pegged his hand exactly. He scanned the cards on the table. He had a straight using the seven through nine and the ten and jack in his hand, but Mike called him. He'd missed it. The board was clear.

He slowly flipped over his cards, revealing his straight to the table, but his face indicated he knew he was beaten.

"Remember when we were talking about strokes and FAST earlier, Jimbo?" Mike said, trying to lead Jim. "We never discussed what the T meant."

"Just flip over your damn cards," Jim insisted, not wanting to prolong his misery any longer than he had to.

"T is for time, my friend," he said, flipping his cards over with a satisfied grin. The king and four of spades. A flush. "As in time to pay me!"

Jim clenched his jaw, pouting in silence. He'd done it to himself, checking when he already had the straight. Mike hit his flush on the river, the card Jim let him see for free. "Mother f—"

"Now, now, can't win 'em all, Jimmy boy," Mike cut him off.

It was Lynn's turn to deal, but Bonnie took the cards and shuffled for her. "Welcome to the table!"

"Would you like to buy back in, Jim, or should we deal you out?" Jay asked.

"Come on Pit-Bull; it's only money," Mike said stacking chips in random piles. "Right?"

Jim watched him, slightly slack-jawed, as Beverly touched his forearm. His eye twitched a little as he reached for his wallet. "Keep it up." He threw another hundred on the table.

"Atta boy!" Mike slammed his hand on the table.

The next few hours were a lot quieter for Jim. He lay back and played only when he thought he could win. He ignored Mike's goading, resisting the chance to reveal who he really was. The rest of the group shared idle chatter about benign topics like their grandkids, gossip in the neighborhood, and last week's episode of *CSI*.

Jim slowly but surely built a fairly large stack of chips. It was Mike's chips he wanted, though, and he seemed to be avoiding playing against Jim.

At the two-hour mark, it was time for a break. Mike made a bad joke about draining his lizard before disappearing from the room. Bonnie and Beverly made eye contact and headed for the back porch.

"Would you care to get some fresh air, James?" Beverly asked.

Would he! He followed along quickly, hoping to vacate the area before Mike returned.

On the back porch, Bonnie didn't waste a second before lighting up a joint. She took a quick drag and handed it to Beverly. They didn't seem to think there was anything wrong with the illegal contraband they were smoking in front of the former cop.

"How is Lynn holding up?" Beverly asked, coughing a little as she exhaled.

Bonnie took the joint back from her. "The shaking is getting worse; this helps, though." She held up the joint before taking another toke.

Jim looked back and forth between them without a word. Did they really think this was OK?

"Her or you?" Beverly said with a snicker.

Bonnie laughed with her. "Both."

"I'm sorry," Jim stepped in. "Is that a marijuana cigarette?"

This was New Jim after all.

Bonnie held it out to him. "Why, yes, it is. I'm sorry, I should have offered earlier!"

"Did I miss them legalizing that?"

"Oh, James," Beverly sighed. She took the joint and took a quick hit before handing it back to Bonnie. "You really do need to lighten up. I'm going to the loo before we start up again."

Beverly left Jim and Bonnie alone.

"So, you want a hit or you going to turn me in?"

Jim considered his options and then conceded. "I'll give it a try."

"There you go!" she said, handing him the joint. "Your first time?"

Jim took a deep drag and coughed. "In about forty-five years."

"Don't worry, I won't narc on you," she smiled. "Can I give you some advice?"

He shrugged, took another hit. It didn't feel like anything, but he knew it would hit him soon. He would need his wits for the rest of the game, so he passed the joint back.

"The people here are good people; they want to be your friends," she said. "I don't know you, but I'm pretty sure your problems are with yourself. Get over yourself, and you'll fit in just fine."

"You some kind of shrink?" he asked.

She smiled. "That obvious? Psychiatrist, practiced for thirty-five years. Wish they would have let us prescribe this."

"Why'd you stop?"

"I got tired of hearing the same problems over and over," she looked down at the ground as she spoke. "And then Lynn got sick, and she became my focus."

Jim knew the feeling. "Can I ask what's wrong with her? She seems fine."

"MS, multiple sclerosis. She'll take her shot tomorrow and be down for a few days," Bonnie said. "I think this poker game is what keeps her going; it's the only thing she talks about all week."

"Oh."

"So don't fuck it up, k?" She patted him on the chest. "Let's get back."

Jim spent the next hour studying the people around him. Maybe it was what Bonnie had said, maybe it was his earlier resolution to try, or maybe it was just the pot, but he was making a genuine effort to understand the group dynamic.

They all seemed happy. There was no reason he couldn't be happy. His gaze settled on Mike. Oh yeah, he remembered why he couldn't be happy. At least not yet.

"Did anyone else put their house in a trust with their children?" Beverly asked as she looked at a freshly dealt pair of cards. "Samuel had mentioned it a while back, and with Ted's sudden death, it really got me thinking."

The concept came from out of nowhere, but Jim knew what she was talking about. Thane had suggested it to Jim when he bought the house. He probably should have done it already; it would be a family trust that included himself, Heather, and Jenny. Should anything happen to him, the house would belong to them, and they wouldn't have to pay estate tax or probate the property.

The table chimed in with various responses. Sam had proposed the idea to all of them, and most of them had done it. They weighed the benefits, and the consensus was that it was a solid financial move to help take care of their kids. He made a mental note to look into it when the case was finished.

The final hand of the night was dealt.

Jim felt like he'd been disengaged from the game for a while. His stack of chips was good. He'd recovered from the initial loss of that devastating first hand and was ahead for the night. So it would have been easy to just bow out when Mike bet twenty-five, but what fun would that be?

"It's twenty-five, that's two-five," Mike said. "Whattaya say, Pit-Bull? You been quiet for a while."

Jim tossed some chips in the pile. "I say you should stop calling me that."

Jay quietly called them while everyone else folded. The first three cards were turned over, ace of hearts, two of clubs, and five of hearts. It was Mike's turn for action again.

"So defensive," Mike said, sliding more chips into the pot. "Twenty-five more."

Jim put his chips in without a word, just a straight face for Mike.

"I will see one more card," Jay said softly, placing his chips in the pot.

The next card was flipped. Another two, this time a heart.

"Check," Mike offered quickly.

Jim followed suit, but Jay chimed in with a bet. "I would like to bet fifty dollars."

Without hesitation or even a glance in Jay's direction, Jim and Mike spoke in unison, "Call."

"I see there is no respect for me at this table," Jay said.

The last card was the ace of spades.

Mike and Jim were locked in a death stare from across the table. Beverly batted her eyelashes at Jim, but he wouldn't avert his attention from his enemy. This would be their final showdown of the night.

"Hundred," Mike said, pushing chips in without breaking eye contact.

Jim furrowed his brow and broke the stare-off. "A hundred? That's a big bet." He reviewed his cards and tapped his chips. "I really hate to lay this one down."

"Been here before, Pit-Bull. You sure you want to come at me again?" Mike took a cigar out of his pocket and rolled it in his fingers. "Didn't work out so good for you last *time*."

Jim looked at his cards again, then across to Beverly. He gave her a quick wink. "I think I've got a read on your poker face there, Mikey. I'll raise to all-in. That's another one-seventy-eight on top."

Mike turned to meet Beverly's eyes. The corner of her lip was curled in a smirk. She raised her eyebrows at him. *What now, big boy?*

"I am still in this hand as well, you know," Jay interjected.

"Yes, Sanjay, you can play, too," Mike said condescendingly. "It's your turn."

The whole table turned their attention to Jay as he counted his stack of chips. "I only have one hundred and five dollars, but I…I call."

"Damn, that's a big pot," Tommy observed.

"Biggest we've had in some time," Beverly replied. "James and Michael seem to bring out the best in each other."

"You boys came to play, didn't you?" Mike stalled.

Jim was growing impatient. "You in or out?"

"I'm in. You overplayed your flush, Jimmy boy." Mike flipped his cards over. "Full house, aces full of twos."

"River again," Jim nodded. "Nice hand."

Mike reached for the chips. "Gotta be in it to win it."

Jay flipped over his cards revealing the three and four of hearts. A straight flush, but no one was paying attention to him.

"Hold on," Jim said, flipping a pair of twos over. "Quad twos. That's four twos."

"Guys?" Jay said.

They continued to ignore him. Mike stopped raking the chips and strained to look at Jim's cards. He looked to Beverly for confirmation, and she nodded.

"Son of a bitch! You checked quads?"

Jim shrugged.

"Guys?" Jay raised his voice.

Mike and Jim turned sharply to Jay and found themselves in unison again. "What?!"

"I have a straight flush."

The table turned their focus to Jay's cards. There was an eruption of laughter. The perfect tension cutter to end the night.

Jim lightened and slapped Jay on the back in congratulations. "Nice hand, little man."

"What a monster!" Mike conceded.

"I was not sure what was happening there," Jay said.

Tommy nudged him in the ribs. "Got caught downwind in a pissin' contest."

"That sounds rather unpleasant," Jay responded.

"A pissing contest I won, by the way," Jim affirmed, a truth that was lost in the commotion. Jim had beaten Mike, and he wouldn't let him forget it.

With that, they traded chips for cash and called it a night.

TWENTY-SEVEN

The dynamic of the excursion changed on the way home. Much to Mike's chagrin, Jim accepted an offer to ride home with Beverly that night.

She didn't invite him in when they got there, though. He was sure that his victory over Mike had earned him another invite for a nightcap. Only a few hours prior, she had practically thrown herself at him, after all.

He asked her if they could go out tomorrow, but she declined. She said she'd check her schedule and get back to him; she was sure something would clear up later in the week.

She left Jim standing outside her front door, confused. He convinced himself he'd misread the earlier signs. He didn't misread anything, though; she had recalibrated her approach. He just didn't know it yet.

"Swing and a miss!" Mike yelled from next door.

The next morning, Jim studied the information he'd compiled so far on the "case." The case, the one he still wasn't quite sure he could prove even existed. The night before had provided a subtle clue he decided was just a small piece of a larger picture.

Sam's seemingly innocuous suggestion that the owners of Shady Place put their homes into a trust had other implications. If an owner died and their home needed to be probated, it could take months or years, but placed in a trust, the home could be sold by surviving members without having to wait.

He could kill the owner and list and sell the property in a fraction of the time.

He could kill the owner.

Jim had already considered Sam a suspect. Outside of Mike, he was the only suspect. He scratched his chin and stared at the wall he'd covered with Post-it notes. He wrote "Trust" on a new note and slapped it on the wall.

His next action was one he thought he'd never take in his life.

New Jim.

He stopped by the house of Michael O'Flaherty, his sworn enemy, and asked him if he wanted to go to the local Board of Realtors with him. He could have called, made Mike come to him, but his cell was still dead.

"A field trip!" Mike was excited to kick their sleuthing into high gear.

Jim drove them to the Board of Realtors and instructed Mike, "Let me do the talking."

Mike was happy to oblige; he was actually happier Jim came to him than he was about the fact that they might be making progress. He was impressed with Jim's connecting the trusts with Sam's evil plot. He had been effusive on the ride over about how impressed he was. Was he a little too excited about the process? Maybe, but he was on the other side of an investigation for once, and it was actually fun to fit the pieces together.

The Board of Realtors was buzzing with activity. A continuing education class had just let out, a class on ethics that the agents were required to take every few years. An affable young administrator with Sarah emblazoned on her name tag greeted them.

Jim never had the patience for pleasantries, so he just jumped right in. "I need some information."

"I've got information," she responded. "What do you need?"

Mike could already sense he was going to have to step in and help but decided to see how it played out.

"A list of everything sold in Shady Place over the last three years or so. I'm in a bit of a hurry."

The entire office stopped what they were doing at the mention of Shady Place. You'd think Jim had called her a bad name.

"Shady Place?" Sarah asked. "What do you need it for?"

"What does it matter?"

She stumbled on the words a bit, obviously uncomfortable talking about Shady Place. "I'm just, well, that's...ummm, Sam Thane's neighborhood. Have you spoken to him about it?"

"It's not *his* neighborhood," Jim said. "He can't have a monopoly—"

It was going exactly as Mike had expected, Jim's sandpaper approach to human relations didn't work in the real world. Maybe when he was a cop, but not now, and not with this young lady.

"I'm sorry, Sarah," Mike cut in, pointing at her name tag. "That's a pretty name. My friend here ain't used to interacting with the public. Let alone such a pretty girl." He leaned in a little closer and whispered, "He spent the last few years in the looney bin."

She lightened at Mike's flattery, even blushed a little. Jim tried to contradict the statement, but Mike shut him down with a single hand. "He's interested in selling his house in Shady Place, and the Realtor he's been talkin' to has been tootin' his own horn a little. We just want to find out if he's blowin' smoke or the real deal. Think you could help us out, pretty Sarah?"

Come on! Jim thought to himself. *Does anyone really fall for that kind of bullshit line?*

"OK, give me a minute. I'll print up a list of all the sales over the last few years with the agents involved," she said, backing away with a big smile.

"You're a doll," Mike said, then turned to Jim. "And you're a real charmer."

"Oh, shut up," Jim said. "You're just preying on someone who obviously has very low self-esteem."

Mike shrugged. "I bet that girl would go to the moon and back for me right now. A little compliment and a smile go a long way, boss."

Sarah returned with a handful of printouts and handed them to Mike. "I didn't catch your name."

"Thank you, little lady," Mike said. "It's Mike, Mike Johnson."

Mike elbowed Jim gently, *told you so.* Jim shook his head, then snatched the papers.

"My grandma's birthday is this weekend," Sarah said. "You should come! She'll be eighty! You guys would be perfect for each other!"

Jim tried to hold back, but laughed loudly in an abbreviated HA!

Mike took it in stride. "Well, thank you, my dear, but I'm seeing someone."

Not a lie, he just wasn't the only one seeing her.

"Thanks, Sarah." Jim held up the papers as he walked away. "Let's go, Casanova!"

Mike nodded to Sarah, then followed Jim outside.

Sarah shrugged. "I thought he said his name was Mike."

†

Jim was still laughing at Mike when they got outside. "It's the hair; it makes you look old. Eighty!"

"Hey! Wait up a second!" An agitated man ran up behind them, flailing his arms. "You were asking about Sam Thane and Shady Place! There's someone you need to talk to. Call this number and ask for Tanya."

He handed Jim a crumpled business card and scampered away.

"Wait a second!" Jim called out.

"I've already said too much!" the man turned to shout back. "Just talk to her!" The man ran into a parked car, recovered, and hobbled away.

"What the hell was all that about?" Mike asked. "Who do you think he was?"

"Barry Watkins," Jim said.

Mike knew Jim was a good detective, but how in the hell did he know that? "How—"

Jim held up the card the man had handed him. One side had a handwritten phone number on it. The other side read Barry Watkins, Realtor, and had a photo of the man.

TWENTY-EIGHT

"We need a map of Shady Place," Jim observed.

Mike thought about it. "Maybe Thane? But we probably don't want to ask him; he might have questions. The HOA?"

"You mean Stern?" Jim asked.

"Yeah."

"Can you ask her?"

"No."

Jim thought about confronting Stern over the recurrent dog shit that continued to show up on his front lawn, but decided against it.

Not today.

She answered the door in her bathrobe, with wet hair. Every other time he'd seen her, she had been put together: hair pulled tightly in a bun, glasses, and pursed lips. Jim was stunned at how different she looked with her hair down. He forgot why he was there.

"Mr. Phillips?" she said. "Is there something I can help you with?"

"Huh?" he replied, shaking off his distraction. "I need a map."

"Of?"

"Right," Jim said. "Shady Place. I need a map of Shady Place."

She put her hands on her hips and pursed her lips.

There she is.

"Mr. Phillips," she said, always so matter of fact with him. "This is my personal residence. If you need a map of the neighborhood, you can stop by the office any weekday between 10:00 a.m. and 4:00 p.m."

"But, Mike," he stopped and sighed to himself. *Mike sent him there.* "Where is that?"

"Just inside the east gate."

He lingered to take her in; she really did look a lot different. Alluring even.

"Will that be all, Mr. Phillips?"

He snapped back to attention and nodded in the affirmative. She closed the door without another word.

Goddamn O'Flaherty.

He stopped by the homeowner's association office on his way and got what he was looking for. When he splayed the map out on his desk, the neighborhood was a lot larger than he thought.

It was sprawling.

Thousands of acres and even more home sites. Cross-referencing the addresses of the "victims" they'd identified might be harder than he thought. At least more time consuming.

His security cameras were monitoring the neighborhood around him on a screen at his desk. When the doorbell rang, he assumed he'd be looking up at a delivery man with his new cell phone, but instead found the lovely Beverly in a sundress smiling back at him.

A pleasant surprise for sure.

"Hey, Bev," Jim answered the door with a smile. "What's going on?"

"I tried calling you, but you're not answering your cell phone."

"It's broken; supposed to have a new one delivered today," he said.

"I have some time before my plans tonight," she said. "Thought maybe you'd want to join me for a drink? There's a nice little wine bar not too far away."

He looked back to his office; he was just getting going. "Yeah, ummm, OK. Why not?"

She frowned a little. "I didn't mean to bother you."

"Oh, no. Sorry, I just got into something!"

She pointed up at the camera overhead. "May I see?"

He took her inside to show her the system he'd created, a split screen with eight separate angles.

"My house, Mike's, the backyards, the street," she counted them off. "Looks like you've got it all covered."

"I don't want a repeat of the other night with the toilet paper," he said. "I can turn the one away from your house if you want."

"No, it's nice to know you're keeping an eye out," she said, looking around the room at his walls covered in Post-it notes. "Maybe you'll catch the vandal who's been shiting on your lawn."

His ears perked up at her use of shite instead of the American shit he would have used. Her accent made him smile inside. After spending most of his life around Philadelphians, who used words like mook and youse, he found the variety of dialects in Shady Place amusing, interesting, and foreign all at once.

Then he realized he'd drifted away again. "I'm sorry, what?"

"The shite," she thought about it. "The dog poop on your lawn…" The way she said "poop" made him smile even wider.

"Right, of course." He nodded. "I need to review the footage;

I've just been so busy. How do you keep up with everything going on here?"

She shrugged. That was life in Shady Place; there was always *something* going on. "That's why people move here, so they can stay active in their twilight years."

She was so matter of fact, but the fact of the matter for Jim was simple. "I've done more this last month than I did in the whole three years since Karen passed."

"James," she said. "You've only been here a few weeks."

"You sure?"

She nodded and smiled. "Shall we go?"

"Somewhere I can get a stiff drink!"

Beverly took one last good look around his office, taking in as much as she could before Jim led her out.

Jim settled for a beer. They told him it was an IPA brewed somewhere close by. He thought he'd give it a shot. It poured out with golden edges and a slightly copper hue. The aroma was hoppy, with a hint of caramel and butterscotch, maybe; it was something sweet he couldn't put his finger on. He could definitely taste the hops and a bit of a diacetyl butteriness. At least that's the description the waiter gave him and what he'd told Jim he should taste.

He tasted beer. He liked beer. It wasn't his go to, but sometimes he wanted something a little lighter. He didn't hate his IPA, but he really wished it was a scotch.

The wine bar Beverly took him to only had a beer and wine license. He could see a sports bar three doors down that had a full liquor bar, but New Jim was adaptable. This is where Beverly wanted to go, so he was in.

The little spot she'd taken them to had an outdoor patio that overlooked a lake, which in Florida can, and most of the time does, mean a man-made retention pond, often with a spurting fountain in the middle to jazz it up a little.

Those were the things Jim noted to himself when they sat down, but his mind quickly drifted to the case he and Mike were working. He needed to tie the list from the Board of Realtors, the map, and the murders together.

Murders. Could even call them that?

"You're somewhere else right now," Beverly said. "Are you thinking about your case?"

"Yes, I'm sorry," he said. "I just get so wrapped up."

She smiled, touching his hand. "It looks good on you; it really does."

"Over thirty years I worked putting bad guys away. Then I retired and spent five years watching my wife…" He shook his head softly. "Since Karen passed, I just haven't had any direction."

He didn't mean to bring Karen up in front of Beverly, but she was part of his being. So much of who he was he owed to her. All the good parts.

"It's been a while since you had something to focus your attention on?" Beverly asked.

"You know, this case may not go anywhere, but I feel like I have a purpose again. A reason to get up in the morning," he said. He continued musing aloud. "Maybe I'll get a PI license when this is all over."

"I peeked at the wall in your office," she said. "Do you really think Samuel could have something to do with it?"

He sipped his beer, then smacked his lips slightly in disapproval. "Nothing surprises me. There's plenty of motivation."

"What would be the motivation?" she asked, brushing a strand of hair from her face. It had been falling in front of her eyes all day. It was by design, so Jim would notice her eyes when she had to wipe it away. If he was paying close enough attention and the time was right, he'd know to brush it aside himself.

"Money," Jim said. "I've seen people kill for much less."

"You think you know someone. Should I be worried?"

He cocked an eyebrow at her and gave her a sly little wink. "Not with me next door."

It was the first sign she'd seen from him that he was gaining a little confidence. "Based on what you've told me, maybe you're the one who should be worried."

"Maybe!" he laughed.

He took a swig of his beer and the two shared a long, quiet moment of eye contact, just in time for the skies to open up. It was a little earlier than usual. The rain snuck up on them and began to fall heavily, sending the duo running for cover under a nearby awning.

"Every day!" he said, shaking his head.

They laughed as they shook water off themselves like wet dogs. The hair had fallen back over her eyes, but she didn't swipe it away this time. Instead, she waited.

Jim delivered.

He pushed the locks from her eyes gently, saying, "Let me get that for you."

Their eyes were locked again, and she bit her lip gently. Jim swallowed. He froze, staring at her in silence. His heart was pounding, but he simply couldn't take the next step.

Sensing the moment was passing, Beverly took it for him. She grabbed him by his head and kissed him. She pulled him out into the rain, and they remained locked in an embrace that sent shivers through Jim.

He wasn't sure how long they were standing there, snogging as Beverly called it, but he did know he felt something. It wasn't the same feeling he'd had with Karen the first time, the last time. It was something different. Something new. Something all its own.

They separated as the rain stopped, and Jim let out a deep breath.

Beverly could see the impact the kiss had on Jim. It was exactly what she was looking for. When they looked up, a group of patrons at the wine bar were applauding them.

Much of Jim's sunburn had subsided, but the embarrassment he felt caused his skin to surpass even the brightest hue he'd worn since the golf course.

He cleared his throat. "Ch-check, please."

The return home found Jim with a new a swagger. Beverly could already sense it in him. He seemed to stand a little taller when he opened her door for her. He was almost puffing his chest out, but not intentionally; it looked natural. A return to prominence for one who had forgotten who he was.

He walked her to her door and gave her a peck on the cheek. "Thanks for today."

"Of course, James," she smiled. "It seems like you may just be ready to come out of your shell after all."

"Yeah, maybe," he smirked.

"Tomorrow," she said, taking his hand. "I'm all yours, all day, if you'll have me."

"I'd like that."

DAVID A BYRNE

They shared another deep kiss. He felt like he was living in a bad romance novel. It was almost too clichéd to be real. A kiss in the rain. A good-bye kiss on his lady's doorstep. If it was indeed a reenactment of a romance novel or movie, it was still rated G, suitable for all audiences, more Nicholas Sparks than *Fifty Shades* of anything.

They broke off their connection, and she went inside. When he turned to head home, he found Mike staring at him. He was standing in his own driveway, smoking a cigar, a sign he was either celebrating or upset. In this case, Jim was certain he knew which.

He threw a wink in Mike's direction before retrieving what could only be his new cell phone from his front porch.

TWENTY-NINE

When he got his phone up and running, Jim had twenty-seven voice mails and seventeen text messages.

Most of the messages were from his daughters, each more frantic than the previous. The text messages included a lot of exclamation points and question marks. The correspondence led right up until a few minutes before Jenny walked in and found her father passed out.

The other messages were from his new Shady Place friends trying to track him down for one reason or another. The last voice mail was from his old captain, a response as terse as the message Jim had left for him:

Phillips, it's Captain Brown calling you back. Tag. You're it.

He prepared to call his old captain, but something on his desk caught his eye.

It was the business card Barry Watkins had handed him the day before.

Tanya Jennings.

He tapped the card on his desk, studying the name and phone number.

He reached Tanya on the second ring. "Ms. Jennings? My name is Jim Phillips. Would you have a moment to talk to me about Sam Thane?"

The line was still open, but the call was silent.

"Ms. Jennings? Tanya? Are you there?" Was she afraid to talk to him? Maybe there was something to this, or maybe they had a bad connection. He kept trying. "Barry Watkins told me I should talk to you…"

On the other end of the phone, he could hear a soft, uncertain voice. "I'm here."

Their discussion was short; she agreed to see Jim in thirty minutes.

Mike prepared as he always did for a date with Beverly. Tonight, it was a light blue button up short-sleeved shirt, cigar in the front pocket, and khaki pants.

He checked his hairpiece and his breath before stepping out the front door. He was headed to pick up Beverly but decided to make a pit stop at Jim's first. He figured they could make plans for tomorrow, and he could remind Jim why Beverly had plans that night.

When Mike raised his hand to knock on Jim's door, it opened before his knuckle could land.

Jim was obviously on his way out. "Mike?"

"Hey, Jimbo," Mike said. "You get that map?"

"Yeah, I got the map."

Mike grinned, knowing he'd sent Jim straight into the lion's den. "I see you made it back in one piece."

"What do you want?" Jim was still ruminating on a suitable payback.

"Well, I was just on my way to my date with Bev…" Mike paused for effect before finishing his thought. "Wanted to see when you'd have a little time to go over the stuff we got from the Realtor place. You call that Tanya girl yet?"

Jim sucked his teeth at the mention of Beverly, exactly the reaction Mike was looking for; a little dig in a friendly conversation.

"No, not yet," Jim lied, then returned the dig. "I was busy with Bev all afternoon."

"Maybe we can call her together?"

"Maybe we can."

"But not now, because I have to go on my date with Bev," Mike reiterated. "Got any more of that B12? I think I'm gonna to need the energy tonight."

Mike patted Jim on the shoulder and turned away.

"Hey," Jim called out after him. "You may have tonight, but I've got all day tomorrow."

Mike stepped in closer. He put his mouth right next to Jim's ear. "You know, I think maybe you should stay away from her."

Jim slowly turned his head to meet Mike's eyes. "Or what?"

It escalated quickly, the two men face-to-face, less than a few inches apart. If he hadn't been so pissed at Mike already, Jim's proximity radar would have had him going over the deep end. He stepped back, squared Mike up, and shoved him. "You'll kill me?"

"What's that supposed to mean?" Mike pushed Jim back.

"You knew I'd figure out people were being murdered, so you brought me into this to keep yourself from being a suspect!" Jim said as he shoved Mike harder.

Mike recovered. "What? You're crazy! Why the hell would I…" He spoke as he pushed Jim again. "I didn't kill anyone!"

"Right, just like you didn't kill Peterson!" Jim gave him another shove. They were standing in the middle of Jim's lawn, circling each other like ravenous animals, ready to pounce. "I should have seen it all along. Pushing me toward the Realtor, but it's you! Admit it!"

Jim knew Mike hadn't killed anyone. He was just angry, and everything he hated about the man in front of him was boiling over.

Mike had had enough. He tackled Jim. The two wrestled on the ground, neither ever really gaining the upper hand.

Jim made several failed attempts at Mike's toupee. "Get this ridiculous thing off your head!"

They took turns insulting each other, Mike claiming he didn't kill Peterson, Jim refusing to accept the claims. They were working something out; maybe it needed to happen, or maybe it was healthy for two grown men to just go at it every once in a while. It's the whole reason they still allow fighting in professional hockey. They were both due five minutes in the penalty box after this one.

They were wearing out. Jim had one hand on Mike's hair, while Mike firmly held it in place with both of his hands. They were slowing and almost to a stop, and then Mike mentioned Karen. "You were too busy with your dying wife to pay attention to what really happened!"

Jim stopped. He let go of Mike's hair, balled up his fist, and reached back to unleash a blow. "You mother—"

"Boys!" Beverly stepped in. She was certain they were fighting over her. It was exactly what she wanted. Better than a box of chocolates or flowers. Genuine hatred toward each other, all because of her. "There's no need to fight over me."

They both turned to look at her. Jim pushed off Mike, making sure to use his entire body weight to get up. He brushed past Beverly and headed straight to his car without looking back, "Have fun on your date."

He was gone.

Beverly offered Mike a hand. "That was interesting."

"Anger issues," Mike said.

Beverly let go as Mike was halfway up, sending him tumbling back down.

"Hey!"

She pointed at his shirt and covered her mouth with her hand. "You've got shite on your shirt."

He looked down and frowned. "I guess I'll go change."

"Please do."

Jim made another call to his old friend Captain Brown on the way to Tanya's house but was greeted by voice mail again.

Tanya didn't have many visitors and rarely left the porch light on, but today, she was expecting company. Jim didn't think anything of the gradual incline from the driveway to her front door. He had no reason to.

He knocked gently. She seemed so meek and quiet on the phone, the last thing he wanted to do was come off as aggressive.

"Who is it?" a female voice asked from behind the door.

"Jim Phillips; we spoke on the phone."

He could hear a handful of locks opening on the door. He looked around the street. It seemed like a nice enough area, but he was sure she had her reasons for the extra security.

The last thing he expected to see when she opened the door was a beautiful young woman sitting in a wheelchair. Before either could get a word out, her security alarm let out an ear-piercing wail. Jim covered his ears as Tanya quickly wheeled her way back into the belly of the house.

"Oh shoot!" she cursed to herself. "Please come in and lock the door!"

She fumbled with the buttons on the alarm keypad. She was becoming flustered; there usually wasn't anyone else here when she screwed up like this. She felt stupid as her fingers flubbed the buttons. Each depressed number led to a beep, but she was putting the numbers in wrong. Or was it too fast? Either way, she was becoming distraught.

Her house phone rang, adding to the chaos. She was breathing heavily and on the verge of tears until Jim stepped behind and softly addressed her.

"It's OK; just breathe," he said calmly. "Take your time and put the code in. One number at a time."

Beep, pause. Beep, pause. Beep, pause. Beep.

The last sound was quickly followed by a new chime affirming the system had been satisfactorily fed a code that allowed it to return to a dormant state.

She sighed and wiped her face with both hands. "Thank you."

He handed her a portable phone he found on a nearby table, which she answered and assured the monitoring service it was another false alarm.

She led him to the kitchen and offered him a cup of tea. Jim offered to make it for her instead, but she insisted she needed to do for herself.

"Please, just have a seat," she said, navigating her kitchen as deftly as an open-wheel racecar driver on a road course.

She wasn't what Jim had expected, and he wasn't sure how to broach the subject matter he'd come to question her about. She offered him sugar and honey, then slid up next to him.

She quickly pulled the cup from in front of Jim and replaced it with her own cup. "Oops, that's Sleepytime tea; you don't want that one, or you'll be crashing here tonight!"

He could see she was capable but struggled with her disability.

"You live here alone?" he asked.

She nodded. "I do now."

Her fiancé wasn't prepared to handle an "invalid." His words, not hers.

He was a dick.

She wasn't sure why exactly Jim was there, but knew it was about Sam Thane and Shady Place. She wasn't really one for small talk, not since the accident, and she wasn't looking for sympathy, so she wasted no time jumping right in. A trait Jim admired.

"It was three years ago. It was my first listing, and I guess I didn't know any better," she explained. "Nice little three-bedroom in Shady Place. I couldn't have been more excited."

Jim nodded along, sipping his tea. "I understand things sell quickly in there."

"That's why I targeted the neighborhood. A friend of my gram's wanted to sell, so she gave me the listing. I thought everything was going to be great, scheduled open houses, put my sign in the yard, and I was ready to go."

She paused to take a sip of tea.

The look on her face told Jim whatever happened was still weighing heavily. He said, "We don't have to talk about this if you don't want to."

"No, it's fine, really." She shook her head as she spoke, almost as if it was in disapproval of what had transpired all those years ago. "The first call I got was from someone disguising their voice and telling me to get out of Shady Place."

"You were threatened?"

"Not really; they just told me I didn't belong there. I thought it was some sort of hazing or a joke." Her face dropped a little, and she furrowed her brow as she continued. "It was the second call, telling me I needed to cancel the listing or else…"

"Or else what?"

"Didn't say," she said. "I have a friend who's a cop, but he told me it wasn't really enough to do anything. The call came from a disposable cell. I called the Board of Realtors and got the same story; nothing they could do." She looked away. The story was starting to bring back unpleasant memories. "Then one night, I get a call to show the house, but the buyer never showed up."

Tanya stared at her hands as she wrung them together. Jim knew better than to try to touch a trauma victim uninvited. Instead, he offered words in an attempt to comfort her. "I can see this is hard for you. You're under no obligation to speak to me—"

"Look, mister. I don't really know what you're here about," she found the strength to meet his gaze. "But outside of my family, you're the first person who hasn't looked at me like I was crazy or a liar in years. I think even my family is just humoring me. If you're willing to listen to my story, I'm going to tell it."

He smiled and nodded. "Please go on."

"When I left, it was pouring. I could barely see the road." She closed her eyes, and she was there, with the rain pounding on her windshield, the whoosh back and forth of her wipers, a bright light gleaming in the rearview mirror. "Next thing I know, there are high beams in my rearview. A horn blaring behind me." She took a quick breath, then continued, "I swear there was a bump, something hitting me from behind or on the side. I don't know, it all happened so fast…"

She stopped and dropped her head into her hands. She was sobbing softly, blaming herself again. Was she just careless? Did she just lose control? Tanya looked up at Jim with tears streaming down her cheeks. "I woke up in the hospital. Three months, they told me. Did I do this to myself?"

Jim hesitantly reached a hand toward her. She didn't recoil, so he rubbed her arm gently. "I'm sure you didn't cause whatever happened. Were there any leads?"

Tanya shook her head no. "I asked about my car, if there was paint or anything, but they had already scrapped it by the time I woke. They told me I just lost control on a wet road."

She sniffed and wiped away what was left of her tears. *No more crying today.*

"Look, I don't know if it was him, but the other Realtors are afraid of him. Even though there's no proof he's ever done anything, no one wants to take a listing in that neighborhood. After what happened to me…no one wants to end up like this."

Jim was reminded of the image of Sam pounding that for sale sign into the yard of the house he'd "converted" from a For Sale by Owner.

"You're a strong young woman," he said, trying to be sincere, unsure what to say. "You're more than just that chair."

He felt like he'd made some profound observation; one she was sure to appreciate.

"Don't do that," she said. "Everyone assumes that's what I want to hear. You don't know me, but you seem to know Sam Thane. If you think you've got something on him and you can take him down, you do that!"

"I will," he said. He wanted to say more but left it at that. He tried to take a sip of his tea, but Tanya pulled the cup away from his open mouth.

"What are you waiting for? Go now; go get him!" She shooed him out the front door, "Don't come back until you've got some results!"

THIRTY

Jim went home from Tanya's house possessed. Her story didn't really help the case, but it inspired him. He spent the night sifting through online tax records, cross-referencing sales, dates, locations, and obituaries. He marked his newly acquired Shady Place map.

He pored over the information until he was bleary-eyed. He copied everything and slid it neatly into a folder. A nod of appreciation; Jim's seal of approval.

On just a few hours of sleep, more a wakeful rest, he drove to the closest police station Google could find, and after waiting forty-five minutes, he presented his case.

His name was Ronald Benjamin, Ronnie to his friends. He was a detective, about half Jim's age. He actually reminded Jim of himself at that age; they even had the same haircut. The similarities Jim was so quick to recognize in this younger version of himself are precisely the reason Benjamin's response didn't surprise him.

"This is pretty thorough," Benjamin said, fanning through the pages of Jim's file. "Are you a PI?"

Jim shook his head. "Detective James Phillips, Philadelphia PD. Retired."

"Retired," Benjamin looked at a few pages a little closer. "Wait, is this all in Shady Place?"

"Yes, there is a direct correlation between—"

"What is it?" Benjamin said, holding a hand up to cut Jim off. "An epidemic of failed life alert bracelets? People falling and they can't get up? It's an old folks' neighborhood!"

Jim didn't like jokes being made at his expense, not by some snot-nosed little runt. "It's an active adult community!" The words startled Jim as they came out of his mouth. He never thought he would defend Shady Place, but there he was. "It doesn't matter what it is. People are dying!"

"Look, Mr. Phillips—Detective." Benjamin realized he'd been callous with a former brother in blue, so he backed off the quips. "I'm sure you were a great cop in your day, but it seems like maybe you've got a little too much time on your hands."

Jim poked his finger hard on the file. "That Realtor is killing them! This poor girl is paralyzed! Why is no one doing anything about it?" He moved his finger upward and stuck it in Benjamin's face. "Follow the evidence, and do your job!"

"Mr. Phillips, you need to calm down. I'll take your file and look it over." Benjamin was growing frustrated with this old man who was berating him. This time waster. He'd always skated a thin line between insolence and reverence when it came to his elders. Today, the former won out. "Maybe you should just go home, play a round of shuffleboard, and enjoy your twilight years. Let those of us who are still cops have our turn. How's about you let me do my job? How's that sound?"

Jim retracted his finger. He had left it lingering in Benjamin's face a little longer than he should have, but he was making a point. It occurred to him that the reaction he was getting was precisely the same one he would have given himself thirty years ago. He was the past, and he was trying to stir a pot that had nothing in it. Benjamin didn't care about some old people he didn't know, who might or might not be dying from unnatural causes.

Jim feigned a smile. "Yeah, sure; great idea. I'll do that."

He left without another word, but the sounds of Benjamin dismissing the "geezer" to a uniformed officer who questioned the interaction followed him out.

He ruminated on what went wrong. He thought about his evidence objectively, conceding what he hadn't wanted to admit. He'd forced it. He was connecting dots that all pointed in one direction.

Nowhere.

He could see the correlation between all the "victims." The family trusts, Thane's sales, often within days of taking the listing, and even the way they all died, just like Mike had pointed out.

That was the thing, though; unless you were looking and making leaps of faith, there simply wasn't enough to go on. Maybe if the autopsies had said something. *Anything*. But that coroner was as useless as tits on a bull.

The only connection he could find was Mike.

He'd brought it up.

He'd identified the victims.

He'd had issues with all of them.

They had all dated Beverly.

Beverly. His mind wandered while he sat at a red light. He blew it with her. He made an ass of himself the evening before. Could he recover? *Probably not*, he concluded. The case was all he had left.

The incessant honk of a car horn behind snapped him out of his stupor. He began driving again, but his mind drifted back to the case.

It wasn't the first time it crossed his mind. Had Mike played him? Did he allow himself to be pushed toward Thane?

As much as Jim wanted to put it all on Mike, that didn't make sense, either. Maybe he was so desperate to feel like he was important again, he just got caught up in the fervor of it all and went with it.

His phone buzzed with a text message. The sender's name alone surprised him; the message confused him. It was from Beverly:

Where R U? Thought we had plans.

THIRTY-ONE

Beverly was standing in his driveway when he got home. He had called her from the road after she sent him the text message. He told her he didn't think they would still be on after the display he and Mike had put on for her last night.

She told him plainly, "Not a word about any of it. No Michael. No death. Just you and me. Now get back here and pick me up."

He'd thought it was over. Why would she want anything to do with him after the childish wrestling match in his yard? But there she was, climbing into his car.

"James," she said, pecking him on the cheek. "I trust with all that ugliness behind us, we can have a pleasant day."

"Yes, ma'am," he said. "Just point me where to go."

"The mall."

His face betrayed him before he ever got the words out. "The mall?"

"Big place full of different stores...people shop there," she said, knowing full well what he meant. "It won't be long; just need to take care of something, then the rest of the day is yours."

He nodded and smiled. "Mall it is. Where is it?"

Jim managed to make the drive to the mall a torturous one for Beverly. He spent the entire trip complaining about how archaic shopping malls had become. Why would anyone in their right mind drive somewhere, wrestle with parking, put up with punk kids and rude clerks, and pay more than Internet prices?

Why? He implored her, but she brushed off his complaints. She considered bringing up his case to distract him, but had already promised it wouldn't be a topic of discussion for the day. Instead, she just let him ramble.

To Jim's credit, everything he said was true. When they reached the mall, it was packed, and they had to park what felt like miles away, a distance that seemed even greater thanks to the sweltering Florida heat. It was the first time he noticed Beverly was wearing a zipped-up sweatshirt over her clothing.

How can she not be melting? Must be a woman thing.

Jim even managed to keep his cool when a pack of teenagers on skateboards whizzed past them, pointing and laughing at him in hushed murmurs. Jim narrowed his eyes and followed their trajectory as they skated away. When Beverly touched his arm, though, he returned his attention to her.

The mall was gargantuan. It was shiny and new, clean and bright. All the modern stores anyone could ask for. There were droves of people of all shapes, sizes, and ages. Mothers toting their children in harnesses, strollers, and even the occasional leash. A brilliant idea Jim thought, wishing the child who'd just run past them screaming had been restrained.

Spry seniors, many decades older than Jim, used the circular layout of the sprawling commercial center to do laps, often in pairs or groups, with weights on their wrists and ankles. The building shielded them from the oppressive heat and any potential nasty weather that may arise.

Groups of teenagers loitered about, their faces buried in electronic devices. Their attention seemed to fall on Jim more frequently than any of the other mall patrons, garnering suspicious scowls from the crusty old man.

"What did you say you needed here?" he asked.

"I didn't," she replied, leading him further into the belly of the beast.

"Fair enough," Jim said. "What do you need here?"

Before she could answer, a long-haired teenager in skinny jeans and a Pantera T-shirt stepped in their path. Jim was sure the kid was wearing the shirt ironically and wanted to chastise him, but the teen spoke first. "You're him, aren't you?"

Jim looked to Beverly. She shrugged. He wasn't sure whether to engage or try to move on. Logic told him the right move was to not engage.

Jim rarely listened to logic.

"I'm who?"

The kid held up a phone with an image of Jim's naked posterior trotting through the clubhouse at Shady Place. "Lobsterman streaks senior party!"

Beverly's eyes widened as she attempted to suppress laughter. She squeezed her lips tightly together. Jim on the other hand, felt no need to suppress anything.

"The hell?"

Beverly touched his arm and whispered to him, "Tommy put it on YouTube."

"Over a million hits, dude!" the teen said, looking back to his friends for encouragement. "You're famous!"

Jim snatched the phone from his hand. "Get out of here, all of you!"

227

"Hey! Give my phone back, old man!" He tried to take the phone from Jim, but he was nowhere near Jim's size or strength, and his attempts fell short against Jim's rigid arm holding him at bay.

"Fetch!" Jim said before tossing the phone into a nearby fountain.

The youth bounded to the fountain to retrieve his treasured lifeline. A teenager without his cell phone might as well be dead to the world, after all.

"Damn kids," Jim said.

"The paparazzi are bound to appear when you're a celebrity," Beverly quipped. "Maybe I can get an autograph later?"

This time, he decided to do the opposite of what his instincts urged him to, and he made a joke. "It won't be cheap. Extra if you want a selfie with me. Just see my assistant for details."

She kissed his cheek. "Oh, you."

"Why are we here again?"

"You'll see in just a moment," she said. "This way." She led him to the open center of the mall. The area played host to whatever seasonal gaiety might be happening at that time of year, Santa, the Easter Bunny, a makeshift haunted house. This time of year, though, it was devoid of holiday cheer, and they found a large group of seniors milling about.

Jim recognized one of them. He definitely lived in Shady Place. Then another and another. He quickly surmised something was amiss. They were in various stages of limbering up and removing sweatshirts and jackets.

"What's this?" he asked.

Beverly checked her watch, then unzipped her sweatshirt. "Be a dear and hold this."

She was wearing a T-shirt underneath that read Shady Place Silversteppers.

They all were.

Before Jim could gain his bearings, the group had taken formation, and some loud pop song he'd never heard before was flooding the central core of the mall. A sense of dread immediately filled him.

The entire group remained still, heads bowed toward the ground as the intro to the song rose in crescendo before cutting off completely. He tried to speak to Beverly, or really anyone who would listen at that point.

What is happening?

Hello?

Anyone?!

The music kicked backed in, and the group exploded in movement around Jim. He froze as they rhythmically spun and dipped around him. Beverly was leading a choreographed flash mob, and Jim was trapped in the middle of it.

He tried to make his way out, but every attempt was thwarted by a new wave of dancers.

They weren't doing anything too fancy; some of them really just moved a few steps here and there, as much as their bodies would let them at this advanced stage, but they had rhythm. They looked good, they were in sync, and they were enjoying themselves. So was the crowd that grew around the dancers.

If he had been on the outside, Jim would have seen quite the spectacle. But Jim wasn't on the outside; he was stuck. He was not enjoying himself. He was, in fact, growing quite angry, mostly at Beverly. He simply stopped moving, nearly throwing the group off step, but they managed to avoid him. He thought about sitting

229

down and waiting until it was over, but instead stood still, frowning, attempting to burn a hole through the back of Beverly's head with his eyes.

As the song reached its end, the group returned to their start positions, heads down, perfectly still, until there was silence.

The crowd erupted in applause, hooting and howling at the exploits of the Silversteppers. "The Silversteppers flash mob was a triumph of epic proportions," the *Shady Place Times* would declare in the next weekly issue, Jim's look of despair caught in the middle as photographic evidence the event had indeed taken place.

The group bowed, then shared congratulatory embraces. Beverly finally broke loose and found Jim stewing by himself around the outside of the group.

He carefully spaced his words out for effect. "What...the... fuck..."

"I supposed I should have warned you." She smiled coyly, wiping a bead of sweat from her forehead. "I thought it would be more fun this way."

"Fun?" He threw his hands in the air. "We have drastically different ideas of what constitutes fun!"

"Lighten up, James. You're going to give yourself a coronary," she said punching his arm. "After your display at the social, I thought you might enjoy this!"

He shook his head, not talking to anyone in particular. "She brings me here, of all places, the god damn mall..."

"James..."

"The mall, Beverly; you brought me to the mall."

"Jim!"

"And dancing!"

"Jim, shut up!" she shouted as he continued trying to speak over her.

She grabbed his face and kissed him. He was still trying to speak when their lips connected, but he quickly surrendered and joined in.

"Gross!"

The teenager had returned.

They broke off their embrace and found he wasn't alone. He had summoned a mall cop, who couldn't have been more than twenty himself and obviously took the role way too seriously. *Surely a police academy wannabe or washout*, Jim thought.

"That's him," the kid pointed an accusatory finger at Jim and waved his waterlogged phone in his other hand. "Dude broke my phone!"

Jim wanted to flee, but Beverly was with him; he couldn't just leave her. A slight squeeze of his hand drew his eyes to hers, and he could see she was thinking the same thing. With a small nod, they took off running.

"Come back here!"

The pursuit took them quickly out of the mall and into the parking lot. Zigs and zags were the order of the day as Jim and Beverly wove in and out of parked cars.

When they reached the sanctuary of Jim's Shelby, they stopped and caught their breath. The rush! Like being a teenager again. Jim had forgotten all about the embarrassment he felt being blindsided by that flash mob.

"I think we lost him," he said.

Beverly agreed, looking around to make sure.

"You make me feel so—" Jim couldn't finish the thought

before she was mauling him, knocking his seat backward.

Just like high school, he thought as they made out feverishly. The only thing that would have made it better was if it was actually his dad's car.

A tap on the window interrupted them. The mall cop had found them. He snapped their photo and informed them that they were banned from this mall forever.

"Joke's on you," Jim shouted through the window. "I didn't want to come here to begin with!"

Beverly chimed in, "Would you be a dear and text me a copy of that? We don't have any photos of us together!"

They laughed hysterically, even as the mall cop escorted their vehicle through the parking lot. Beverly pointed out that the man sitting beside her, James Phillips, was in fact now an outlaw.

Even if it was only mall law.

T HIRTY-TWO

His trip to the mall with Beverly left Jim with an unrestrained stupid grin that Beverly had never seen on him before.

"Something is different about you, James Phillips," she said, touching his hand.

Was it? He thought about where he was mentally. Maybe he *was* different. It reminded him of a promise he'd made to his daughters.

No, not that one, another one.

When they reached a stoplight, he pulled out his cell phone and typed a group message to Heather and Jenny.

Just one word:

Alive.

THIRTY-THREE

The day Jim spent with Beverly was magical. He didn't use the word lightly, but he fell in love that day.

Despite the fact that she ignored six calls from Mike, which was certainly endearing, it wasn't with Beverly.

Jim had fallen in love with Shady Place.

The neighborhood was more vibrant than usual. There were more people than usual. This weekend, Shady Place was hosting the National Pickleball Open Tournament. The event brought vendors, participants, and spectators from all over, and even featured a charity golf event. A hole in one on seventeen would snag you a new car!

Beverly showed Jim a side of Shady Place he'd never seen before. They perused booths with everything golf, tennis, and pickleball. Fashion, clubs, balls, rackets, you name it. A lot of them were giving away free swag. Jim's head had begun to peel from his burn, making it the joke of the day to suggest a hat for the next time he hit the links.

Usually, that kind of attention would have caused Jim to unleash a barrage of vitriol in the direction of those who dared poke the bear. But for one day, he took it in stride. All he had to do was look down at the hand cupped in his or at the face smiling next to him, pointing to this and that. They laughed and joked the day away.

He began to realize Beverly was constantly finding new ways to challenge him. The insult restaurant. The flash mob. Pitting him against Mike. She was trying to draw him out, and it was working.

The unexpected side effect was Jim's newfound affinity for Shady Place. Not the people, but what the neighborhood itself had to offer. The capper, what really pushed him over the edge, came in the form of a collection of golf carts.

There must have been forty of them. All different shapes and styles, from hot rods to sport-utility vehicles. Jim was slack-jawed in awe. One simple word was all he could muster. "Wow."

"You like them?" Beverly asked.

He smiled. "They put your clunker to shame. Might have to get myself one after all."

"Maybe like that one?" She pointed to one that bore a striking resemblance to his beloved Shelby GT.

He moved around the cart slowly, tilting his head to look at the details. "It's nice; not a Shelby, but…wow. It's really nice."

"You like her?" The car's owner approached. "A bit of an amalgamation. Not a Shelby, but there's some nods in that direction." He leaned in to whisper to Jim, "Don't tell anyone, but I souped this baby up; eighty-five horses."

"How fast?" Jim returned the whisper.

"I've hit 120 on an open stretch; thought I was going to die."

Jim didn't say a word, just turned and smiled at the man. They didn't need to say anything else, just a simple nod.

"She for sale?" Jim asked.

"Not this one, but here's my card," the man said. "Give me a call next week; maybe I can build you one."

Jim was giddy. A schoolgirl rolling in puppies would have

been less excited than Jim. He held it in, though, for the most part.

Beverly could tell he'd fallen hard for a glorified toy car. "Shall we move on, James?"

He took one last good look, then joined her. He made it less than fifteen feet before spinning around and snapping a photo. "For reference."

"What does a girl have to do to get that sort of attention?" she asked, batting her eyelashes.

"Racing stripes would help."

As the sun went down, Jim and Beverly found a comfortable piece of sod on a sprawling parcel of a lush Shady Place park. The lawn was covered in a sea of blankets, each containing its own set of Shady Placers there to view that night's Movie in the Park.

This week, it was *As Good as It Gets*, the Jack Nicholson–Helen Hunt feel good laugher about an old misanthrope who finds love and a new lease on life when he decides to step outside of his comfort zone.

It would have been a good opportunity for Jim to hold a mirror up to himself. Maybe Beverly had planned it this way all along. It would have, of course, if Jim and Beverly hadn't spent the first thirty minutes rolling around groping each other and necking like teenagers.

It was the second time they'd done this today. And the second time they had an audience.

Why don't you kiss me like that, Herman?

Look at them go!

Harlot.

The comments continued, but no one stopped them. Beverly

ran her hand up Jim's leg and found exactly what she was looking for. His little officer was at salute. She wondered if Little Jim was a detective, too. If he could find the right spots. Regardless of his skill level, he was ready to go.

So they did.

Jim drove Beverly's golf cart as fast as it would go. He assumed the party was on hold until they got back to her house. "You know, these things really are convenient. I think I'll call that guy next week."

"Mm-hmm," Beverly said, unzipping his pants as she leaned her head down toward his lap.

"Whoa, hello?" he said, looking down at the top of her head.

He took a deep breath as she took control of his shaft. His eyes shot wide open, and he muttered, "Ohhhh…"

To say Jim was surprised would be the understatement of the century. There she was, challenging him again. This time, his ability to operate a moving vehicle while being pleasured.

He failed.

The cart swerved erratically, nearly off the road. Beverly popped up and lifted her eyebrows at Jim. "You may want to be a little more careful when I've got you in such a…precarious position, James."

He may have failed initially, but not again. "Challenge accepted," he muttered to himself.

"What?"

He shook his head and shrugged his shoulders, *I didn't say anything.*

Jim skidded off the driveway and onto Beverly's lawn. That's where he left the cart, but she didn't care. They were going at it like they were running out of time. They backed into Beverly's front door so hard, she hit her head and swore a procession of words Jim didn't recognize, but from their order and her tone, he was sure they were the worst she could conjure.

She took a moment to catch her breath and unlock the door, but the reprieve was short. They immediately resumed their snogging all the way to the bedroom.

"Why don't you put on that little black number you had on before," Jim suggested. "When my head was lodged firmly up my ass."

"Excellent idea. Why don't you make yourself comfortable?" she said, slipping out of the room.

He ran his hand across her bed. Black and red faux silk adorned her king-size bed. There were no frilly pillows or lace. Only a stitched fleur-de-lis in the middle of the comforter. To Jim, it was elegant; he was sure it had some meaning. In reality, she just liked the French flower and thought the colors were sensual.

"There's Cialis and Viagra in the nightstand, next to the lube, if you need," she called to him from her closet.

"No need," he replied. "I'm good to go." And he definitely was.

"Then just grab a few condoms. Same drawer. I'll be right there."

He was good to go, but a few condoms, plural? Maybe he would need a pill. He opened the drawer and found more than just a few pills or condoms. It was a treasure trove of deviance. Lube, condoms, personal massagers (Jim refused to even think the word dildo, let alone say it out loud), and a few items he wasn't quite sure what they actually were, something with studs and a string of plastic balls.

He retrieved the condoms and left the rest; he'd have to ask her about the other "goodies" later.

When she returned, he finally got a good look at the skimpy outfit she'd put so much effort toward squeezing into.

Idiot, he thought.

It was an all-over lace baby doll. Sheer and lacy. It tied at the front just over her supple bosom. Of course he'd noticed them before, she always dressed to entice, but they were never this readily... available. She propped herself against the closet doorframe and bit her lip.

"Well?" she asked.

Jim was never so present as he was in that moment. He summoned her to the bed with one finger curling toward him. She quickly obliged, and they picked up where they'd left off.

She pulled his shirt off violently, indifferent to how many buttons she sent flying across the room. She kissed his chest gently, moving down toward his stomach, her hands following. He was embarrassed by his gut, but she didn't seem to mind as she dug into the flesh of his chest with the claws of a jungle cat. Jim winced but dared not stop her.

He reached his hand under one of the pillows behind him, trying to grab hold of the headboard, but found something else instead.

He couldn't tell exactly what it was. It was coarse but had a rubbery surface underneath. Maybe some sort of fake animal. It could you even be a dead animal, he thought. He wouldn't put anything past Beverly after what he'd seen in the drawer. He rubbed it around in his fingers, then pulled it into the light to see just what he had found.

"What the fuck is this?"

Beverly's attempts to pleasure Jim were futile at that point. He had gone flaccid in an instant, and she had no clue why.

When she lifted her eyes enough to see what he had, she couldn't help but laugh. "Oh, no."

Jim was holding Mike's hair with two fingers, as far away from his face as his arm would allow. His mouth was curled in disgust as though it were emanating some pungent odor only he could smell.

"Is this…?" He threw the toupee across the room. "Oh god, it's his hair!"

"I believe it is. I bet that's why he was calling all day."

He jumped off the bed, wiping his hands on anything he could find, but he was convinced Mike had been everywhere and touched everything. There was nowhere he could turn and not see Mike's stupid face staring back at him, each version smiling and saying, "Hey, buddy!"

"James! What are you doing?" She patted the bed. "Come back here!"

"I…I can't." He shook his head. "He's everywhere I look. He was just here. Did you even wash the sheets? Never mind, don't answer that."

"Jim, please," she pleaded. "It's nothing serious, just serious fun. Now come back over here; we're not finished."

"Fun?!" he exclaimed. "All this is fun to you? I'm not really into having *fun*! You know, I was starting to think I could really fall for you!"

"James, sweetheart." Even if he came back to bed now, she was over it. "I've buried three husbands already; I'm not really—"

"Forget it," he said, storming out of the room.

Beverly sat in the middle of her bed, half naked and confused, wondering what the hell had just happened. Before she could think too much, Jim slid back into the room.

"I think the night is over, James."

"Oh, don't worry; it is," he said. He bent over and picked up Mike's hairpiece. "But this; this belongs to me."

THIRTY-FOUR

The last twenty-four hours had sent Jim on an emotional rollercoaster. Disappointment. Visceral high. Cavernous low. The ride was nauseating.

He was resigned to the fact that anything he thought he could have with Beverly was a pipe dream at this point. Jim had never been good at sharing, and a love triangle was the last place he wanted to start. Mike could have her; they deserved each other.

Serious fun.

She could cram her fun up her ass, he thought.

Jim resolved to just throw himself into the case against Thane. He poured over the evidence he'd gathered, but wasn't seeing anything new. It was all just too circumstantial. Just a collection of seemingly interconnected happenings.

He rubbed his head in frustration. Stubble was beginning to permeate the surface of his usually smooth dome. He didn't like it, he would have shaved it clean days before, but the sunburn prevented him from even considering it. Instead, his head was crusted with skin flakes and prickly bristles. He was contemplating methods for attacking his unruly scalp when his phone rang.

The caller ID flashed a familiar name: Captain Brown.

"Hey, Cap," Jim answered, placing the phone down on his

desk on speaker.

"Jim!" His former captain sounded genuinely happy to speak to him. "How the hell are you, you old son of a bitch?"

"I'm still alive." He wasn't sure whether to address the son of a bitch comment, an obvious attempt at familiarity, or get right to it. Per his usual course, he skipped any banter and pressed forward. "The O'Flaherty case…"

The captain's voice lost its joviality and returned Jim's formal tone. "I see you're just as chatty as ever. Last time we talked about that, you told me you never wanted to hear his name again. Then you scratched the shit out of my desk, remember that?"

"Your desk?" Jim asked.

"The mahogany desk in my office." He was wasting his time. "The one your badge dug a deep gash…it was a three-thousand-dollar desk, man…"

Jim couldn't care less about some desk from another lifetime. He waited in silence until Captain Brown spoke again.

"Hello?"

"O'Flaherty, was there anything in his testimony about Peterson?" Jim asked, noticing movement on his security monitors.

He clicked on the small image housing an unsuspecting octogenarian absentmindedly walking an oversized standard poodle. The dog was sniffing around Jim's yard, but its actions were innocuous, for now.

"Yep, that little weasel Spitzer he had working for him," the captain said. "He admitted to killing Frank. Took the full weight of it. Some beef O'Flaherty didn't even know about. What brings this on now?"

"Nothing in particular," he lied. "It's just been nagging at me lately. So O'Flaherty didn't do it?"

"He did a lot of things, but that wasn't one of them."

Jim was only half listening; instead, his attention was focused on the dog squatting in his front yard and the steaming pile of shit it was dropping.

"You've gotta be fuckin' kiddin' me!" he shouted.

The man's face turned toward the camera. Had Jim shouted so loudly he'd actually heard him? The man tugged at his dog's leash and led him away as quickly as old legs would allow.

"I know you really thought he did—"

Jim didn't let Brown finish his sentence. "Not you. Thanks, Cap. Tell Kyra I said hi."

Click. He ended the call unceremoniously.

He considered bursting through his front door and scooping the turds off his lawn, then chasing the man down and returning them to him. Or worse. What could he do that would be worse? He could hold the man down and make him—

No. He stopped the locomotive before it went completely off the rails.

He was going to be smarter. He clicked on his computer a few times and retrieved a CD from his desk drawer.

There's no way she can ignore this!

Jim stood on Linda Stern's doorstep with a satisfaction he hadn't felt in a while. He had let the destruction of his lawn by unfettered defecation go on far too long. Maybe he couldn't prove Sam had murdered anyone in Shady Place. But today? Today, he had evidence of exactly who had taken a shit on his lawn.

Linda was shocked to find a Ziploc bag with something thick and brown dangling in her face when she opened the door. It was attached to Jim's extended arm. The arm was attached to Jim's shoulder, which led up his neck, upward a little further to his face, a face that wore the biggest, most satisfied, ear-to-ear, tooth-bearing, most on-point, pun-intended, shit-eating grin the man had ever sported in his life.

"Mr. Phillips!" she shrieked. "Is that feces?"

"Damn right it is, Stern," he trumpeted. "And it's fresh!"

This was exactly the kind of behavior she had come to expect from Jim Phillips. She had to bob her head back and forth to dodge the bag he swung in her face. He was trying to make a point that she obviously wasn't getting.

"I didn't even yell at him, Stern," he exclaimed. "Here's the evidence; it was some really old guy. It's all right here!"

He thrust the CD in her face. It contained all the complimentary video evidence she would need to take action. While she appreciated that he was no longer shoving the bag of dog crap in her face, she still had no clue what he was going on about.

"Mr. Phillips, explain yourself," she demanded. "This behavior is unacceptable!"

"I caught the guy, the one whose dog has been shitting on my lawn," he beamed. "Watch the video. You can see him, big ass poodle or something. Here's the shit, too." He reached in his back pocket and pulled out a folded piece of paper. "And here, take this. I did some research; you can test dog shit for DNA and link it to the dog who left the pile! I was thinking you could test every dog in the neighborhood, and when they leave a pile lying around, we fine the owner! What do you think?"

She was hearing his words and actually appreciated the idea, but wheels were in motion for something bigger involving Jim Phillips already. "Please wait here one moment, Mr. Phillips."

"Sure, OK," he said, placing the bag on the ground.

She disappeared inside briefly, then re-emerged holding an envelope. "I'm glad you came here today. You saved me a trip to your home."

She handed him the envelope.

"What's this? Another fine?"

"No, Mr. Phillips," she shook her head. "It's the agenda for the next homeowner's association meeting."

"Oh, right. I have to propose a rule change for the DNA thing," he nodded in agreement. "By the book, Stern; maybe you're not so bad after all. Is there a form or something I need to fill out?"

"I don't think you understand," she said. "The topic of whether or not you should be allowed to remain in Shady Place is on the docket."

"Wait, you're kicking me out?"

"Mr. Phillips," she tried to level with him, fearing it was futile. "It's nothing personal, but your behavior simply does not fit what we are trying to be as a community in Shady Place."

"You can't do that!"

"We most certainly can," she said. "Did you ever read the covenants and restrictions?"

All Jim had was a soft laugh to himself. He shrugged his shoulders and shook his head softly. "Who gives a shit, anyway? You've got much bigger problems than me in this neighborhood."

He turned to walk away, but she called him back. "Mr. Phillips, please retrieve your bag of feces."

"Oh no, Stern," he said, smiling widely. "That's for you."

THIRTY-FIVE

There was no date yet, but Jim was certain he was finished in Shady Place. And so it was. To celebrate, he bought himself a twelve pack of beer and decided he simply didn't care.

He spent some time going over what he had researched for the case, but nothing had changed. It still wasn't enough. If Sam was doing anything, there was no proof.

The Phillies were on ESPN at seven. They weren't particularly good. In fact, they'd gone backward every year since they won the World Series in '08 and finished dead last the season before.

It didn't matter, though. They were the Phillies; they were his team, and he would root for them every time they took the field. They were playing the Braves, another bad team. Maybe he'd get to savor a small victory after all.

He settled in, a frosty beer with a freshly popped top in one hand and the remote for the television in the other. The national anthem had barely made it out of an up and coming pop star's mouth when there was a knock at his door.

I should have known, he thought. Why would he be left alone? Since the day he'd moved in, he felt like he could count the waking minutes on one hand that he'd be left absolutely alone to his own devices.

Tommy stood before him, staring at his feet like he'd done something wrong. "Got a minute? Got something I gotta talk to somebody about."

"Sure, champ." Jim was surprised to see Tommy. Of all the interruptions and interlopers who'd intruded on his peace and quiet, Tommy was never one of them. "Beer?"

Tommy accepted the offer and joined Jim on the couch.

Champ.

The moniker made Tommy cringe.

Tommy had spent a lot of time in his life answering fan mail addressing him as such. There weren't as many these days, but he answered every letter and every e-mail, and he always included the same line:

Keep your hands up, Tommy "Champ" Griffin

He didn't have any other nicknames. Just Champ. A lofty title. He had lost a fight, and he wasn't the only champ. But someone said it once early in his career, after a Golden Gloves bout, and it had stuck. He'd always thought The Alabama Slamma would have been more appropriate, but we don't get to choose our own nicknames.

He hadn't fought in over twenty-five years, but he did what he could to stay in the public eye. The occasional commercial, public appearances, or sports card shows for autograph sessions. Every year, his fan base shrank, a lot of them dying off. But he worked at any chance to keep his brand going.

Whatever he wanted to talk about that evening took a back burner to the baseball game on the screen. "My man! You got the Braves game on!"

Like many southerners, Tommy was a Braves fan. They were the team of the southeast for a long time. They moved to Atlanta when Tommy was already a young man, but Hank Aaron had long been a favorite, and adopting the Braves was a smooth transition.

"I have the Phillies game on," Jim countered.

"That's right, you're a Yankee," Tommy remarked, knowing the implication would dig deeper than just calling him a northerner.

"Screw the Yankees."

Jim's comment solicited a smirk from Tommy. Both their teams had been beaten in the World Series by the Yankees in the last twenty years, so there was no love lost over a little venom spit toward the Bronx Bombers.

"They gonna be right there at the bottom with the Phils and Braves this year, anyway," Tommy suggested.

Jim grunted an approval, and they watched the game in silence. Tommy's thick meat hooks picked at the label on his beer bottle. He was more focused on scratching the paper away from the smooth surface than what was transpiring in the game.

The occasional sigh from Tommy garnered a peek from the side of an eye from Jim. He never actually questioned the releases; instead, he took great measures to try not to mention that Tommy had stopped by for some unknown purpose.

Tommy's attempts to broach a topic of conversation were thwarted several times by exciting plays on the field. A catcher legging out a triple. *Did you see that? Kid's got some wheels!* A bad strike call. *Hometown call; ump's blind!*

The third time, Tommy waited for a commercial. "So…" he started to speak, but was quickly shut down.

"I gotta take a leak," Jim shot off before disappearing into his bedroom to use the master bath. He called back from beyond the doorway, "Help yourself to another beer; I got plenty."

Tommy was growing frustrated. He may have taken a lot of

punches to the head, but he could see what Jim was doing. So, he grabbed two more beers, returned to his seat, and paused the game. When Jim returned, Tommy thrust a new beer into his hand and asked him to listen.

And so he did.

Tommy confessed to Jim something that only a few people in the world knew about him. He was in a relationship. One that scared the hell out of him. It was the best thing that had ever happened to him, but it could jeopardize his standing in the sporting community. He did, after all, still have a name to protect. A brand.

He could command forty dollars an autograph, fifty for a photo op, and even more if he inscribed a message on something special. All these years after the last time he set foot in the ring, he still made a fair amount of money.

Tommy told Jim a lot of things about the inner workings of his daily life and his marketing strategies, but he was beating around the bush at getting to the point. He could see he was losing Jim. The look in his eyes said he was getting tired of seeing a frozen image of a taco with a Dorito shell emblazoned across his television.

"I'm ramblin'," Tommy said. "Reckon you want me to get to the point, and I'm fixin' to, but I need you to tell me this ain't gonna leave this room."

"I don't even know what we're talking about, so your secret is safe," Jim said glibly, hoping to end the torture Tommy's prattling was inflicting upon him.

"Jim, it's got me all tore up inside," Tommy said. He had yet to pop the top of his new beer, but he was already nervously picking the label off. His label-less first bottle was wantonly relegated to the coffee table with no more than a few sips missing.

Tommy's sincerity, the redness of his eyes, the slight tremble in his voice, were beginning to push through Jim's shell. Whatever Tommy needed to tell him was serious, at least to him. He sighed and leaned toward Tommy to give his full attention.

"Before we go any further here, tell me something," Jim said. "Why come to me? I'm the last person most people here would trust with a secret. Although your timing is impeccable…" He trailed off on the last sentiment, saying it more for himself than Tommy's benefit.

Tommy laughed at Jim's observation; he was right, Jim should be the last person to confess anything to, but here he was. And this was why: "You'll tell it to me like it is. That's all. You don't give no shits about what nobody thinks, so you'll tell me straight up what I should do."

Jim couldn't help but laugh a little. Tommy was right, he never minced words and was rarely reserved enough to hold anything back.

"All right, big guy," Jim said. "What's rattling around in that head of yours that's got you so tore up?"

Tommy took a deep breath. Before Shady Place, he'd had a very different life. He'd had a wife and two kids. It was the way life was supposed to be. You grow up, you get married, you have kids. That life isn't for everyone, though. It was a lot easier when Tommy was on the road or training for a title fight. The life of a prizefighter was busy and provided enough distractions to keep what a preacher had once told him was a demon at bay.

When his career was over and the travel slowed, he and his wife were forced to actually spend meaningful time together. It was hard; it was too hard. He didn't love her, not like he was supposed to. She knew it and didn't hate him. They were best friends and parents of two wonderful children. She had managed the money well, and they were happy to split it evenly and go their separate ways.

He spent his nights alone for years after that, but no more alone than he'd spent the sixty years prior.

"I been seein' someone in Shady Place goin' on two years now. Nobody knows about, but he's my world—" He caught himself; he hadn't meant to say "he" yet. Maybe Jim hadn't heard it or thought it was just a slip of the tongue. He kept going, "It's a thing nobody would think was happenin' and it could ruin my career. It's the only thing gets us to fightin'…"

"This is about you and Patel?" Jim asked matter of factly.

Tommy dropped his beer bottle to the floor; good thing he hadn't popped the top yet. "Shit, sorry. I…" He fumbled to retrieve the bottle from beneath his feet, purposely not looking up as he spoke. "You already knew?"

Jim picked up the bottle and forced Tommy to look up at him with a simple, "Hey." When he looked up, Jim locked eyes with him and offered him a warm smile. "I'm a detective. I've known since the first time I saw you two together. The subtle touches on the arm, how quickly the two of you always team up, and the way he reacts when you make a joke at his expense. We all do it, poke fun at each other, but when you tease him, it hurts him. You know what really gave it away, though?"

Tommy shook his head and whispered softly, "What?"

"The way you look at each other."

Tommy let a few tears slide down his cheeks before brushing them away quickly. "What do I do? He's gonna drop me if I don't come out to the world, but I could lose everything!"

Jim shrugged. "I don't care."

Tommy huffed in frustration. "Really? That's all you got for me? You don't care? You really are an ass—"

251

"Whoa, hold on," Jim cut him off before he could finish the insult. "I mean I don't care that you're gay or that you're with Jay. I was a fan before I met you. I'm a fan now that I know you. I don't care. Neither should you."

"I could lose endorsements or signin' gigs."

"So?"

"What if I lose fans and people hate me?"

"Fuck 'em."

"Fuck 'em, that easy?" Tommy said.

"Yeah," Jim smirked. "These days, you'll probably make more fans than you've ever had. Remember that kid who played for the Rams? Top-selling jersey for a while; never even took the field in a game that counted."

Tommy was contemplating. Of course he knew Michael Sam; he'd watched the whole media circus surrounding the brave young man's journey. He always wondered inside if it had all been a publicity stunt, but felt guilty letting the thought even cross his mind. He'd done what Tommy had never had the balls to do. Maybe it was jealousy. Someone could just be who they were without concern for their image.

"You're right," was all Tommy said.

"I'm always right," Jim responded with an air of confidence that assured Tommy he believed it to be true. "Now can we please watch the rest of this game?"

"Yeah," Tommy said. He was shell-shocked. He never thought Jim Phillips would be the voice of reason in his life, the one who would tell him exactly what he wanted to hear, what he *needed* to hear.

Jim zoomed through the commercials. "Staring at that taco

for so long made me kind of hungry. Anyone deliver tacos around here?"

Tommy smiled at Jim. "I don't think so, but I'll order you a pizza."

"Sounds good. You want a meat lover's?" Jim smirked again.

"Come on," Tommy responded.

"Too soon to joke?" Jim asked, holding his hands up sheepishly.

"You can get your own damn pizza now," Tommy said, but he appreciated the sentiment Jim intended and offered him a gracious smile for his efforts.

🌴

"That was fast," Jim said when the doorbell rang.

It was too fast for the pizza Tommy had ordered less than fifteen minutes earlier. And it wasn't.

It was Jay.

"Patel?" Jim said. "What are you doing here?"

Jay was fumbling for words, rubbing the back of his neck and struggling to make eye contact. It was the first time Jim had ever heard him speak with less than perfect diction. "Well, I…uhhh, I just wanted to…you know. Well, see, there is a big pickleball tournament tomorrow…" He nodded to himself, confirming that was the angle he was trying to go with. "I was hoping you would come and root me on."

"Really? That's why you're here?" Jim cocked an eyebrow at him.

Jay looked toward Mike's house and nodded softly. "Of course. It would mean a lot to me."

Jim knew he was lying, but he decided to throw Jay a bone. He was interested in finding out the real reason he was there. To Jim, there were two possibilities; really, two individuals: Mike or Tommy.

"Why the hell not?"

"Really? Thank you, you are a very kind man," Jay said. "I knew everyone was wrong about you."

Jay shook Jim's hand and smiled widely. He continued to linger, looking to his feet for an answer, but finding none. He glanced toward Mike's again. Jim tracked Jay's eyes in time to see Mike quickly disappear into his garage. He had his answer.

"Something else?"

Jay pointed to Mike's house. "I heard what happened between you two, my two friends, and I would like very much for you to make up."

"What's he got on you?" Jim asked. "It's gotta be something; that's what he does. He gets something on you, and he uses it to take advantage."

Jay turned his gaze back to Mike's house. He wasn't sure how to answer. Mike was peeking around the corner of his garage door for a cue to come over. The street light reflected off his naked head that usually wore the hairpiece currently hiding in Jim's desk drawer.

"Let me ask you," Jim leaned in, half-whispering for exaggeration. "Is it about you and Tommy?"

"You know?"

Jim opened his door wide enough for Jay to see Tommy sunken into his sofa.

Jay's eyes shot open wide. He was so focused on the task at hand, he'd failed to notice Tommy's golf cart in the driveway. "He told you?"

"I already knew," Jim said. "He just wanted someone to tell him it was OK."

Jay lowered his gaze. "Did you?"

"I told him to be himself. Same goes for you."

"It is why I left India. They are not so accepting of such things," Jay confessed. "You are a good man, Jim Phillips."

"What's taking so long?" Tommy shouted, looking back over his shoulder. "Jay? What are you doing here?"

Jay looked to Jim for permission to enter and received a nod of approval. He turned back to Mike before crossing the threshold. "He already knows, Mike! You are on your own!"

Mike was standing in his driveway, anxiously looking toward Jim's door. He was deflated by Jay's words, standing alone with a hangdog look. Jim leaned out far enough to make eye contact and shook his head. "Just get over here."

The pizza had finally arrived, but Jim passed the responsibility off to Jay before he would be allowed to cross the threshold. "Take care of this; I'll join you in a few."

Jay collected the pizza and headed inside. "What are we watching? I do hope it's cricket!"

Jim had resigned himself to the fact that he was never going to have a moment to himself until his exile from Shady Place took effect. The first night he tried to sit down and relax by himself, he ended up with a full house.

"Hey, Jimbo." Mike strode up to Jim's door as if their last contact hadn't concluded in a wrestling match the previous night.

"Make it quick, O'Flaherty," Jim said.

"Whoa, hey, come on now!" Mike said. "Can we go in your office?"

Mike closed the door and immediately went to work on Jim. "I'm here to be honest with you. I want to come completely clean."

"That would be a first," Jim snarked.

"Fair enough, but I'm serious." Mike was genuinely trying to level with Jim. "You know I like Bev, and I've been trying to date her, but she just won't be exclusive."

No shit.

"I didn't bring you this case because I cared about the people who were dying," he said, pointing to the list of names plastered across Jim's office wall. "The truth is…" He hesitated. "I was scared. I knew the guys Bev was dating were dying, but she's like a drug, man. Whatta they call that? When you do somethin' you know's bad for you? Like smokin'…"

"Cognitive dissonance." Jim was cold with his words; he still wasn't sure where this was going.

"Yeah, right, that," Mike pretended like he knew it all along. "I've been lookin' over my shoulder for years, then there you are. First thought I had when I seen your face? *I gotta get the fuck outta here!*" He laughed and slapped Jim on the shoulder, but Jim still wasn't a willing participant in the conversation. "More I thought about it, figured you'd either turn me in or keep me safe. Well, I'm still here, and I ain't dead. That's sayin' somethin'…"

"It's always about you, isn't it?" Jim asked. "It doesn't say anything other than that I want to be able to keep an eye on you. You're not telling me anything I don't already know. I'm sure you're scared. You're a spineless coward."

Mike didn't know what to say to get through to Jim. "I'm not in the program anymore!"

"What?"

"I couldn't take it anymore," Mike said. "When my wife ditched me, I took off. I hit a stash I had back in Philly. Cash, fake IDs, the works. Then I headed to Florida."

Jim's mouth fell open slightly as he processed Mike's words. He held a finger up as if he was going to make a point, then tapped his chin gently with it instead. "You left the program, came here, and somehow I end up next door to you."

"Funny if you think about it, really." Mike smiled, trying to crack Jim's sullen façade.

No, it is most certainly not funny.

"You think we can move past everything, maybe try to solve this case?" Mike asked, extending his hand to Jim. An olive branch.

"I know you didn't kill Peterson," was all Jim could muster.

Mike smiled widely. "That's the closest I'm ever going to get to an apology from you, ain't it?"

"Take it or leave."

"Take it!" Mike exclaimed. He turned his back on Jim to examine all the notes splattered across the wall. "So, the case…"

"Case is dead."

Mike turned. "What? What about that girl? Tanya?"

"I talked to her; there's nothing there," Jim said, shuffling papers on his desk. "I took it to the cops, and they laughed in my face. I'm missing something, Thane is not that smart. Is he?"

He tailed off, he was questioning himself more than anything else. Was he being outsmarted by Thane? The Realtor? He might as well have been a used car salesman with that shit-eating grin he wore all around the neighborhood.

"It just so happens that's the other reason I wanted to talk to you," Mike said smugly. "I had an idea, if you don't mind getting your hands a little dirty."

"I'm listening."

"Sam has an office right here in Shady Place. Maybe there's

some evidence there?" Mike said, wringing his hands together. "But we'd have to break in."

Without a word, Jim reached into the top drawer of his desk and retrieved what looked like the pelt of a dead rat. "You might need this."

It was Mike's hairpiece.

"I'm good; you can keep it." Mike was ready to shed his safety blanket and let the world see his true form.

"I'll drive," Jim offered.

As they left, Mike pointed back to the living room. Jay and Tommy were eating pizza and watching Jim's television. "What about those two?"

"Let them enjoy themselves." Jim waved them off. "It's a big day for them."

When the door closed, Jay looked over his shoulder. "Jim? Mike?" he called out. "I think they left..."

Tommy shrugged. "Why don't you grab us a few more beers? Jim gonna leave us here, we might as well thank him!"

"Should we save some pizza for them?" Jay asked.

Tommy shook his head. "Nah, I paid for it."

"Actually, I paid for it," Jay pointed out.

Actually, Tommy had given Jim twenty dollars to pay for the pizza. He shook his head and chalked it up to Jim being Jim. What's twenty bucks between friends, anyway?

T HIRTY-SIX

They made short work of the trip to Sam's office, Jim ignoring any posted neighborhood speed limits; they were nothing more than suggestions, anyway. He figured he was already on the way out, so what was the worst they could do to him?

1 Shady Place Drive.

The office was near the guard shack at the front of the neighborhood, but far enough away they could park out of view of the guard. Jim assessed the windows and the door lock. "I don't see an alarm…"

He crouched down and examined the lock, running a finger over the keyhole.

"Just a basic cylinder lock," Jim said, producing two small pieces of metal.

The tools for the job were simple: a tension wrench and a pick. Jim was practiced in a few methods of lock picking, a skill he utilized on a number of occasions during his time on the force. This was the easiest type of lock, a simple pin and tumbler design.

"Keep a look out," Jim said.

Mike leaned over to see what Jim was up to. "Whatcha doin' officer?"

"Just a little B and E," Jim said, fitting a pair of latex gloves over his hands. "And it's 'Detective.'"

"Gloves? What about me?" Mike asked.

Jim shrugged. "Guess you can't touch anything."

Mike frowned and sulked until Jim tossed him the extra pair of gloves he had in his back pocket.

He could have used an electric pick or a more aggressive pick design and simply raked the lock. It was a method that left the picker hoping for the best, instead of employing any true skill. He liked the challenge of the simple tools. The ability to feel and hear the pins click into the shear line.

The process was simple, but puzzle-like in nature. It was the aspect of building a case he loved the most. Putting the pieces together until they made sense. This was no different.

He inserted the tension wrench and turned it to create a ledge that could catch the pins and lock them into place with the pick.

The tension wrench was nothing to see, a flat piece of metal that turned at a ninety-degree angle at the end. The pick was one of a handful in the set, hinged into a pocket-sized multi-tool design. Each pick had its own tiny variances, with different teeth and angles for different jobs. This job was simple. Jim selected the pick with a slightly hooked end and went to work.

With the tension wrench already in place, Jim slid the pick in and tuned out the outside world. He needed complete focus so he could hear the pins lock into place. He hushed Mike's incessant questions with a sharp look and a finger to his lips.

The constant sound of the cicadas chirping all around them had melted into a soothing melodic tune to Jim's ears, allowing him to focus only on the task at hand. He was able to move the pick deftly through the pins, locking them in place one by one, each delivering a gentle satisfying click, confirming it had fallen into its place on the shear line. Like a master locksmith, Jim had tricked the lock into thinking the key it was meant to mate with was safely entwined.

Easy peasy.

Or so goes the version of the story Jim would have you believe. If you asked Mike, they were there for hours.

In reality, Jim had fumbled with the lock for nearly thirty minutes. The incessant questions he fought off from Mike were his offers of help and questioning whether they should just forget it. Not Jim, not today; he was determined to shake off the rust and solve the puzzle.

The only thing Jim had left in Shady Place was this case, and he'd be damned if he was going to let a simple pin and tumbler lock beat him.

"Let's just go," Mike pleaded. "It's been thirty minutes—"

"You got somewhere to be?" Jim cut him off. "Past your bedtime maybe?"

Mike huffed. "I just don't wanna get caught."

They were, after all, committing a crime. Jim shrugged him off and turned the tension wrench too hard, almost snapping it off in the lock.

Shit!

OK, Phillips, breath in, focus, and let your fingers do the work, Jim thought to himself.

That's exactly what he did. Mike was prattling on behind him about what would happen if the police caught them and tried to look into his background. They might take him away! They might even lock him up! Jim wasn't listening, though, he was so focused on the lock and the pins falling in place that when the last one clicked, and he turned the tension wrench to retract the cylinder from the doorframe, all he could do was breathe a sigh of relief.

261

"Got it."

"About damn time," Mike said, turning the handle and brushing past Jim.

The Shady Place Realty office was small. It didn't need to be big or extravagant. Everything about it was tailored to the needs of the clientele Thane had made a healthy living catering to. It began as an art form, but had evolved into a simple science. The customers didn't need anything fancy or overly technical; they just wanted ease and comfort.

It was all by design. A design cultivated over a decade of working with a particular kind of customer.

The walls were lined with stock images of active seniors enjoying themselves outdoors. Tennis, golf, swimming, or some nighttime escapades at the clubhouse or out under the stars. It was an enlarged version of the brochure that had disintegrated in Jim's fingers for all those years prior to his transplantation.

The waiting area consisted of a small sofa that was plush but firm enough that sitters wouldn't sink in so far they couldn't rise again without assistance. Never let the customer feel helpless or confused. A small coffee table had an oversized neighborhood map under glass; it was adorned with golfing, senior living, and home and garden magazines. A forty-two-inch television was angled where it could be seen well from almost anywhere in the office. Thane had learned over the years that wives and the occasional husband dragged their significant others out while there was some sporting event they were dying to watch, but had sacrificed their afternoon to be there.

The desk was smaller than you'd expect. Big enough for separation, but it allowed him to get close enough to point out minute details. A computer rested on the corner of the desk, with an oversized screen. The text on every program was set to a large enough font, it could surely be seen from the moon.

The small kitchenette was there primarily to offer beverages: tea, coffee, or water he would ask. It was not a yes or no question. No wasn't allowed in his office, so every question, every option, was aimed at eliciting a dialogue with open-ended questions. Sales 101.

But Sam had never taken any marketing or sales classes; he learned from experience and taught himself well.

The place was in immaculate order, no clutter to be seen. The only items that seemed out of place were the unhealthy number of pens everywhere, explained away by the fact that not having a writing utensil handy would never be an excuse to not close a deal. The last, possibly most important, items were littered about the office. They were curious but indispensable. The coffee table, the desk, the kitchenette, even the file cabinet tucked in the corner held small plastic cups with Shady Place Realty emblazoned on the side. Each cup housed a small collection of eyeglasses.

Readers.

Losing one deal to a potential buyer not having his glasses had prompted Sam to buy not one or two sets of simple reading glasses, but an entire case. A hundred pairs. There were at least twenty pairs littered around the office. The remaining awaited their turn in the box they had originally arrived in, tucked snugly under the counter in the kitchenette. It may have seemed overkill at the time, but over the years, more than thirty pairs had walked out the door.

Every inch of Sam's office was aimed at closing the deal. Jim remembered sitting across from him at the desk all those years ago and saying no. In retrospect, he should have been proud, but he'd still ended up in Shady Place. Thane had still won in the end.

That would be the last victory he would ever have over Jim Phillips. Armed with only the flashlights on their phones, they searched the office.

"What are we even looking for?" Mike asked.

Jim scanned the open office space. "Anything suspicious. Check the file cabinet; I'll look in the desk."

Jim looked through the drawers of the desk. He was tempted to toss the place the way they used to back home when they had a warrant to search some scumbag's property. But the surreptitious nature of this excursion wouldn't allow him the satisfaction.

"Cabinet's locked," Mike said, tugging on the different drawers, each of which gave slightly, but none opened.

"I got it," Jim said.

"Oh, no." Mike threw his hands up. "We don't have time for you to pick another lock."

Jim reached into the drawer he was searching and produced a small key, tossing it to Mike. "Here…jackass."

Mike trailed off, mumbling about how long it had taken Jim to open the outside door. Why was he a jackass? *You're the jackass*, he thought.

As Mike fingered through every folder he could see in the vertical file cabinet, Jim was coming up empty. He frowned. He couldn't shake the nagging feeling he was missing something.

Would Thane really leave anything here?

Of course he would. He's arrogant.

Where are you hiding?

Jim bumped Mike out of the way and ran his fingers over each of the files, but quickly concluded there was nothing worth further examination.

A quick search of the kitchenette turned up nothing.

The bathroom was a bathroom.

Nothing behind the pictures.

His gaze turned upward. It was your run of the mill drop ceiling. Two by two tiles across the entire office.

"Maybe there's something up there," Jim said, pointing up.

Mike followed his finger upward. "The ceiling? I think you're reachin' now, Jimmy boy. I think it's a bust."

Jim ignored Mike's voice of reason and climbed on top of Thane's desk. He could reach the tiles just enough to push on them, but he'd never be able to see what, if anything, might be hidden in the small cavity they protected.

Consternation grew in Mike as he watched Jim hop down from the desk. He was frantic; it was an unfamiliar look on Jim. He grabbed a small trash can, but it was too flimsy. There was no way it would hold his weight.

But the unsuspecting chair nestled in the opening of the desk? *That* would suffice.

Despite Mike's objections, Jim placed the chair firmly on top of the desk and stepped up.

"Doesn't seem like a good idea…"

Jim waved him off. "Just hold the chair."

Jim stood atop the chair and pushed gently upward on a ceiling tile. It moved with ease up into the spacious void above the rows of tiles. The chair got him high enough that he could stick his entire head into the opening. He surveyed the area with his flashlight, but could only see insulation and air conditioning ducts.

"See anything?" Mike called up to him from below.

"No, it doesn't…" He focused the light on something gray a few tiles away. "Hang on; what's this?"

From below, it looked as though Jim was a headless body floating above the desk. As he spoke, he kicked out with a leg, looking for the arm or back of the chair to climb up further.

"What are you doing?" Mike asked, dodging Jim's flailing foot.

"Just need to get a little higher," he said as he looked back down trying to find purchase with his foot. *Got it.* He used the arm of the chair to thrust himself a little higher into the ceiling, disregarding the continued protests from Mike.

The thought crossed his mind that Michael O'Flaherty was concerned for his well-being, a turn of events he never could have foreseen. The added height allowed Jim to reach both arms into the ceiling cavity; he regained his bearings and attempted to focus the beam of his flashlight on the spot he thought he saw something, but found nothing.

He could have sworn he saw something. It was gray; it was right there a minute ago. He moved the flashlight slowly around the empty chamber, but there was nothing. He did a one-eighty to face the opposite direction, his feet fumbling clumsily below, rocking the chair.

"Just come down; you're gonna break your neck!"

He looked down again to make sure he had solid footing and stabilized the chair. "I'm fine." He turned his gaze back upward and found the gray object he'd been searching for.

A small gray squirrel greeted him. *Tick-tick, tick-tick.*

Jim's eyes opened wide as the squirrel reared back in fear. He let out a shrill, blood-curdling cry that reminded Mike of a scream queen from a B horror flick.

Typically, a small rodent wouldn't frighten Jim, but he had just read a news article about a renegade squirrel terrorizing a Florida retirement community. It had attacked three different residents within a two-day period and was still on the loose. The odds that this was the same squirrel were infinitesimal, but the mere chance had given Jim enough of a start to upset the precious balance holding him in place.

They had created an intricate ecosystem, the desk, the chair, Mike, Jim, and the drop ceiling above, but the sound so startled Mike, he yanked on the chair leg, pulling the entire apparatus apart.

The chair tumbled over backward to the ground, leaving Jim dangling above. But only briefly. Mike tried to react quickly and grab Jim's legs, but the ceiling panels were no match for the weight of a full-grown man.

Feeling the support below him evaporate, Jim grasped for anything he could get his hands on. The four panels around Jim gave way and joined his rapid descent toward the floor.

When all was said and done, Thane's temple of salesmanship had been unceremoniously defiled. The ceiling had been eviscerated, its entrails spilling down to the floor below.

It was as if an explosion had rocked the area. Pens, reading glasses, ceiling tiles, and insulation were splattered across the room. Mike and Jim were splayed on the floor on opposite sides of the desk.

Jim was certain he had taken the brunt of the fall, landing squarely on his back on the desk before bouncing down to the floor. He rolled to his left just enough to see Mike lying on his back on the other side of the desk, motionless. "You OK?"

Mike was whispering something inaudibly, but Jim wasn't listening. His attention turned to the notebook strapped to the underside of a drawer. *Bingo.*

"I found something!" Jim proclaimed unstrapping the notebook. "Mike, I got something…"

Mike whispered very softly, "Help me…"

"What? I can't hear you," Jim said, squirming his way closer.

Mike had read the same article as Jim and now found himself face-to-face with the miniature terrifying beast. It was perched on his chest, staring at him. Mike would swear its eyes were glowing red, and it was foaming at the mouth. He convinced himself if he stayed still, it might not attack. He knew what happened to those poor people and that squirrel was still free. Now it had found its next victim. Him.

The squirrel was rapidly waving its tail back and forth, peering deep into Mike's soul, when Jim's head emerged from under the desk.

"Oh shit!" Jim cried out, jumping upward sharply and banging his head on the undercarriage of the desk.

Kuk kuk kuk, the squirrel cried out before throwing itself at Mike's face.

Mike rolled as quickly as he could, barely averting the furry demon's assault. He struggled to find his footing, but managed to rise and take a defensive position.

Jim watched from under the desk, rubbing a small gash on the top of his head.

Mike squared off with the squirrel. They stood a mere three feet apart. He crouched over, arms spread wide, palms open, then wiggled his fingers, ready to tango with the tiny rodent. He was trying to remind himself how much bigger he was than this creature, but a feeling of impending doom was creeping up inside him.

The squirrel continued to *kuk* at Mike, furiously wagging its tail in an angry vibration. It mirrored Mike each time he tried to move.

"The hell?" Jim murmured just loud enough to draw the squirrel's attention.

"You're on your own!" Mike shouted as he attempted to run to the bathroom.

But the squirrel was quicker, overtaking Mike and climbing his leg, then up his shirt, until it reached his head and began scratching his face. Mike backed into the bathroom and stumbled to the ground. He grabbed the squirrel with both hands and tried to pull it from his face, delaying the attack just long enough for Jim to swoop in and trap the furry menace in a small trash can.

They locked it in the bathroom, with the trash can temporarily holding it at bay. No sooner had they pulled the door shut, was it attempting to scratch and claw its way free.

"You read that article, right?" Mike asked.

Jim nodded in the affirmative, catching his breath.

Mike joined his nod. "Then we're good here?"

Jim continued to nod as he reached under the desk to retrieve the notebook he'd spotted during the fracas. He picked up the chair that had fallen and plopped down in it with a heavy sigh. "At least I found something."

Mike looked over Jim's shoulder as he flipped pages.

It was all there. Each page was devoted to a different name with a list of physical ailments that might be exploited. Jim shook his head with every page turn. He stopped on a familiar name.

Ted Williams: Heart Condition.

"We got him," Jim said softly.

"Yeah?" Mike asked. He was squinting; he couldn't see what was on the pages, but Jim's reaction said all he needed to know. "Let's take it and get out of here."

"We can't take it," Jim said. "It would be inadmissible in court, and he'd know we were here."

Mike looked around. "He's going to know we were here…"

Jim extracted his phone from his pocket and began snapping

photos of the pages. He paused on the last page with writing on it. He hadn't made it that far before.

"Oh shit, look."

Mike squinted again, but his eyesight wasn't what it used to be. Luckily, there were readers strewn across the floor all around them. He read the words aloud. "Beverly Stanton: Nut Allergy. Son of a bitch. She was right."

Jim snapped a photo of the page. "Bev?"

"This was her idea. She mentioned his office."

Jim leaned under the desk and returned the notebook to its hiding place. "She was right, and she might be next. Let's get out of here."

"What about this mess?"

Jim assessed the catastrophic scene before them, then smirked. "Open the bathroom door...then run."

Jim waited outside while Mike psyched himself up enough to open the bathroom door. He considered holding the front door shut and forcing Mike to go toe to toe with the demented critter inside. He owed Mike at least one for sending him to Stern's house alone, not to mention, it was only moments ago that Mike had tried to abandon him and make a break for the bathroom. He would have been justified. Instead, he held the door open long enough for Mike to run out, trapping the squirrel inside. New Jim was merciful. Or maybe he was just keeping score for a later date.

The squirrel stared at them through the glass front door, twitching its tail and kukking away.

The two men looked at each other, then back to the ferocious creature, before teaming up for a bout of raucous laughter.

THIRTY-SEVEN

Doctor's wishes be damned. It was time for a celebratory cigar. He wasn't sure Jim would let him smoke in his beloved car, but he tried anyway.

Mike produced two cigars from his shirt pocket and offered one to Jim. "We've earned it."

"Why not?" Jim said, rolling down the windows.

Mike clipped the ends of the cigars. "I got a theory about you, Phillips."

"This should be good."

Mike lit his cigar. "I think you've never had friends, so you don't know how to do it."

"I have friends!" Jim responded.

Mike offered to light Jim's stogie. "Your kids don't count. I bet when she was still here, you spent all your time with your wife. When she died, you spent all your time alone. Sound about right?"

Jim considered Mike's words; he'd never really thought about it. "What's your point?"

"James Phillips," Mike said with the sincerity of a teen in love. "Will you be my friend?"

Jim slowly turned his head and scanned Mike's face until he laughed and slapped Jim on the shoulder. "Not askin' for your hand, man. Just offerin' to be your friend."

Jim thought about Mike's proposal. Could they be friends? It was too late. "Maybe we could have been friends…"

"But?"

Jim pulled the HOA agenda from his back pocket and handed it to Mike, who pulled on the readers he'd taken from Thane's office and read in silence.

"Why?" Mike asked.

"Guess Stern has a hard on for me," Jim shrugged, puffing on the cigar. At least he had one victory to hang his hat on that night.

Mike rubbed his chin. "You're gonna fight it, right?"

"I don't really care anymore. I just want to put this case to bed," Jim said. "You can keep your Shady Place. If the marshals find you, it won't be because of me."

"What about Bev?"

"All yours…" Jim's phone rang. Speak of the devil. "There she is now." He answered on speaker. "Hey, Bev. I'm with Mike; your tip was spot on—"

She cut Jim off, wheezing into the phone, "Can't…breathe… Sam…"

Jim asked, "What about Sam?"

She gasped for air on the other end of the line.

"Hold on, Bev," Mike shouted. "We'll be right there!"

The line fell dead.

Neither Jim nor Mike had a key to Beverly's house. She had a hide-a-key under a planter a few feet from the front door, but she'd never shared that fact with them.

Mike tried the handle to no avail. "It's locked!"

They both feared the worst when she failed to answer their fervent pounding on the door.

"Get out of the way!" Jim pushed Mike aside and kicked the door open.

Beverly was swollen when they found her. She was turning blue, gasping for air. A half-eaten plate of cookies was resting on her nightstand.

"The cookies; I bet they're from Thane." Jim smelled one. "He knew about her nut allergy!"

Mike sifted through the contents of her nightstand, shuffling around salacious goodies. "I thought she had an epi-pen in here…"

"Kiiiittttch…" she couldn't get the word out, but they knew what she meant.

Jim made quick work of tracking down the epinephrine that could save Beverly's life. He jammed it into her leg and depressed the plunger.

THIRTY-EIGHT

They were a sight to behold, Jim and Mike, sitting in the waiting room while nurses and doctors attended to Beverly. They were ragged. It had been an unexpectedly long night, and it wasn't over yet.

Jim sported a dried spot of blood on the top of his head; it wasn't bad enough to need stitches, but the area around the cut was already beginning to rise and work its way from red to bluish-purple. Mike's face showed a much more pronounced assault. Tiny claw marks tracked from his nose to forehead, a few on his eyelids showed he was lucky to have sustained only superficial damage.

"Notice she called me?" Jim asked, touching the tender spot on his head.

Mike cocked his head to Jim. "Yeah, well, she slept with me…a lot."

"You and everyone else," Jim retorted.

"Come on, man; she's dyin' in there," Mike responded. "Besides, I thought you were done with her."

"I could have, you know," Jim said, talking over Mike. "But I turned her down."

The two continued to bicker back and forth long past the arrival of Beverly's doctor. She was younger, tasked with the overnight ER shift. It was a particularly slow night, so she simply watched the duo battle over the virtue of the woman she had just treated. She found the interaction fairly amusing, a welcome distraction. Alas, the intercom informed her she was needed. She cleared her throat, and the men looked up.

"Miss Stanton is stable and awake," she said. "And she's asking for you."

"Who?" Mike asked.

Jim nodded, "Yeah, who?"

They waited in anticipation as she dragged out the answer. "Well, I believe she asked for…" A pause for effect. "Her boys."

Even footing still. After the way Jim treated Beverly the night before, she still considered him one of her boys. For Mike, it was status quo, never stepping forward or backward. Their relationship simply was what it was, and he would have to accept that. If it wasn't Jim, it would be someone else. He would never be her one and only.

Though he had stepped out, Jim's competitive nature forced him to strive for victory. Even if he was finished with Beverly, he still wanted her to choose him over Mike.

But was he finished with her?

Maybe not, but for now, he'd lost no ground in a competition he'd removed himself from. She did, after all, call him when she was in peril.

She was attached to a bank of monitors, with a bag of fluid dripping antihistamines intravenously to help reduce the swelling. She tried to remove the oxygen tubes from her nose when they entered—they shouldn't see her this way—but she had to speak to them. Her voice lacked its usual vigor, almost to the point of a whisper.

"I'm going to be OK," she said softly. "They said I can probably go home in the morning."

Mike patted her on the arm. "What a relief!"

"We'll get that bastard," Jim said calmly. "What was he doing there, anyway?"

"Cookies." she shrugged. "Not the first time. I didn't think anything of it."

Mike leaned in closer and spoke quietly. This information was for her ears only. "We found something in his office, a notebook!"

"He knew about your nut allergy," Jim said.

"Of course he did, that bastard..." Her breath was strained. "He tried to kill our friends. He tried to kill me..." she coughed occasionally for effect. "You have to stop him. You have to take him out."

Jim nodded. "I think we've got enough evidence for the police to listen now."

She tried to sit up, but was too weak. "That's not good enough. You have to make him pay..." She touched both of them gently on the arm. "Do it for me?"

Mike was hooked. "Of course, we'll take care of him."

"We'll take care of it," Jim said. "You get some rest now."

"My boys." She shook her head and smiled. "You saved me. Thank you both. I know you'll make this right."

They left her, but stopped when they were just out of earshot. Jim was pondering. He could see Beverly through the open door checking herself in a compact mirror.

"So, what's the plan?" Mike asked.

After one last look at Beverly, she was rubbing something into the puffy skin under her eyes, he pulled Mike away by the arm. "I'm going back to the cops."

"What about what Bev said?"

"Be smart here. We're civilians, not vigilantes," Jim said. "The police can handle Thane. You just lay low; no reason to draw attention to yourself. In a few weeks, I'll be gone, and it'll be like none of this ever happened."

That was the end of the conversation.

⁂

Jim should have gone to sleep and resumed in the morning, but it wasn't in him to rest while there was still work to be done.

Jay and Tommy had fallen asleep in each other's arms on his sofa during the night's escapades. All of the beer he had purchased was gone; the discarded bottles covered his coffee table. All he could think was *Coasters!* But he had other concerns and let it slide, allowing their slumber to continue.

Jim went to work preparing his new evidence. Sure enough, surveillance footage showed Thane arriving at Beverly's house and leaving just before she called Jim.

There you are.

The notebook. The video. The attempted murder. Sam was toast. It was late, probably too late to bother Detective Benjamin. No matter. Jim was up, and he was twice the man's age. He dialed and waited.

The conversation was brief and unfulfilling.

This is Benjamin.

"Benjamin, it's Jim Phillips."

Isn't it past your bedtime?

"He tried again; this time, he put someone in the hospital, but if we hadn't stopped—"

Who? That realtor? What happened? You have proof?

"My neighbor nearly died from an allergic reaction to nuts.

He gave her cookies with nuts in them. He knew she was allergic…"

Jim already knew exactly how the rest of the conversation would go. He could hear how the words sounded coming out of his mouth.

An allergic reaction? You've got to give me a little more than that.

"Motive, means, opportunity! It's all here!"

Coincidence and circumstance.

Jim pled his case. He relayed all the facts, the video, all the details they found in the notebook. The notebook. The one Jim had found in Thane's office. The office he illegally broke into. As soon as he mentioned it, he knew he had lost.

What were you doing in his office?

Jim retreated, left the line open in silence.

I talked to your old captain, and he assured me you're the real deal. You may be onto something, but this Thane guy has no record and strong ties to the community. In this case, nothing short of a confession or a smoking gun will do.

"You're absolutely right," Jim said, realizing what he had to do.

Good, now go relax and enjoy retire—

Jim hung up on him. He was finished with the conversation and had no need for civilities with the condescending prick who reminded him too much of himself. He immediately dialed again.

He informed Sam he was ready to list and made an appointment for the following afternoon. Three didn't work for Sam, but four would. A power play, Jim was certain of it. The salesman was sharp and had his own little games.

But Jim knew all the games and would be ready for whatever Sam Thane tried to throw at him.

THIRTY-NINE

Jim spent the whole night in his office preparing for Thane's arrival. His plan was to coerce a confession, expose the villain's wrongdoing, and leave Shady Place a safer neighborhood than he had found it.

He gathered supplies for their meeting: a copy of the surveillance video, a tape recorder, his map, the photos of the notebook, and his gun. There was no telling how Sam would react. He had to be prepared for anything.

As the sun rose, exhaustion finally began to take its toll. He had to get some rest. When he emerged from his office, he found Tommy and Jay still sleeping on his sofa.

He woke them and shooed them away as Jay reminded him about his pickleball tournament later that day. It had slipped his mind in all that had come up, but he promised Jay he'd try to make it.

Tommy hugged him on the way out; an awkward moment, with the large man nearly enveloping Jim. A simple handshake would have sufficed, but Jim's candor and guidance meant too much to Tommy to settle for less than a warm embrace.

A shower, then bed; that was the plan. The wound on his head was tender under the heavy flow from his showerhead. Jim liked his showers hot, and he liked the water to blast his skin. It soothed his body and mind. His skin would shine like a newborn babe, pink from the excessive heat. But Jim had been forced into cooler than usual showers for days thanks to his sun exposure, and if not for the nasty gash he'd suffered the night before, he may have been able to return to the comforts of his boiling pot. Maybe YouTube was right; maybe he was the Lobsterman.

Nevertheless, his mind was elsewhere. It was swimming with thoughts of Shady Place. Part of him was already beginning to lament Stern's edict. He had somehow made friends and was beginning to find a place. So, he would do it for Shady Place. For his friends.

Screw Benjamin. He was on the brink of solving the case, and Sam was going down.

His mind continued to wander, even after he'd finished showering. He didn't want to move. Not again. And the girls… Jenny and Heather were going to be so disappointed in him. Despite the way he behaved around them, he wanted their respect and adoration.

He climbed into bed a little after nine, still thinking of how he would break it to the girls, considering the jokes he'd use to make light of the situation. He lost himself in the different scenarios, predicting their reactions.

Where would he go? He could take turns staying with them. Or he could travel.

This was what Karen had wanted, not him; maybe it was a blessing.

This went on for hours, Jim's mind wandering instead of resting. He couldn't say when he actually fell asleep, but it was a heavy, deep sleep.

It wasn't until the doorbell rang that Jim awakened. The sun had moved across the sky into the later afternoon.

He awoke groggy and confused. Was Sam there already? It was three forty-five. The Realtor was early, but he wasn't ready yet. He had yet to lay out the traps he would use to snare his prey.

Jim was equal parts relieved and annoyed to find Mike standing before him when he opened the door.

"I was headed to the pickleball finals. Jay's goin' for the championship," Mike announced. "You in?"

Jim checked the street; no Sam. "You gotta go. Thane is coming over."

"What?" Mike questioned. "Now? What about the cops?"

Jim shook his head. "No good. All circumstantial."

"What are you gonna do? Can I help?" Mike asked.

Jim looked down the street again, and then spoke softly. "Let me worry about that. This may be my last act as a Shady Place resident, but as God is my witness, there's no way I'm leaving here without taking that son of bitch down. Now go home so you don't get caught up in any of this."

He closed the door in Mike's face.

Rude.

Mike turned to leave but decided not to. Instead, he waited in his driveway. His guts screamed at him that something was going to go wrong at Jim's house.

By the time four o'clock had come and gone, Jim was ready for his guest. A tape recorder was nestled safely under his coffee table, his gun hidden in the top left kitchen drawer, and two separate folders with damning evidence laid peacefully on the coffee table, waiting to be revealed.

At 4:05 p.m., his phone buzzed with a text message: *Appointment ran over, few minutes behind, be there ASAP. Sorry.*

Jim was certain it was another power play. Thane always had to have the upper hand. He was probably a block away just letting the time pass, keeping Jim at bay. It was about the illusion of being so important that it was no big deal to make a customer wait. But it was a big deal; Jim took it as another slight. A simple, but elegant ploy had only garnered more ire.

Sam's excuse was valid. He was fifteen minutes late because he was meeting with an insurance adjuster. It seems a squirrel had nested in the ceiling of his office and caused a number of panels to collapse.

"The place was trashed, but only a few hundred dollars' damage," Thane said. "But you should have seen the baby squirrels. Those little guys were so cute. I'm a sucker for animals. You like animals, Mr. Phillips?"

It seemed as though Jim's tracks had been covered at Thane's office. It had a nest; that's why it was so aggressive! A protective mother. His first inclination was to inform his accomplice that they were in the clear. The thought itself gave Jim pause; why did he care if that human turd knew? Because Mike was his *friend*. That thought gave him even greater pause. This place was seeping into his bloodstream.

Despite his elation over the narrative he'd created playing out exactly as he'd hoped, he kept his response simple and disinterested. "Oh? That's curious."

"Not even worth the deductible, but I think I'm going to keep one of the squirrels if animal control will let me."

Thane's inane banter had Jim questioning the evidence. Was this guy really a killer? This kid wanted to adopt a baby squirrel only hours after trying to kill Beverly.

It's always the ones you'd never expect came to mind. He was probably going to dissect it. The markings of a sociopath, a true killer.

"Tea, coffee, beer?" Jim offered, showing Thane to the sofa.

He politely declined, then held up a folder of his own. "I brought some listing paperwork for you to look over. If you're ready, I think I have a buyer lined up already."

"Just put your paperwork down for now," Jim said, joining him on the sofa. "I'd like to just talk for a minute first."

"Sure," Thane placed his folder down between Jim's two conspicuously placed folders. "What's up?"

Jim tapped one of his folders with an extended digit. "I've been doing a little research, and it looks like you're the only Realtor doing any business in Shady Place. Impressive."

"It's my niche, why waste your time with the rest when you can have the best!" He was like a recording.

He's a monster, Jim thought. Sitting there so smug, so self-assured. "Tell me again about the living trusts…"

"Oh, well, you don't need to worry about that now, but maybe for your next house," Thane explained. "You create the trust in case anything happens to you; then your kids don't have to probate or pay estate taxes because they are already members of the trust. Just a little trick to help save some money."

In case something happens to you. That was all Jim heard. Was Sam openly threatening him now? The gall.

"And it makes it easier for you to take the listing, no probate," Jim said. "You get a lot of estate sales? I mean, you have to in a neighborhood like this, right?"

Sam wasn't used to this type of questioning; it was highly unusual. "Well, I guess, the kids usually use me because I sold the house to their parents."

"Right, right, makes sense," Jim nodded. "Seems like a lot of people dying around here lately."

Thane was slow to answer. Now he was trying to size Jim up. "It is an older demographic. Comes with the territory—"

Jim stepped over his words. "Like Ted, for instance. Crazy he had another heart attack so soon after the first one."

"I know!" Thane said. "I guess those things happen, though."

"You were there right before it happened, weren't you?"

"Yeah, he seemed fine."

"Yes, he was fine," Jim said. "Then just like that. So sudden sometimes. Did you know Beverly almost died last night?"

He appeared genuinely surprised. "Really? Bev? What happened? I just saw her last night!"

I know you did.

"Allergic reaction from some cookies," Jim said. "I figured you would have known that already."

"She was fine—"

"When you left?" Jim finished his sentence for him. "Just like Ted?"

Thane stood up. "We aren't talking about listing the house anymore, are we?"

Jim turned on his television, and the surveillance footage of Thane filled the screen.

"What's this?" Sam asked.

"I set up cameras outside the house after it was vandalized. Funny what you catch sometimes," Jim said.

"And there I am," Thane said. "Such a handsome devil! Is that last night? I just told you I was there."

Thane was trying to diffuse what he saw escalating into a tenuous situation with a little humor, but failed to see just how

284

serious Jim's accusations were.

"But you didn't tell me the why," Jim said. "Why were you there? Why did you bring her cookies? Especially cookies with nuts in them! You knew she was allergic to nuts!"

"Cookies?" Thane stared at Jim in silence, hoping for some sort of explanation, but got none.

Silence as a tool.

Sam continued. "What are you trying to get at here? Do you think I tried to *kill* Bev? I thought maybe you were mad because I was sleeping with your girlfriend or something."

Sleeping with her. Another notch on the bedpost for Miss Stanton.

Jim continued to stare, clenching his jaw at the young Realtor.

"I can't help it all these old ladies like me," Thane continued. Convinced there was no chance at a listing, he might as well take Jim down a peg. "Guess you old men just can't satisfy them the way I do, but I would never kill—"

"Sit down!" Jim pushed Thane back down on the sofa, sticking a finger in his face. "You tried to kill her, just like all the others!"

Jim was stronger than he'd expected. "Can you hear yourself right now? Are you actually accusing me of trying to kill her with nuts?"

"We found your notebook!" Jim tossed the two folders in Thane's lap, spilling the contents. "Let me know if we missed anyone."

Sam sifted through the loose pages, growing more and more confused. "Notebook? What is all this? I don't understand what's happening right now…"

"I'm sure that's how your victims felt," Jim blurted, his fist clenched tightly in a ball, ready to strike at the slightest provocation. "Just stop denying it! The evidence is right in front of you. You kill them, then you list their houses. You greedy son of a bitch!"

Thane jumped to his feet and threw up his hands. "I didn't kill anyone, you psycho!"

He was convincing, but he was, after all, a salesman. Jim had had enough. He lunged at Sam. "I'll show you psycho!"

He fell backward over the sofa with Jim's full weight on top of him. The two tussled on the floor wildly, bouncing off of walls and knocking barstools and anything else so callous as to be in their way to the floor. Jim pushed off of Thane and rushed to the kitchen.

His safety valve was in place. Thane had chased him into the kitchen, but stopped dead in his tracks when Jim trained his Glock on him.

"Whoa, hang on now," Thane said, inching closer. He'd had enough of this old man's bullshit antics. His own pigheaded adrenaline was pumping so heavily, he didn't have the sense to stop.

The sprier young man was on top of Jim before he could parry the attack, knocking the gun out of his hand. The sidearm bounced a few feet away into the foyer. Thane tried to hold Jim in place. He was trying to calm him down, but Jim was pulling away hard.

"Damn your old man strength!" Thane shouted in his face.

Jim shook loose, swatting Thane's hands away and diving for the gun, knocking him to the ground. "I'm not old, god damn it!"

He thought he was free, but Thane reached out and grabbed his foot. Jim stumbled and hit his head on the kitchen counter. The hit was hard, leaving him dazed and sending him collapsing to the ground. He was down, but not out. He was disoriented, but through bleary eyes, he could see Sam bolting through the front door.

Mike was still standing in his driveway when Thane made his frantic escape through the front door. He recovered quickly, gently closing the door before make a concerted effort to look casual on the way to his SUV.

"Hey, Sam," Mike called out to him. "What's goin' on?"

"Sorry, Mike can't talk!" Thane said ducking into his vehicle. Once inside, the effort to stay inconspicuous vanished. He threw the SUV in reverse, tires screeching as he backed out, sending an unsuspecting pedestrian diving to the ground.

Jim burst through the front door, waving his gun. "Get back here, Thane!"

"What's happenin'?" Mike made his way through Jim's yard.

There was a surprising amount of foot traffic on the street. Jim lowered his gun, tucking it into his belt. "Call the cops! He's getting away!"

The pursuit was on, with Jim pulling out quickly and sliding in behind Thane on the road. The two sped through the Shady Place streets at breakneck speed, nearly forty-five miles per hour.

But their high-speed chase was derailed as quickly as it began. The event in Shady Place that day not only included the National Pickleball Open Tournament but an open golf tournament as well. There were pedestrians on both sides of the road, and every crosswalk and golf cart crossing was overflowing with residents and visitors enjoying the warm summer afternoon.

Sam's eyes were trained on Jim in his rearview mirror. He honked his horn, but his attempts to hurry the crowd were futile. *The tournament.* He had completely forgotten about it with the fury the squirrel unleashed on his office the night before and the basket of crazy Jim had unleashed on him just minutes ago. He calculated his options, checking his mirror again. Jim was steadfast; somehow, it felt like he was staring straight into Sam's soul from the Shelby behind him.

Before Sam could make a decision about his next move, Jim was exiting his car and approaching on foot.

Shit!

He followed suit and jumped out of his SUV. Jim stopped, locking eyes with his quarry. They stood staring at each other. The moment was brief, both men weighing their options, but it was the younger who would act first. Thane took off on foot, directly into the crowd of pedestrians, hoping to lose Jim in the horde.

The pursuit continued on foot, with Jim yelling for Thane to stop and Thane telling him to give up. There would be no quit in Jim, though; this was his endgame. He still wasn't sure what he'd do with Thane if he caught him, especially if the police weren't nearby. The two shook off the curses of the unsuspecting masses as they pushed through.

Jim was in familiar territory when they reached the vendor section of the event. The display of custom golf carts was just ahead, and Thane was headed right for them. Jim would have loved the opportunity to stop and admire the custom Mustang cart again, but didn't have time. As quickly as the thought crossed his mind, he found Sam coming right at him in a custom Hummer cart he had just highjacked.

Jim dove out of the way, taking three unfortunate souls down with him. He recovered quickly and spotted his favorite cart, the custom Mustang. He would get to do more than just admire it this time. He jumped in the driver's seat and smiled, savoring the fact he was going to get to ride that bad boy after all.

"Jim! Couldn't stay away?" the owner was still trying to get the words out when Jim floored it. "What are you doing?!"

"Police business!" Jim shouted as he vanished into the crowd in hot pursuit, scattering innocent bystanders in his wake.

Jay woke that morning in Jim's living room and was quickly sent on his way.

I should not have drunk so much last night, was all he could think on his ride home to prepare for what he hoped would be an extended pickleball adventure. He spent the morning hydrating and trying to overcome the headache and queasiness so common after a night of drinking.

A heavy, greasy meal is never a good plan before rigorous physical activity, but Tommy assured him it was either that or to just start drinking again, a prospect that nearly induced vomiting. That would come later.

In the midst of his first-round match, Jay found himself barely able to stand. The heat of Florida was usually no match for a native of the tropical subcontinent of India, but that day, in his condition, the humidity, the hangover, the greasy food, it was all taking its toll. And it was all coming back up.

He was granted just enough of a reprieve to release everything inside him in a nearby garbage can. He was lucky to make it to the receptacle in time, but the relief he found was all that was necessary to push through. *Puke and rally.* He'd heard Jim say it the night of the social, and it seemed appropriate now.

And rally he did. He chugged two bottles of water and chewed a mint, then went back to work.

The rest of the tournament flew by for Jay. With Tommy in the stands cheering him on, he wasn't just winning; he was destroying his opponents, winning nearly every point along the way. Late in the afternoon, only one opponent stood between him and the trophy, the trophy that indicated he was, indeed, the best pickleball player in the country. At least on that day. In the sixty-five-plus age bracket.

It had been a back and forth match, the toughest of the day by far. He leaned over, breathing hard, sweat dripping down his nose to the court below his feet. He looked to the crowd, where Tommy gave him a knowing nod: *You got this.*

"OK, Patel, this is it, game point."

He wiggled his hips, gracing the crowd with the signature move on each serve, then raised his racket over his head and tossed the ball in the air. It was hanging there forever, slowly descending as Jay prepared to whack it toward his opponent. Just before he made contact, it happened.

"Look out!" Thane shouted, hurtling through a parting sea of spectators just to Jay's left.

He still managed to strike the ball, but his balance was thrown, and it was intercepted by Thane's cart, striking only a few inches from his head.

"Watch it!" Thane shouted at him.

"Noooo!" Jay shouted in frustration, a frustration that would grow exponentially as Jim emerged from the crowd, still in hot pursuit of Sam.

"Hey, Jay," Jim nodded as he passed by.

"Jim?" Jay's confusion quickly gave way to a shooting pain in his foot as Jim ran it over on his way by. He screamed in agony, dropping to the ground to grab the source of the discomfort.

Jim waved to him from the cart as it disappeared as quickly as it had arrived. "Told you I'd make it!"

Jay spat unspeakable words at Jim in Hindi until Tommy was at his side, consoling him.

Sirens in the distance indicated Mike's call had summoned the police. At some point, this runaround would end, and it would all get sorted it out. One way or another, the chase was nearing its end.

"Just stop, Thane!" Jim shouted as he closed the gap. He was piloting the faster cart, and the fifteenth fairway offered the first open stretch since the pursuit had begun. "You can't get away; the cops are almost here!"

"Leave me alone," Sam roared back. "I didn't do anything!"

Jim had to hand it to him; he was maintaining his innocence through it all. He probably still didn't think he'd done anything wrong. He was sick.

They scurried across the fairway, through the rough, over a cart path, and with one sharp turn, Thane's cart bounded through a small row of hedges and was suddenly airborne. The cart threw itself over an embankment and landed with a thud on the street running congruous to the fifteenth hole.

Seconds later, Jim's cart blasted through the bushes, nearly landing on top of Sam. The street looked familiar to Jim. It should. They had landed directly in front of Mike's house, as he and Beverly stood dumbstruck by the actions unfolding before them.

Neither golf cart was operable. Thane made the first move, jumping off the cart and heading straight for Jim.

"Enough!" he shouted. He was finished with this nonsense. Jim Phillips's shenanigans had gone on for too long. It was his turn to become the aggressor.

Seeing Thane coming, Jim reached for the gun he'd tucked in his waistband, but not quickly enough. Thane pounced, knocking Jim out of the cart and sending the gun sliding across the street.

It all happened so fast, and Mike was unsure what to do, if he should intercede or even how he might go about doing so.

"What is wrong with you?!" Sam shouted maniacally.

He jumped on top of Jim and began pounding him into the pavement. "Why..." he punched. "Won't..." another punch. "You..." He grabbed Jim by the shirt and shoved him hard against the ground. "Stop?!"

Jim was weak but undeterred. "Just admit it...you did it for..." He coughed. "The money."

"Get off him!" Mike shouted, running toward Thane, but he stumbled as he approached, tumbling toward them, until he tripped over Jim's feet, his momentum casting him several yards past the skirmish.

"You too?" Thane asked, before turning his attention back to Jim. He raised his fist for another blow, but something changed.

A dazed Jim watched Sam's face morph from angry determination to concern. "Oh god, Bev, no!"

"Huh?" Jim mumbled. His question was answered in the form of two gunshots. Shots that would echo through the streets of Shady Place for years to come.

Thane's concern turned to confusion and shock as blood began to leak from his chest. He gasped for air, rocked backward slightly, then collapsed forward onto Jim.

His mouth was next to Jim's ear as he mumbled something indiscernible, then breathed his last breath.

FORTY

Her body was still weak from the anaphylactic shock that had nearly killed her the night before, but like everyone else in Shady Place, the approaching sirens drew Beverly to the street.

She found Mike standing in his driveway, pacing nervously, and questioned what was going on in their sleepy little neighborhood. Surely, it involved Jim, she thought, and hopefully Sam. It wasn't so long ago that she was lying in a hospital bed, the result of his late-night visit to her home.

Mike confirmed her suspicions; both Jim and Thane were involved. He wasn't sure what was going on, but Jim had urged him to involve the police, so it must be serious. They had been gone awhile, and his concerns were growing; he wasn't sure where they were.

And then he knew exactly where Jim and Sam were.

Beverly watched the action unfold quickly. The golf carts soaring through the air and crashing before them in the street. Sam attacking Jim. The gun sliding across the street, slowing to a stop only a few feet from her. Mike trying to play hero, but failing to alleviate the brutal assault Jim was receiving.

Her attention drifted to the gun again. She hadn't fired one in a long time, but something had to be done. It was heavy in her hands. She checked the safety. *Off.* Her former husband had taught her all about safe gun practices before an unfortunate hunting accident took his life. She'd sworn off the messy devices ever since. But now...now it was a necessary tool.

She had always been a good shot, but she decided to step a few feet closer anyway, just to be sure. Squeeze don't pull. That's what he'd taught her, smooth, straight back squeeze; a pull could jerk the firearm, sending your shot offline. Even just a little was too much.

Two smooth squeezes. Two loud bangs. Two shell casings sprinkled on the ground at her feet. One dead Realtor.

Jim gently lowered Beverly's trembling hands. They were so tightly gripped on the gun, he had to pry it from her fingers.

Her lips were quivering as she stared forward, mumbling to herself, "I had to do it."

Jim wrapped her in his arms. "It's OK. It's over now."

"He was going to kill you," she said, devoid of emotion. "I had to."

Mike gently nudged Thane's body with his foot before joining them. "I think he's dead."

"Go inside; I can handle the police," Jim whispered to Mike. "No reason to risk them looking into your past."

Mike was reluctant to leave them alone. Even though Jim had told him he was finished with Beverly, incidents like this tended to bond people. If he left them now, he might as well push them together. But Jim was right; if he stayed, it might not matter at all.

Beverly repeated her mantra to Jim softly. "I had to."

"I know, I know; it's OK." He embraced her warmly.

Handling the police was no problem for Jim. He told them to talk to Detective Benjamin. Thane had assaulted him, so he pursued him. He was uniquely qualified for such a task. Maybe he was a little overzealous in his chase, but he didn't do anything wrong.

Beverly's actions were justifiable. And that's the way it was ruled. Justifiable homicide.

Beverly spent the evening at Jim's side as he was checked for a concussion. It was precautionary, but he had taken a number of nasty blows to the head. The battery of tests cleared him of any serious danger, but his face was a reminder just how rough the last few days had been.

It was quiet on Shady Oak Way for the next few days. Everyone seemed to be lying low after what was being called The Incident.

Mike's driveway was conspicuously empty. Beverly spent the weekend recovering, then continued to dodge previously coordinated engagements, the follies, tennis. Whatever it may be, it just wasn't important after what had happened.

Jim got what he had wanted all along: silence, peace and quiet. But at what cost? He had grown to anticipate the company of others in Shady Place. Distraction by interaction. Now he was left to his own devices, and he didn't know what to do with them.

The Phillies played the Braves all weekend, which made him think about Tommy and wonder what he was doing, but he knew already. As soon as the pickleball tournament ended, Tommy and Jay were headed to Jacksonville for a sports card convention. Forty bucks a pop for an autograph.

He thought about a round of golf, but it reminded him of the time he'd gone with the guys. Guys he didn't care about as recently as a few days ago, but now longed for their company. What was Mike doing? They hadn't spoken since the cops left and Beverly took Jim to the doctor. He concluded Mike was probably putting the same effort into killing time as he was.

In all his years on the force, he had never killed anyone. He'd only fired his weapon a few times and winged one perp. His partner was gunned down on the street, but Jim wasn't there. For all the bodies he'd been around over his thirty years, this was the first time he'd been so close to the action.

His time alone helped it sink in, but it was beginning to weigh on him. Thane's last words kept creeping to the front of his mind. They were so faint, and he was so woozy, the only thing he was sure of was the length. Three words or three syllables.

Imbabur?

Thimbleturd?

What did he say?

A quick call to Heather led to a family dinner and a welcome diversion. They were so close now, he really should be spending more time with them. They teased him about the shape of his face, but that quickly ended when he reminded the idiots he'd garnered them in the apprehension of a crazed killer.

He confessed to his family his days in Shady Place would be over soon and he would be homeless, a fact he divulged over dinner to the chagrin of his loving daughters. Loving to the point of wanting him close, but not that close.

Itfusmer…no. What did he say?

It was the slowest time had passed for Jim while he was in Shady Place, and it was all leading up to Tuesday night's homeowner's association meeting. The one where a Stern-led board would decide Jim's fate.

F ORTY-ONE

For lack of a better description, Jim was calling it his trial. His *This Is Your Life* moment. Why should he be allowed to stay in Shady Place? The day dragged on slowly. The meeting wasn't until seven that evening, at the clubhouse, but he'd been awake since six in the morning. Early for Jim. He chalked it up to nerves.

Itfusfur?

Jim was still swirling phrases in his head. He decided to purge his house of any trace of the scoundrel. The Post-its, the files, the map, all of it. Maybe if he removed the reminders, he could free his mind of the words that were tormenting him and actually focus on mounting some sort of defense.

But Jim could never just let something go. The words whirled around in his head, tempting him. Another puzzle to be solved. He started in his bathroom and worked his way through the house, collecting Post-it notes. There were dozens, half thoughts jotted down so he didn't forget anything. In his office, there were dozens more, mostly interconnected words, names, addresses. Victims. O'Flaherty. Thane.

Thane. What did he say? It was right there; he knew he was close to figuring it out. He closed his eyes and focused on that moment.

The look on Thane's face when he realized Beverly was about

to shoot him. Bang, bang. Thane fell forward onto him, and he whispered…

Jim opened his eyes and rubbed his chin. His brow had furrowed. It was furrowing so hard, his mother would have warned him about his face freezing in such an awful expression. A few clicks on his computer only sent him searching deeper.

The website for Florida's department of business was fairly easy to navigate. He'd been there before to verify Thane's real estate license. He looked at the company, Shady Place Realty. He was the broker, the only agent registered with the company.

That wasn't it.

ENTER SEARCH: florida division of corporations.

Shady Place Realty, LLC.

Thane said he had a partner; who was it? He had expected to see Samuel Thane and some mystery person, but what he found was another limited liability corporation. Which was owned by another. And that one? Owned by another as well.

Someone was going to great lengths to distance themselves from Shady Place Realty and Thane. But why? Why would anyone care who owned a real estate company in an old folks' neighborhood?

The last LLC was out of state, more precisely, New Jersey. Their website was less friendly, but a few clicks and a few dollars later, Jim had the info he needed on Jersey to Florida, LLC. It occurred to Jim that a lot of Philadelphia professionals took up residence in the suburbs of South Jersey. Cherry Hill, Moorestown, Vorhees, just to name a few, were frequent havens for commuters, including some of the city's most notorious criminals.

Jim considered the possibilities. Could he have missed something so obvious?

He continued to dig. The company was unsurprisingly owned by another corporation, a refrain that was becoming increasingly annoying. The addresses had all been dead ends. Post office boxes at various Pack N Ship companies. It was the type of shell game a seasoned wrongdoer with something to hide would execute to distance themselves from the malfeasance.

His web browser was flooded with tabs. A trail of a half dozen companies that led to one final resting place. A dead end. Jersey to Florida LLC was held by Your Legal Team LLC. An online legal company people used as their registered agent with a given state so people wouldn't be able to find out who they were on the Internet. Instead, they would need a warrant or subpoena. Something that would have been easy for Jim if he was still a cop. But he wasn't.

A dead end. He rolled back in his chair, frustrated. He stared at the screen, but he wasn't looking at anything in particular. He was more staring through it, contemplating his next play.

ENTER SEARCH: jersey to florida llc.

Grasping at straws rarely leads to a respite from sinking into the depths below, but every once in a while, you grab hold of something big enough to hold onto. He sifted through several pages of seemingly unrelated subjects, mostly related to forming corporations in Florida or New Jersey.

Halfway down the third page, he found a thread, so he gave it a little tug. It was a public record of a transaction. A home sale. The company had been the seller of a house in Cherry Hill, New Jersey some years back. Digging deeper in the public record, he found the property had been deeded to the company, not sold. And there was a name.

Thane's words crystallized in his mind, but he could hardly

believe what he was seeing.

He ran his mouse over the name several times, highlighting it, then clicking away.

Surprise or disappointment. Among the spectrum of emotions one is forced to cope with, those were the two he was wrestling with at that moment. He continued wrestling with how to feel all the way up to the point he was standing on his neighbor's doorstep with his finger gently on the doorbell.

Regardless of how he felt, he knew what he had to do.

FORTY-TWO

Stir-crazy would describe what it was like being cooped up the last few days. Feeling trapped in the house, but not wanting to go out. The Incident had taken its toll. When the doorbell rang, it was a welcome disruption to the monotony.

The door opened to Jim looking to the street, still contemplating just what he would say. He turned, offering a strained smile.

"Hey, Bev, how are you holding up?"

She waved him inside. "I'm still pretty shaken. I thought you were supposed to be at the homeowner's meeting tonight?"

"Nothing left to say."

She was making herself a cup of Earl Grey, wearing an anxious expression. For Jim, it would be a cup of coffee. The pain in her eyes showed just how distraught she still was. She was getting ready to start a new book; she'd read four since cloistering herself.

He declined an offer of cream or sugar. "Black is fine."

She clinked a spoon, mixing a bit of milk into her tea. "So, what brings you over? I haven't heard from you since…since that dreadful afternoon."

"Sorry, I was trying to give you some space," he said. "But I suppose maybe support would have been better?"

She shrugged, sipping her tea. "I'm a big girl."

"Over thirty years on the force, I never actually killed anyone." He shook his head softly. "I've heard it gets easier after the first one. Maybe that's why it was so easy for Thane."

"Oh, James, can we not talk about that awful man?" she asked.

He forced a tiny smile. "You know, he mumbled something to me before he died. I've been thinking about it since. It sounded like gibberish at the time, but I couldn't shake it."

"Oh?" she said.

"Yeah, this afternoon, I was cleaning up from the case, figured I should start packing if I'm going to have to move soon anyway, you know?"

She nodded. "Are you sure you shouldn't plead your case? Perhaps with all that's happened, they'll let you stay."

"A few weeks ago, he told me he had a silent partner in his business. Did you know that?"

She turned her back on him, looking out her kitchen window. It pointed at Jim's house. "A partner? You mean in his real estate company? I thought he worked alone."

"Silent partner," he said, he hadn't touched his coffee. He was observing her closely as she opened a drawer. "I did some digging. A lot of digging, actually."

Beverly gently placed her tea on the counter. A switch flipped inside. The pouty damsel in distress was gone. Her eyes were narrowed as she listened to Jim. He didn't really need to go any further, she knew exactly what he had found.

Her hands deftly withdrew the contents of a clear vial, filling a syringe to capacity. She was tuning out Jim's in-depth description of his journey through the information superhighway that had led him to one conclusion.

"You played it brilliantly, Bev," he said in summation. "Having Mike lead me to Thane's office to find the notebook you planted there; the only thing you left out was where to look. It wasn't until this afternoon when I figured out what Thane said, though…"

She squeezed the syringe in her hand as she spun to face her accuser, concealing it behind her back. "I was growing weary of pretending to be upset over that sniveling little worm. Whatever did he say to you, James?"

"It was her."

The two stared at each other in silence for a moment. She was considering the ramifications of Jim's discovery. Had he uncovered enough information to be of any concern to her well-being?

It didn't really matter.

Arrogance and hubris are branches of the same tree and bear similar fruit. She decided to harvest her bounty and take a confident bite. "At least he died knowing."

Jim was surprised by the sudden change in attitude. She dropped any semblance of pretense, so he figured he might as well join her.

"The masterstroke was giving yourself the allergic reaction," Jim said, rising from his seat. "Guess you were never really at risk, though. You knew Mike and I would come running, didn't you?"

It *was* a masterstroke. She smiled knowingly. "Mike is a duffer. But you? I knew my knight in shining armor would rescue me. I didn't even touch the cookies until you kicked in my door."

Her smugness sickened Jim. He'd dealt with sociopaths before, but he'd nearly slept with Beverly. He'd thought he was falling in love with this woman. What dawned on him at that moment cut him to the core. "Did he actually kill any of them?"

"I didn't think he had it in him, but when he killed Ted…" She wistfully observed, "I thought maybe we could have been in on it together all along. Then you started sniffing around, and I knew I had to end it."

"How many?"

She tapped the handles of several different knives before selecting one. "More than you'll ever know." She pulled a large knife from the block and sighed. "As much fun as this has been, I grow weary playing catch-up with you, James. Kudos on your deductions, but this is where your journey ends."

"You know, it's funny; I told my kids I'd die in Shady Place," Jim said, taking a step toward her. "Let me guess? Potassium chloride? That's how you made them look like heart attacks."

"Just too smart for your own good." She raised and lowered her hands as though they were scales, weighing the pluses and minuses of each tool she might use to dispatch Jim. "Decisions, decisions. Did you try to rape me or was it a heart attack as you so astutely observed? Do you have a preference, dear?"

"Will you at least tell me why?" A stall tactic. *Keep her talking, Phillips.*

She rolled her eyes at him. "What do you want to hear? I did it for the money? Wouldn't that be convenient. I got a cut of every deal Samuel closed. And believe me, he was a closer…" The double entendre landed as intended, conjuring images of Thane and Beverly in Jim's head. "But, no; I have plenty of money. It was nothing more than boredom and opportunity. They all made it so easy."

"Boredom?" This vile woman killed out of boredom. Jim's ability to restrain himself from leaping across the room and strangle her was waning.

"All the men in here are the same, chase a pretty girl, hope to get her in bed, then fall in love. Boring. All of you men are boring. Killing them was exhilarating. The most alive I've ever felt. The first one was an accident." She whispered the next bit. "I killed him with sex. That's what you missed out on James."

She gyrated her hips to emphasize just how simple it was for her.

"What about Tanya?"

"Who?"

She probably didn't even register for Beverly, just a footnote in the wake of the quiet chaos the narcissist had left behind. "The young real estate agent, the one who was paralyzed…"

"Oh yes, the speed bump. She should have left when I told her to." She smiled, recalling the blustery night she ran Tanya into a ditch. "It's too bad, James Phillips; you were never boring."

A consolation prize?

"You know I won't go down without a fight," he stated.

"Guess you tried to rape me," she said. Her cool demeanor was chilling as she approached with the knife.

Jim leaned his chin toward his chest. "OK, guys…"

His words unleashed hell on Beverly's house, and her front door was kicked in for the second time in less than a week. Officers poured in through the opening.

Beverly attempted to stave off the wave of policemen who descended upon her, cursing Jim as she flailed about with her knife. The standoff was brief. She was disarmed and pinned on the floor before she could draw any blood.

"You get enough?" Jim asked Detective Benjamin on his way out.

The detective nodded in the affirmative. "Sorry I doubted you." Benjamin offered Jim his hand to shake, but all he received in return was a shake of the head.

"You son of a bitch!" she called to Jim as she was dragged out of the house. "I would have slept with you!"

Now that was a real threat...

FORTY-THREE

The victory should have been sweet. That woman had been so good at what she did that she almost got away with it. If not for Jim, she would have. He should have been reveling in the triumph, rejoicing with the grateful Shady Placers who sang his praises.

Beverly was not well liked in Shady Place. Sure, the men positioned her at the top of the list for her looks, but there was no love lost among the women. With her gone, all was right in the world again.

Jim took umbrage at how callously the life that was lost was being dismissed. Samuel Thane had been a human being. From what Jim had deduced, that human being had in fact done no wrong. No, instead of taking any solace in the fact he'd removed what amounted to a serial killer from Shady Place, Jim was racked with compunction.

Thane's death was ultimately his fault. He let Beverly lead him by the nose right down the path that ended with the demise of an innocent. He didn't like Thane. Not because of anything Sam had ever done, simply because Jim harbored an unreasonable distaste for salespeople.

But he was a human being…

The refrain played over and over in Jim's head as he ignored phone calls and visitors. He sequestered himself in bed. He was so disgusted with himself, he couldn't eat or sleep.

He was a human being…and you killed him.

Perhaps he was being too hard on himself. He let the occasional moments of lucidity allow for self-exoneration. Yes, he'd played a hand, but it wasn't him. It was the architect. That woman. She laid a trap, and he fell into it. It was only fitting that she finished the job herself.

The thought of her standing there, hands trembling, tears welling her in eyes. Crocodile tears. He was sure theater group could be counted among the list of Beverly's extracurricular activities.

Beverly didn't win the war, though. Jim did. He got her; she was going to jail for a long time. When the police tossed her house, they found all they needed to put her away. He should be happy. Maybe someday he would be.

For that day, and many after, the effects of his actions and the consequences rendered were crushing Jim from the inside. It was the same when Peterson died; Jim let it eat at him for weeks.

His grief, coupled with his impending expulsion, left Jim on the brink of self-destruction. The self-inflicted mental anguish, sleep deprivation, and starvation resulted in his mind and body being taxed to the point of total exhaustion.

On the second day, he succumbed to the weight of it all…

And he slept.

The last time Jim was conscious was a Thursday. When he opened his eyes again, it was Saturday morning. Fingers of sunlight reached through his blinds and tickled his face, coaxing him from a comatose slumber.

He was groggy, confused about where he was, *when* he was.

Consulting his phone for the date and time enlightened him enough to know he had to get out of bed. The vacant feeling in his intestines told him he had to eat something.

Bacon. Eggs. Coffee. The sizzle, the grease popping in the pan, the aroma. Collectively, it was almost enough to sate the pangs ravaging his insides.

When his partner and best friend Frank Peterson had died over twenty years prior, it had taken weeks for Jim to recover. This time, the loss of Samuel Thane took only days.

With a full belly, he would turn his attentions to finding a new Realtor, another byproduct of the nasty business that had transpired since his arrival less than a month before.

He'd managed to get himself kicked out of Shady Place. He'd have to sell the house and find a place to live. Jenny and Heather had helped him sell the place in Philly, but he didn't want to involve them if he didn't have to. They forced the Philly sale on him; this was his own doing.

I wish I could just stay.

As much as he hated to admit it, he liked living in Shady Place. Maybe if he had played things differently. Maybe if he had been a little nicer to Stern. Maybe if he had actually read the rules and regulations.

A lot of maybes, but it was too late.

Idiot.

The doorbell rang, as it had so many times since his arrival. He'd been ignoring the blasted thing for days.

But today was a new day. He was back from the other side.

Stern was waiting expectantly when he unsealed his tomb. All of Jim's newfound vigor and excitement were immediately dashed. She was wound as tightly as ever, her hair pulled back so far, Jim believed it was preventing the skin from sliding off her face and revealing the concealed features of a demon escaped from hell.

His head dropped at the sight of her.

"I'm not going to fight you," he glowered. "I'm looking for a Realtor now, since, well, you know…"

"And a good morning to you, Mr. Phillips," she said. "About that, may I have a brief moment of your time?"

"You've gotta at least give me time to find another place," he pleaded.

She smiled. "Please, Mr. Phillips, I'd like to have a civil discussion with you."

She actually smiled; there were teeth and everything. No hint of the hellion he was sure had darkened his doorstep to expel him from Shady Place and into the depths of hell. He eyed her suspiciously, considering barring her ingress, but he allowed the fiend access anyway.

He was civil, offering her coffee. She liked hers black, too.

Black to match her heart.

"Like I said, I'm not planning on fighting you," Jim explained. "I know I missed my chance for that. I'll be gone as quickly as I can."

Examining her features, he was certain he could see the makings of horns trying to push their way through her scalp.

"That won't be necessary. That's actually why I'm here," she said, trying to coerce eye contact from Jim as he stared at her forehead.

While Jim was cleaning up the Beverly mess, the homeowner's association was meeting. He knew this. He had chosen to finish what he started instead of pleading his case to stay, a sacrifice he would never regret.

According to Stern's recounting of the events that transpired that night, he had missed quite the show. In his absence, a strong case was presented for removal.

Discharging a firearm. *They were fireworks.*

Unauthorized decorations. *Wrong.*

Unpermitted placement of a sign. *OK, yeah.*

Drunk and disorderly behavior. *Check.*

Public nudity. *Yeah, check that, too.*

Even a parking ticket. *Oh right, forgot that one.*

He knew the charges. It was a few more than three strikes when you added it all up. What Jim hadn't counted on was the answer to the question, "Does anyone have anything to say on Mr. Phillips's behalf?"

In fact, three someones had something to say.

🌴

There weren't many people at the Shady Place homeowner's association meeting that month. A lot had happened, and there was clamoring of police gathered on Shady Oak Way again that night.

The seven-member board presented the room with an agenda. It was mostly variances and sign approval petitions. A few financial updates. The consideration of a new landscaping company for the neighborhood. And one potential expulsion from the neighborhood. Something that had never actually happened in the history of Shady Place.

Linda liked firsts. Everything had to be by the book, but to set a precedent while following the letter of the law was something she would savor.

Outside of the board, there were only a handful of people in the room. The few who had requested variances and signs got the first attention and left after their petitions were accepted or rejected. By the time the end of the meeting had rolled around and only one item remained, the room was nearly barren save a handful of interested residents who would never miss a meeting and three amigos waiting to defend the final member of their foursome.

Jay spoke to the board first, and it went something like this:

"Hello, my name is Sanjay Patel. You probably know me as Jay, national champion of pickleball. James Phillips is a very stubborn and cantankerous man. He can certainly rub you the wrong way. Jim's behavior upon his arrival at Shady Place was very unbecoming of a resident, and perhaps he should have been tossed out weeks ago. Despite all that and the fact that he broke my foot, James Phillips *is* Shady Place. He is one of us now and deserves to stay."

Jay finished by reminding the board members of Jim's heroics. "And he stopped a serial killer. Thank you."

Tommy followed directly behind Jay.

"Y'all know me, but y'all may or may not know I'm gay. Jim helped me share that little tidbit with the world. He told me it was OK, and it is. Any y'all got a problem with that?"

He waited, no one did.

"He helped give me the confidence to be out and proud. Sure, the man's cranky. He likes hollerin' at strangers for no damn reason. Maybe he got a hard time followin' the rules, but that man is Shady Place. Just like all the rest of us; me, Jay, Mike, all y'all."

Tommy stepped back, but Mike nodded for him to say one more thing. "Oh, yeah, and he caught a serial killer, y'all. Gotta count for somethin'!"

When it was Mike's turn, he made a spectacle of it. He dragged a chair in front of the board and stood on it so he towered above everyone in the room.

"My fellow Shady Placers. I'm Mike Johnson. I've known Jim Phillips for over twenty years. I'm not gonna recap all the stuff youse already know about him. I'm going to tell you about a man who grabbed me and pulled me up from a dark, dark place in my life. When my wife left, who saw me through it? Jim Phillips. When I was ready to throw it in and just give up on life, who wouldn't let me? Jim Phillips. If youse need something, anything, the shirt off your damn back, who's gonna give it to you? That's right, Jim Phillips."

He kept going for another ten minutes about how great Jim truly was; they just hadn't seen it. Then he told them about Karen and why Jim was so sad and cranky. How he and Jim were close friends who solved the murders together (he couldn't let Jim have all the credit, after all). They weren't just close friends, he told them. They were best friends.

It was all bullshit, of course, but Mike did bullshit so well.

Mike reminded them one more time of the serial killer Jim had captured, reiterating he had helped, of course, then waited for the cascade of adulation.

Linda recounted Mike's speech as closely as she could recall it. "I believe at the end, he was awaiting applause. I believe Mr. Johnson has seen too many movies. His speech was rather rousing, and while Samuel did end up being another victim, your actions were virtuous nonetheless."

She smiled at him again. He was reminded of the woman with her hair down who had opened the door to him at her house. That was of course before she scolded him for being there to begin with, but he shook that thought off.

She looked like a different person when she was smiling.

"What does all this mean?" he asked.

"Despite your heroic actions, I moved to have you removed from the neighborhood," she said. "Rules are rules, after all."

He blinked. Apparently, he'd misread the room. Her horns were poking through again. And was that a pointed little tail he spied sneaking up behind her?

"But I only have one vote," she went on. "And while I was disappointed to have to use it to cast you out, my fellow board members found it prudent to ignore the rules and deny the motion. It was a six to one vote, Mr. Phillips. You may stay in Shady Place if you so choose."

He was convinced she was playing a cruel trick on him. Her eyes had lit up, and she continued to brandish a smile at him, but her demeanor and inflection never changed.

"You fuckin' with me?"

"I assure you, Mr. Phillips," she said blushing and averting her eyes. "I am not…frickin' with you."

He laughed at her use of the word frickin', then slammed his palm on the counter. "I could kiss you!"

She looked up at him, locking eyes, then stepped out of character. "You could."

He did.

It didn't end there, though. Jim found a way to get over the hurdle that kept him from sealing the deal with Beverly.

⁂

By the time Linda emerged from Jim's front door, she had regained her proper appearance, but something was slightly off. Her shirt was untucked ever so slightly, and her glasses rested just a tiny bit down her nose. She tried to pull her bun as tight as the community had become so accustomed to seeing, but one of her bobby pins had managed to disappear in Jim's bedroom.

Jim escorted Stern from his doorstep to her golf cart. It was all very formal, no touching, no eye contact, only an interaction between the president of the homeowner's association and a resident after one very long house call. Not one word was whispered about what had just transpired inside.

As she mounted her cart, Ruthie and her little pug Doug meandered down the sidewalk in front of Jim's house. He watched with great interest, his brow furrowed.

Ruthie attempted to pull the grunting little guy along, but he insisted on paying a visit to Jim's lawn. It was one of his favorites. He sniffed the grass, circling a spot that seemed just right, before squatting and eventually relieving himself. As he did his business, one of his hind legs trembled rhythmically in unison with the vein throbbing on Jim's forehead.

One of Jim's eyes twitched as he observed, mumbling to himself, jaw clenched, "I'm standing right here."

Jim took a step forward, but Linda touched his arm gently. "Mr. Phillips…"

Ruthie already had a bag in hand, ready to scoop as Doug finished. Without a word, it was gone, and she nodded to Linda.

"Good morning, Ruthie," she returned.

Jim jogged after her. "Hey, wait up!"

Linda and Ruthie shared a moment of terror, fearing the worst from Jim.

"I just wanted to say I'm sorry for yelling at you the first time we met." His delivery was surprisingly contrite. No throbbing vein, twitching eye, or furrowed brow. Just a soft smile.

"Of course; thank you," Ruthie smiled back. "Have a nice day!"

"I did look over the information you brought me on the DNA testing," Stern confessed. "If you would kindly propose it at the next HOA meeting, I think we might be able to put it to a vote."

Jim smiled and nodded triumphantly. "Maybe I'll do that."

She winked at him and mouthed, *Call me.* He tried to play it cool, but the corners of his mouth were reaching for his ears.

Jim had failed to notice Mike sidle up beside him.

"Hey, buddy!"

"Damn it!" Jim jumped. "You scared the shit out of me, O— Johnson." He was still getting used to not calling him O'Flaherty, and it was even harder in an alarmed state.

"Good day, Mr. Johnson," she said, backing out of his driveway. "Mr. Phillips, don't forget to pay your fines."

And with that, she was gone. Jim continued watching until she was out of sight.

"Linda gave you the good news?" Mike asked.

Jim failed to suppress the grin plastered on his face when he turned his attention to Mike. His newly anointed "best friend" was unable to contain his excitement when he realized something more had happened between Jim and Linda.

"It was more than just the news!"

Jim looked away coyly; he was actually blushing.

Mike laughed and punched him on the arm. "I gotta hear about this. Tell me, she's a freak, right? I bet she—"

"Shut up; I'm not talking about this with you," Jim said.

But Mike kept pushing. It was a subject he'd been curious about since the first time he saw Linda Stern. Jim's elation quickly turned to annoyance.

Just as quickly, the annoyance turned to concern. "Oh shit."

Mike followed Jim's gaze to find a government issue Crown Victoria sliding into Jim's driveway.

A young woman exited the passenger side, hiding her eyes behind a pair of aviator sunglasses. A maroon sport coat over a collared button-down shirt, dark jeans, and a pair of Louboutin heels were accented by the badge fastened to her belt. Her sidearm joined the party when she parted the jacket to put her hands on her hips.

Her partner watched from the car, chatting into a cell phone. She looked up and down the street before settling on Jim and Mike.

"Jim Phillips?" she asked.

"Lookin' at him," Jim said.

She lowered her glasses, nodding approval. "Deputy Marshal Edwards. The office said you called about a person of interest in the neighborhood."

Mike's eyes shot open wide and turned with laser-sharp focus to Jim's suddenly sheepish face.

"I actually meant to call you, but we had a bit of a stir-up around here the past few weeks," Jim conceded. "I think I may have been mistaken."

"Mistaken?" she questioned. "So you didn't recognize someone in protection?"

Mike began backing away slowly, "I'll see you guys later."

"Wait a minute," she barked, stopping Mike in his tracks. "You look familiar."

"I get that a lot," he smiled.

Jim instinctively took a step between Edwards and Mike as she reached slowly toward what he thought was her holstered gun. Instead, she reached in her pocket and procured a photograph. "Was this the man you saw?"

Jim stepped closer and took the photo, then he cocked his head a little and nodded softly. He handed the photo to Mike with a wink. "Actually, yes. Yes, it is."

Mike gave it a quick glance, then shared a moment of relieved eye contact with Jim.

She took the photo back and stepped closer to Jim. "We're not supposed to share any information with civilians, but since you already knew, we relocated him."

"Wait," Jim shook his head. "He's not dead?"

"Detective Phillips," she said. She knew who he was. "We take our jobs very seriously. After the message you left, we took that little panic attack as an opportunity to move him and Lisa."

"Ted Williams," Jim pointed to Mike. "I told you that name was fake!"

Mike conceded, shrugging his shoulders and rolling his eyes.

The marshal's partner joined them. Jim's exploits in taking down Thane and then Beverly had made the local news, and they wanted to shake his hand and commend him for a job well done.

Of course, everything they told Mike and Jim about Ted was hush hush. "So keep it to yourselves."

They left Jim and Mike alone. Jim was hoping Mike would let it go, that he wouldn't mention the fact that Jim had obviously called the marshals on him. It was so long ago, and so much had changed.

"Ted was in the program," Mike said, shaking his head incredulously.

Jim grunted in response, holding out hope it would end with that, but it didn't, of course.

Mike sucked his teeth and turned to Jim. "You called the marshals?"

"The first time I saw you," Jim said, refusing to look Mike in the eye. "Obviously, I changed my mind."

"Obviously," Mike retorted. He continued to stare at Jim expectantly. An awkward silence ensued, Jim's favorite kind, until Mike observed, "Guess you forgot to tell them."

Jim changed the subject. "So, Stern said you stood up for me at the HOA meeting. Best friends?"

Jim slowly raised his right arm, his hand in a loose fist. Mike recoiled. Was Jim going to hit him again? But then Jim opened his palm and extended a hand for Mike to shake.

"Thanks."

Shaking it, Mike winked. "Don't mention it."

When he retracted his hand, Mike squirmed uncomfortably before succumbing to an itch in his pants.

"Problems?" Jim asked, raising an eyebrow.

"Just be glad you never ended up sleepin' with Bev."

Jim laughed, slapping Mike on the back. Just another reason to be glad he'd never closed the deal.

"So, what now?" Mike asked.

He hadn't thought about it. Maybe he would look into getting his private investigator's license, join a softball team, or learn to play pickleball. Jay would love that. Pursue a relationship with Stern, Linda. The possibilities were endless.

Fifteen years ago, he would have had an easy answer. Catch O'Flaherty. But he did that. Eight years ago, his job became to take care of Karen. That was finished, too. For the last three years, he'd focused on feeling sorry for himself. But to what end? He never liked not having any direction. An hour ago, he thought he had to find a new place to live. But now he had a new lease on life.

He simply wasn't himself for a long time.

Now, Shady Place was home.

Home.

He never liked saying the words he said next, but for once in his life, he was OK with what they meant. The possibilities were endless.

Jim shrugged. "I don't know."

CKNOWLEDGEMENTS

Joops Fragale for all your help with the cover and story tips.

Todd Murata, you made me do all the work, but helped me flesh out the story and characters through our chats so many years ago.

Virginia at FirstEditing for cleaning up my mess.

Mom for loving everything I've ever written even when I don't.

Dad for your undying support and never-ending flow of "Dad Grants."

Ashley for putting up with me and not losing your mind. Your love, support, and persistence made this book possible.

I wish I had the space to list out every one of you who have touched me and made this book possible through your support (and sometimes nagging) throughout the process. I could fill a volume with your names and stories about all of you.

Lastly, my late grandmother, Carol Jean Harris, some of your exploits were an inspiration for this work and will surely rear their heads up in future tomes. RIP

www.ingramcontent.com/pod-product-compliance
Lightning Source LLC
Chambersburg PA
CBHW031214120726
47905CB00002B/329